PRAISE FOR THE NOVELS
OF JULIA HOLDEN

One Dance in Paris

"Julia Holden's books draw me in from the very first page, and I find myself not reading them so much as living them. Enchanting and delightful, yet poignant and real, *One Dance in Paris* is one great read!"

—Jen Lancaster, author of *Bitter Is the New Black*

"Poignant, funny, bawdy, and glamorous all at once. I'd certainly book a ticket to Julia Holden's Paris."   —Zoe Rice, author of *Pick Me Up*

"A novel capturing the real Parisian *atmosphère* is a rarity worth noticing. Julie Holden's irresistible sense of humor and amused portrayal of us, the 'bizarre' French, make *One Dance in Paris* a perfect treat for all the Francophiles out there."   —F. G. Gerson, author of *21 Steps to Happiness*.

"Fast-paced and delightful, *One Dance in Paris* sparkles like the City of Light itself."   —Kristen Harmel, author of *The Blonde Theory*

A Dangerous Dress

"Watch out! Julia Holden is addictive. I couldn't put down this infectiously funny, oh-so-glam romantic novel!"

—Meg Cabot, author of the *Princess Diaries* series and *Queen of Babble*

"For anyone who understands the power of clothes, it's an appealing read."

—*The Kansas City Star*

continued...

Also by Julia Holden

A Dangerous Dress

One Dance in Paris

Julia Holden

New American Library

New American Library
Published by New American Library, a division of
Penguin Group (USA) Inc., 375 Hudson Street,
New York, New York 10014, USA
Penguin Group (Canada), 90 Eglinton Avenue East, Suite 700, Toronto,
Ontario M4P 2Y3, Canada (a division of Pearson Penguin Canada Inc.)
Penguin Books Ltd., 80 Strand, London WC2R 0RL, England
Penguin Ireland, 25 St. Stephen's Green, Dublin 2,
Ireland (a division of Penguin Books Ltd.)
Penguin Group (Australia), 250 Camberwell Road, Camberwell, Victoria 3124,
Australia (a division of Pearson Australia Group Pty. Ltd.)
Penguin Books India Pvt. Ltd., 11 Community Centre, Panchsheel Park,
New Delhi – 110 017, India
Penguin Group (NZ), 67 Apollo Drive, Mairangi Bay,
Auckland 1311, New Zealand (a division of Pearson New Zealand Ltd.)
Penguin Books (South Africa) (Pty.) Ltd., 24 Sturdee Avenue,
Rosebank, Johannesburg 2196, South Africa

Penguin Books Ltd., Registered Offices:
80 Strand, London WC2R 0RL, England

First published by New American Library,
a division of Penguin Group (USA) Inc.

First Printing, July 2007
10   9   8   7   6   5   4   3   2

REGISTERED TRADEMARK—MARCA REGISTRADA

LIBRARY OF CONGRESS CATALOGING-IN-PUBLICATION DATA:

Holden, Julia, 1959–
    One dance in Paris/Julia Holden.
        p.   cm.
    ISBN: 978-0-451-22080-6
        1. Young women—Fiction.   2. Americans—France—Paris—Fiction.   3. Showgirls—Fiction.
4. Dresses—Fiction.   5. Mothers and daughters—Fiction.   6. Paris (France)—Fiction.   7. Chick lit.
I. Title.
PS3608.O4832O54 2007
813'. 6—dc22   2007004856

Set in Granjon • Designed by Elke Sigal

Printed in the United States of America

PUBLISHER'S NOTE
This is a work of fiction. Names, characters, places, and incidents either are the product of the author's
imagination or are used fictitiously, and any resemblance to actual persons, living or dead, business establishments, events, or locales is entirely coincidental.
    The publisher does not have any control over and does not assume any responsibility for author or
third-party Web sites or their content.

For my mother

Acknowledgments

With profound thanks to my editor, Kara Cesare, for the wonderful collaborative process that led to this book; to my fabulous agent, Bill Contardi, for his faith and guidance; and to Carolyn, for her brilliant suggestion. To my dear Parisian inspirations, Fabrice and Brigitte, and, again, Françoise. To Laura, for reasons she doesn't understand, and, especially, to my Rachel, who inspires me most of all.

*S*ometimes, *the less you're wearing, the more you're hiding.*

That's one of the lessons I've recently learned. Here are a couple of the others:

Showgirls are not strippers. And, *A headliner is not a showgirl.*

The nakedness, showgirls and headliners are all coming. But before I could comprehend any of those things, I had to get out of Somerville, Massachusetts.

You already know Somerville; it's the run-down, beat-up town where Matt Damon and Ben Affleck lived in *Good Will Hunting.* Slumerville, as many of us natives call it. Scumerville.

Some may resent my perpetuating the unfortunate low-class reputation under which Somerville labors. The mayor's office will remind you that Somerville is a City on the Move, and that they've made great strides in Urban Revitalization. In fairness, they have. Just not on my block.

Maybe it's personal. Admittedly, I've done a few things over the years that might have alienated the powers that be in Somerville. But it would be awfully small-minded of them to withhold all that progress from an entire street on my account—so perhaps the blight that persists in my immediate vicinity is just a coincidence.

I've tried to give Somerville the benefit of the doubt. For instance, not long ago, the city opened a new dog park with considerable fanfare. Jack and I jogged over to the park, which was a very fine-looking place, and which made a very fine first impression on both of us.

Unfortunately, the second impression it made came in the form of an unleashed shar-pei with eczema who attempted to hump the living daylights out of poor Jack. Thanks a lot, Somerville.

Jack is our dog. He's a Jack Russell terrier, which my dad bought because he liked the dog on *Frazier*. My dad named him. Lest you think naming a Jack Russell terrier "Jack" was a clever postmodernist statement, it wasn't. It was purely lack of imagination.

My dad's name is Jack, too.

The shar-pei incident is fairly representative of what it's like to be one of us, as opposed to one of them. *Us* being people who grew up here, whose parents grew up here, whose children will probably grow up here, too. *Them* being the snooty big-money pseudo-intellectual brats who descend on us annually to take advantage of Somerville's cheap rents and proximity to the snooty big-money pseudo-intellectual institutions of higher learning that have us surrounded. Southeast is Boston University. Southwest is Boston College. Farther west is Brandeis. East is MIT, and North is Tufts.

And then there's Harvard.

Harvard hugs Somerville the way an Adams House freshman clings to his floozy rent-a-date on his big night out at the Hasty Pudding. In Somerville, we're constantly confronted by Harvard and its minions. They infest our rental properties, our Laundromats, our bars. They would infest our bedrooms, too, if we let them.

Living under constant siege from Harvard, Somerville girls have an unenviable choice: never date, become a collaborator, or subvert from within. Over the years, several of my classmates have attempted the latter, planning to play Mata Hari with the affections and grade point averages of the Ivy League boys. But Harvard is a powerful foe, and inevitably, sleeping with the enemy leads these girls to cross over to the dark side. Consequently, I've followed a hard and fast rule: I don't date Harvard guys. Ever.

Nonetheless, although I hate to admit it, we need Harvard—at least, we need Harvard Square, which wouldn't exist without Harvard. We depend upon it for our pizza and our ice cream. For our black-and-white movies at the beloved Brattle Theatre. And, maybe most of all, we rely on Harvard Square for our jobs.

Harvard Square is like a giant outdoor red-brick shopping mall. It has Gap, Abercrombie & Fitch, Urban Outfitters, Talbots, Ann Taylor, Express, EMS, HMV, CVS, Starbucks, Au Bon Pain and Baskin Robbins, not to mention countless wireless stores, banks, stationers, bookstores, restaurants, cafés, bars, and everything else you can think of. In other words, it offers a never-ending supply of sub-minimum wage jobs requiring no skills whatsoever, making it the perfect environment for someone with no college degree, poor interpersonal skills, and a bad attitude in general. Namely, me.

Harvard Square also has the advantage of being within walking distance of Somerville. For me, that's not just an advantage, it's a necessity, as I don't possess a valid Massachusetts driver's license. I used to have one. Sure, I've been caught speeding on the Mass Pike a few times, and yes, I was clocked going 98 on the last occasion. Possibly my blood alcohol was a little high the night I drove home from the Plough & Stars and was pulled over by Officer Heggarty, who cut me no slack whatsoever despite the fact that I was coming from a good Irish bar. Still, I managed to keep my license until last fall, when I had that unfortunate misunderstanding about the man's car.

I was going to give it back. Really, I was.

To understand the misunderstanding, you must know something about me.

I am tall.

Very tall.

My passport says I'm six feet tall. More precisely, I'm six feet and five-eighths of an inch tall. But the only people who add fractions of an inch to their height are those who wish they were taller. I'm not one of those.

I got the passport after my driver's license was yanked, because I needed an alternate form of ID. I'm not smiling in my passport photo. I wasn't smiling in my driver's license photo, either. I don't smile for photos. Pretty girls smile for photos; the rest of us, why bother?

Not that I'm hideous or anything. In fact, I suppose if you break my features down one by one, everything sounds passable. I have dark hair, almost black, shoulder length, not incredibly thick but thick enough. I have big eyes that are also almost black, and my eyebrows are fine without tweezer or wax. My cheekbones are even a little on the high side. Then again, my eyelashes, nose and lips are all pretty average, and my skin is downright pale. I have a long neck—at my height, what did you expect?—and narrow shoulders. *Narrow* is actually a good word for the rest of me. Also *gawky, gangly* and just plain *skinny*.

In fairness to my body, it does have curves. They're a little hard to see, though, stretched out over so much vertical space. By any measure accepted in American popular culture, my boobs are too small, although at least they have the virtue of being nicely shaped. I have narrow shoulders, a narrow waist, narrow hips. No butt to speak of. My arms, hands and fingers are long and skinny. A kinder word might be *slender*, but like the umpires at Fenway, I calls 'em the way I sees 'em. Skinny.

My legs are very long, and, I suppose, are not half bad. Probably owing to all the running I do. I've run ever since the seventh grade. I never ran track, though. It's bad form to cut class and then show up for track practice. In any event, throughout my high school years I was much more interested in drinking and smoking. Both of which I've given up, except for the drinking. And why attend class or run laps when I could be letting the air out of the tires on the expensive cars belonging to the expensive Harvard kids who were invading my neighborhood?

I wasn't interested in running for the discipline, and certain not for the glory. I just liked to run. Still do. But not around a track. My routes are determined by the randomness of traffic lights; whichever way the light is green when I reach the corner, that's the way I go. It's a lovely directionlessness, and it takes me away from every lousy aspect of my lousy life.

When I started running, I wore whatever cheap sneakers my dad brought home for me. Nowadays I favor New Balance running shoes, which are made in Massachusetts. They're very reasonably priced, particularly given the way I shop. I run to the nearest New Balance outlet and trade in my old pair for a new one. They don't actually take trade-ins, but silly outlet stores leave the boxes out for you to pick what you want, and don't have employees bring you the shoes. As long as I can find a pair that fits, I lace up the new ones, leave my old pair in the box, and off I go. Trade-in. They've never complained, which is another way of saying they haven't caught me doing it yet.

Finding running shoes in my size, or any shoes for that matter, was next to impossible until I reconciled myself to buying men's shoes. My feet are big. Bigger than big. Size 11 big. Like the rest of me. Too big. Too long. Too tall.

I can pinpoint precisely when I started running. I was thirteen

years old, and in seventh grade. After school, twice a week, I took ballet class. Notwithstanding that I'm the first to admit my lack of apti-
tude for just about everything, I was actually quite good at it. Only
then came the day that the head of the ballet school, Miss Lynch,
would not let me put on toe shoes. All the girls in my class were about
to start wearing toe shoes, which is a crucial milestone at which little
girls enter the painful but exquisite grown-up world of real ballet.
Without putting on toe shoes and learning to dance on pointe, a girl
can't do virtually any of the glorious things the world associates with
the word *ballerina*.

My dad had paid for the shoes, which weren't cheap. But the day
everyone else in class received their toe shoes, Miss Lynch handed me
back the money and sent me home with a note. Here is what it said,
in its entirety:

Linda has grown too tall for ballet.

At age thirteen I was already five foot eight. In toe shoes, you get
up on the very front of your toes. Doing so probably would have added
another six inches. I would've dwarfed my classmates, towered over
any potential partner, loomed over my instructor. Miss Lynch didn't
know what to do with a girl my height, so she sentenced me: *too tall for
ballet*. And sent me home, never to dance again.

No wonder I ran.

Now you know enough to understand the misunderstanding about
the man's car.

I was working as a waitress at Casa B's, which is my favorite restaurant in Harvard Square. Its real name is Casablanca. I can't afford to eat there, but if I could, that's where I would eat. It's also my favorite because the Brattle Theatre is right upstairs.

I am not a skilled waitress. I'm the first to admit it. I confuse orders. I get distracted eavesdropping on the Harvard senior boys trying to talk their way into the pants of the freshman girls, and I forget to pick up and serve orders when they're ready.

So, had the man at table fourteen left me no tip, or told me I was a lousy waitress, or even tried to get me fired—all of which have happened to me more times than I can count—I would have given him back his keys. But that's not what happened.

He was a grad student. At the *Divinity* School, of all places. He also wore a bad toupee, which has nothing to do with the incident but which I take delight in telling you. He and his other Divinity friends had been at table fourteen for almost four hours. They finished their food in the first hour, and his friends stopped ordering drinks after the second. The toupee kept drinking, though—Cosmopolitans, no less—while he and his friends had a vacuous discussion of the theological underpinnings for America's refusal to sign the Kyoto Accords on global warming. I kid you not.

They were still yapping at closing time. Past closing time. The rest of the staff started putting chairs up on the tables and vacuuming around number fourteen, trying to get the three Divinities to take the hint. Nothing. Finally my colleagues ganged up on me. Because it was my table, it was my responsibility to get them to leave so we could turn out the lights and call it a night.

"Time to pay up and go home, fellas," I announced.

Toupee turned and looked up at me. And up and up. He swayed a little in his seat. "Listen, Stretch," he finally began.

Incidentally, why do people uniformly feel at liberty to call attention to a tall person's height? Toupee was drunk, and an idiot to boot—but sober and otherwise intelligent people do this all the time. Respectable middle-aged librarians who would never dream of calling someone *fat* or *ugly* or *short* to their face have no qualms whatsoever about saying *Goodness, you're a tall one.*

I ignored Toupee and looked imploringly at his friends. "It's way past closing. Time to go home."

Toupee stood up. He was a short man. Maybe five foot four. He tried to look me in the eye, but I could see that doing so hurt his neck. Instead, he settled on staring at my chest, such as it is. "Sure," he slurred. "Let's go home. You and me, Stretch. I'll give you something to wrap those long legs around."

I didn't hit him. You'd think the police would've counted that in my favor.

"Get out," I said.

His friends paid the bill and hustled him out. They left me a dollar tip on a ninety-four buck tab.

A dollar, and the keys to Toupee's Volvo.

There they were, on the seat where he'd been parking his brains. I picked them up and put them in my pocket. Had Toupee or his friends come back for them, I would've handed them over. But they never came. Presumably, the friends assessed his inebriation and drove him home. Or maybe he slept in the gutter. Either way, we finished cleaning the place, turned out the lights, locked the doors, and the keys were still dancing in my pocket.

He called me *Stretch*. Twice. And then there was that crass bit about my *long legs*.

When I got to the street, the Divinities were nowhere to be seen.

I took the keys out of my pocket and pushed the *unlock* button. The parking lights on a late-model Volvo S40 blinked twice. The car cost more than I make in a year. More than I've ever made, in any year. In any two years.

I could've walked home.

Stretch.

I will say this: there's plenty of leg room in a Volvo S40. Even for a girl who is six feet and five-eighths inches tall.

rdinarily, I sleep in. Whenever my current unskilled sub-minimum wage job involves working the late shift, which is frequently, I have nowhere to go in the mornings. When I'm unemployed, which is also frequently, again, I have nowhere to go in the mornings. Either way, I sleep.

Jack sleeps in, too. My dad, not the dog. He spent his entire working life as an engineer on the T, shuttling commuters from Quincy Center to Harvard Square and back again, then from Alewife to Braintree and back when they expanded the line in the '80s. To and fro, hither and yon, there and back again and again and again, the same closed loop of train tracks for over thirty years. The endless repetition would've driven some men crazy, but not Jack. My dad is the steady type. A plodder, actually. Dull. Going around in circles and never getting anywhere didn't bother him a bit. At worst, all those years of rumble and squeal made Jack a little deaf. Ever the optimist, he chose to view that minor impairment as a plus: it helped him sleep, which he figured he'd earned after three decades on the early shift.

When Jack—my dad—retired last year, Jack—the dog—barked him awake before dawn every morning for the first two weeks. Although my dad is fundamentally a lazy man, he finally caved and installed a doggy door. It was either that or bloodshed. So now, every morning at five sharp, the dog pops out his little door, squirts all over every shrub he can kill in our tiny little backyard, hops back inside, and doesn't wake up again until one of the humans does. Some days we all sleep until noon.

The Somerville Police, however, obviously do not sleep until noon. Not Toupee, either. By six a.m., the Volvo had already been reported stolen, *and* been found, *and* every Dunkin' Donuts for miles around must have been empty, because what looked like a whole battalion of bad-natured cops had my house surrounded. I doubt that many troops were required to capture Saddam Hussein.

Between my dad's tinnitus and the dog's empty bladder, neither one budged when Officer Hardy pounded on the door.

Fortunately, court opens early in Somerville, and even more fortunately, I landed in front of Judge Hastings. Judge Ames is a by-the-book hardass, and Judge Griswold is just a cranky old bastard. Neither of them would have been happy to see me again, and either would've thrown a whole law library of books at me.

Have I mentioned that this was not my first trip to court?

The bailiff called my case. "People of the Commonwealth of Massachusetts against Linda Stone."

I looked up at Judge Hastings. Unlike Ames and Griswold, I could handle Hastings. Because she is a woman. From experience, I knew that all I had to do was trot out my standard line about my mother, and she would pack me off with a sympathetic smile and six hours of community service.

"I'm not buying that line about your mother."

Uh-oh.

"It's not a line," I said. "It's the absolute truth."

"I know it's true. I've read your file." She lifted a folder and hefted it. It was even thicker than I remembered. "One time too many." She dropped the folder, and it landed with a *splat* on the bench. "You can't use that as an excuse for the rest of your life."

Maybe not, but up to this moment, it had worked just fine, thank you very much.

"I know," I said sheepishly. Anyway I hoped it was sheepishly. But I guess I don't do sheepishly very well. What with all the speeding violations, and that DUI thing, which I could *swear* Officer Heggarty said wouldn't appear on my record, and now the unfortunate little incident involving Toupee's Volvo, which I refuse to think of as *grand theft auto* no matter what that prosecutor said, because there was nothing grand about it, I only drove the car a half-mile home, and besides, it was hardly theft, more like a very short-term loan—what with all of that, Judge Hastings simply wasn't interested in my poor pathetic motherless child routine anymore. She lifted my license for a year, *and* sentenced me to thirty days of community service, *and* ordered me to pay a five hundred dollar fine.

I almost asked her if she knew where I could steal five hundred dollars. Almost, but not quite.

What can you say about a twenty-five-year-old girl whose mother died?

In case you don't know, that is an allusion to *Love Story*. Which I don't recommend, even though it, too, is the story of a townie-girl in the neighborhood of Harvard who comes from an environment not entirely unlike mine. I don't recommend it because it's sappy and sentimental, and I am neither. In case you couldn't tell. Besides, in that book, the *girl* died. Here, the girl—me—is just fine, thank you very much. It's my mother who died. Not to mention that I'm twenty-six, not twenty-five.

I don't remember her. She died before I turned two. Cervical cancer. She was tall, too. She must have been, because Jack is only five foot six, and he wears size eight shoes. I must've gotten the height, and these big old feet, from someplace. I guess someplace was Maggie. Jack has only two photos of her, or at least he has only shown me two. One of them is fuzzy, and the other is half obscured by a lovely rendition of Jack's fingertip. The fuzzy picture is of the two of them. Even sitting down, she is visibly taller than Jack. In the fingertip shot, she is conspicuously pregnant: a long telephone pole of a woman with what looks like a bowling ball stuffed under her shirt. I guess I was the bowling ball. So the photo is proof. I am her daughter. She was my mother.

Maggie Stone. Margaret, if you want to be technical.

That's about it.

All I know, I mean. About her. Not that I have ever been that curious.

I suppose I asked questions once or twice. But I gave that up pretty quick. Either Jack wasn't telling what he knew, or he genuinely knew virtually nothing about the woman he had married.

"She just showed up one day."

"Where?"

"The park."

"Which park?"

"Prospect Hill."

"What were you doing in the park?"

"Sitting."

"What was she doing?"

"Walking."

Incidentally, because Jack is hard of hearing, we tend to shout at one another. So, to the uninitiated, this conversation would have sounded like an argument. In fact, we argue plenty, but not this time.

"Where did she come from?"

"No idea."

"Didn't you ask?"

"Nope."

"Why not?"

"She didn't want me to."

"Did she tell you that?"

"Nope."

"So how did you know?"

"I knew."

That's it. Tall Maggie Stone shows up in Somerville, Massachusetts on a cold day in March. The year is 1979, and Maggie is thirty-seven years old. Where she came from, Jack doesn't know. What she did before, Jack doesn't know. What they talked about that first day in Prospect Hill Park, or any other time for that matter, Jack doesn't recall, or won't say. All I can tell you is that within three months they were married, a year later I was born, and before my second birthday she was dead.

"One more thing."

"What?"

"I loved her," Jack shouted.

He did. I can see that. "Did she love you?"

My dad is not an introspective man, but he thought about that for at least four or five seconds. "I think so," he concluded. "I hope so."

"Did she love me?" The words surprised me. I hadn't formed that question in my head; it just asked itself.

"Of course she did." For an instant, Jack's expression was the saddest I had ever seen. Then he turned angry. "Why would you ask that?"

I just shrugged my skinny shoulders—her skinny shoulders, I suppose—and turned and walked away. In my room, I pulled off my sweats, tugged on a pair of running shorts and a ratty old Red Sox T-shirt, laced up my latest New Balance trade-ins, then headed for the front door. There's a nine-step stoop in front of our house, but going down, I took it in three, three steps at a time. Long legs, and years of practice. By the time my foot hit the pavement I was already running, on my way to wherever the traffic lights would take me, to nowhere. I remember it was chilly that day, with a little mist falling, classic New England weather. I was cold in just a T-shirt and shorts, and the cold felt good. I picked up the pace and the blood started to pump in my ears. Not loud enough to drown out the echo of Jack's question, though. "Why would you ask that?"

Because she left me. That's why.

I admit it, you caught me in an introspective moment there. But don't get any wrong ideas. I've had maybe three introspective moments in my entire life.

Until that package showed up and changed, well, everything.

The package came on a Wednesday. It hadn't arrived by four thirty in the afternoon, because I would've seen it on my way out the door to work. My latest dead-end job was doing an unskilled impersonation of a waitress for the five-to-closing shift at the Crew Bar on Kennedy Street. The Crew attracts underage undergrads from Eliot and Kirkland Houses, which are right next door, and CEO wannabees from the Business School, which is just across the Charles River. The bar is directly opposite the Kennedy School of Government, but I've never seen anybody there from the K-School. I guess they're too busy figuring out how to save the world, or overthrow it, to drink pints of Sam Adams and get sloppy obnoxious drunk. Which is what the B-School guys and the college kids do, routinely.

If you just looked in the window, you'd be convinced the Crew is a gay bar, because the entire clientele is always one hundred percent male; the waitresses are the only estrogen in the joint. Sadly, though, the crowd seems to be overwhelmingly heterosexual. Not that I have anything against straight men. In fact, every person I've ever had sex with was a straight man. My problem with the drunkards at the Crew is not their sexuality, but their juvenility. If that's a word. We are talking about a population whose collective idea of flirting is to grope your ass. *My* ass.

On top of which they are abysmal tippers.

Pretty much the only thing that made the place bearable was the bartender. Kyle is from Somerville, too, but from the Tufts side, whereas I'm from the Harvard side. He's not a smart guy, but at least he's honest about that, unlike the phony brainiacs who fill the bar, and Cambridge in general. The scar over Kyle's right eye from the bar fight I started in Braintree gives him a rugged Harrison Ford kind of look, before Harrison Ford got old and creepy with Ally McBeal. Kyle and I used to date. To be slightly more accurate, we used to have sex together, whenever it was mutually convenient. We don't date anymore, or have sex, either. But he's still a pretty good guy, nice enough to look at, way more tolerable than the Harvards, and, big plus, he's as tall as I am.

Let's be clear: I don't discriminate on the basis of height. When it comes to dating and relationships, I am an equal opportunity destroyer. I have ruined relationships with boys and men of every height. But it's a relief to be able to look a guy in the eye.

Mostly, I think the problem is mental—and it's in the guys' heads, not mine. Men don't know how to be shorter. It makes them feel inadequate. To the point where it actually hurts their sexual performance. Which, between us girls, is a real drag. If I could find a shorter man who was self-confident enough to maintain an erection, trust me, I'd keep him.

Some tall girls try to compensate by slouching, which annoys the piss out of me. You're still tall, sweetheart, now you're just tall with bad posture. I may not like who I am, but at least I stand up straight.

Around ten p.m., Kyle waved me over. "You busy tonight?" he asked. Which I know from experience is Kyle's way of saying he'd really like a blow job. Lately he'd been sleeping with Jenny Oliver, whom I went to junior high school with and who's been a slut even before she knew what sex was, but I guess they were on a break. Or maybe Kyle was on a break and just hadn't bothered to tell Jenny. He did his best to flash a killer smile, but his parents were Puritan Revivalists who believed braces were the devil's work and consequently his smile was not Kyle's best feature.

"Busy."

"Doing what?" He had to shout over the barroom din. I wondered if a lifetime of pulling pints would leave Kyle with hearing loss, the way the trains had done to Jack. Men need to find quieter jobs.

I looked around. "Working."

"Coulda fooled me." Kyle looked at me, I looked at him, and in that instant he knew to a certainty that Mr. Big was on his own tonight. He shrugged and went back to making drinks.

Incidentally, why do men name their penises? And under what delusions are they laboring when assigning the names? Because notwithstanding that Kyle was at least my height, a more accurate moniker would've been Mr. Slightly Smaller Than Average. In fairness, he knows how to use it—but let's call it what it is, and let's not call it what it's not.

The bar may have been jammed at ten o'clock, but by midnight the place had emptied. It was early May, and final exams were only weeks away. To a Harvard boy, drinking is like having a mistress: he enjoys his night out, but he knows he's going to be married to his grades for the rest of his life. By twelve thirty, Kyle turned out the lights and locked the door. I could feel him turn in my direction for one more try, but I was already heading down the block and away from him. I waved over my shoulder and kept walking.

Some nights I run home, just because, but that night I strolled. The weather was lovely—as good as New England gets, in that sweet blink of spring that every so often manages to wedge itself between the long cold wet winter and the long hot sticky summer. Usually I avoid Harvard Yard on principle, but this time I walked through, confident that the undergrads would be either cramming or sleeping and that I would have the quad to myself. As I walked past the statue of John Harvard, I gave him a lecherous wink. Years ago, one grossly inebriated night in my late teens, I sat on his face. Harvard Security was not amused. Although I suspect old John quite enjoyed himself.

Anyway he didn't complain. And he did have stamina, which I admire in a man.

By the time my saunter ended at our front stoop, it was one a.m. I bounded up the steps. When I reached the top, it jabbed me in the stomach. The package. It was long and flat, and the mailman had shoved one end of it into our mail slot and left the rest of it sticking out like a nasty child's tongue.

I yanked the parcel out of the slot, unlocked the door and then slammed it behind me. Neither Jack nor Jack stirred. I turned on the foyer light.

The package was two-and-a-half feet long, about ten inches wide, and two inches thick, but it weighed almost nothing, as if someone had mailed an empty box. It was wrapped in brown paper, and every millimeter of seam was meticulously sealed with Scotch tape. It was addressed to me, in a large, loopy, extravagant handwriting I'd never seen. For just an instant, I had the insane thought that it was from my mother. But my mother was dead. The thought went away.

I looked at the return address. It said:

> *D. Belle*
> *7 Josephine Lane*
> *Las Vegas, Nev. 89109*

I didn't know anyone named *D. Belle*. I didn't know anyone in Las Vegas. I had never known anyone in Las Vegas, never been to Las Vegas, never even *thought* about going to Las Vegas.

I hurtled upstairs and turned on the light in Jack's room. From under the covers, Jack growled at me. The dog, not my dad. How the dog breathes under there, particularly given what sometimes comes out of my dad, I'll never know.

"Shut up, Jack," I said to the dog. "Wake up, Jack," I said to my dad.

He turned toward me and opened one eye. "What."

"Who is D. Belle?"

"What."

"Who do we know in Las Vegas?"

"What."

"Who in Las Vegas knows me??"

"Oh." Jack closed his eye. He had never really woken at all, and now, despite the bright light and my hollering, he was instantly and fully asleep.

Leaving me to open the package all by myself.

*D*on't ask me why the package intimidated me, but it did.

Imagine that you grew up and spent every moment of your whole life in a plain gray box, with nothing to do, no one to see, nowhere to go. Then one day, without warning, there's an earthquake, and one side of your plain gray box splits open. Right outside is a lush green valley, the sky is brilliant blue, incredible birds of every imaginable color sing songs of such stunning beauty that somewhere nearby, angels are weeping. Is your first reaction *Ooh, ahh, how wonderful?*

No way. Your first reaction is *fear.* Followed closely by *What the fuck is that?*

Somehow, holding that weightless package in my hands—which, I kid you not, were trembling—I could feel the earthquake coming.

I walked to my room, turned on the light, and sat down on the bed. Instead of ripping off the brown paper wrapping immediately, I looked around the room. It was a lot like me, which is to say nondescript. The only thing on the walls was the faded Red Sox pennant Jack hung there before I was born. My closet door was open, and the clothes inside were plain and formless: skinny boy jeans, tanks and Ts and sweatshirts, whatever my Harvard Square short-term employers had left over that would vaguely fit me. I've never cared about clothes, never wanted to wear anything fancy or even nice. Pretty clothes are for pretty girls.

In part, I surveyed the room because I wanted to remember it— as if I already understood that everything was about to change. Also, though, I was buying time. Time to get over my fear.

Finally I opened the package. It wasn't easy, between my shaking hands and that hermetically sealed Scotch-tape job. Finally I dug out a jackknife, slit the brown paper and removed the box inside. There was a thumb slot on one side, and the lid of the box opened like a long narrow door. Carefully, I opened the cardboard door.

Inside was . . . a feather. A long, perfect peacock feather. I picked it up and turned it in my hands. In the harsh light, it glistened blue and purple and green and gold; it was probably the most colorful object that had ever been in my room. It was beautiful. For quite some time, I just looked at it, captivated by its iridescence. Honestly, it probably took a full five minutes before the thought occurred to me:

Somebody sent me a *feather*?

I looked again in the box, and saw what I had initially missed: a small envelope taped to the side. I removed the envelope. It wasn't sealed, but still I held it up to the light in an effort to discover its contents before I actually opened it. All I saw was the silhouette of something about three inches square. I took the something out of the envelope.

It was a photograph. A snapshot, really, because "photograph" sounds posed and professional, and this was neither. It was black and white, and it had a scalloped white border. It was a little out of focus, probably taken with a cheap camera or by a poor photographer, maybe both. I suppose such a bad picture should not make your heart skip a beat, but the instant I looked at the image, that's what mine did. BUMP-bump. BUMP-bump. BUMP . . . ba-DUM-bum-bum.

The photo depicted two young women, girls really, maybe eighteen years old, if I had to guess. They were leaning against a car, an old Chevy, and you could tell from how high their hips hit the car that both of them were tall. Extremely tall. Leggy, too. One wore a halter top and shorts, and at the end of her long legs her big feet were encased in white canvas sneakers. Her hair was pulled back in a ponytail, and her face was almost but not quite pretty. I did not recognize her, and she isn't the one who made my heart stumble.

The other girl sported an enormously tall headdress constructed of rhinestones and peacock feathers. Her feet, even larger than her friend's, still looked delicate in beautiful, glittering high-heeled sandals. She wore a dress unlike anything I had ever seen. It was barely a garment at all, composed almost entirely of narrow bejeweled straps and strategically placed feathers. There was more bare skin than dress—lots more—but the dress itself was hypnotic; I could barely tear my eyes away from it to study the rest of the picture. The girl wearing the sparkling miracle of a dress was pointing her right arm at something out of the frame to her left, and both girls were looking in the direction of her pointing hand. Because her arm crossed in front of her torso, I couldn't be sure, but it appeared the dress did not cover the young woman's breasts.

I studied the dress again. It was beautiful and shocking, simultaneously sexual and like something out of a fairy tale. It transformed the girl wearing it into something more than human—an unimaginably tall, slender, exotic goddess. My breath was literally taken away. Briefly, ridiculously, I wondered what it would be like to wear such a dress. Then I looked at the girl's face, and I forgot about the dress.

Although I couldn't be sure because of the headdress and because the photo was in black and white, it appeared that her hair was dark, perhaps black. She had big dark eyes, and perfect eyebrows. Her cheekbones were a little on the high side. Her lashes, nose and lips were pretty average. Her skin was pale, much paler than the other girl's. And her head, adorned by that huge peacock crown, rested on a long, slender neck.

Which is to say, she looked like me. Not a little like me. Not sort of like me. She looked *like me*. Or, put another way, I looked *like her*.

I wondered if there was any caption or inscription on the snapshot. I turned it over. On the back, printed diagonally, was a date: JULY 1960. I did the math. Assuming the girl in the picture was eighteen, she would have been born in 1942.

Jack, my dad, met Maggie, my mom, in 1979. According to Jack, she was thirty-seven when they met. Meaning she was born in 1942.

It was a tiny snapshot, taken from a distance, slightly out of focus. And it had come from a total stranger in a strange land. But in that instant, I knew.

I was looking at my mother.

*Y*ou might assume I immediately woke my dad and confronted him with this incredible discovery. You would be wrong.

First, there was no point. I had already tried, to no effect, which confirmed that Jack and Jack were in their Sleep Zone. The Boston Pops could be blaring the 1812 Overture outside our windows, but if Jack and Jack were in the Zone, even the live cannons wouldn't wake them.

Second, I didn't want to be disturbed. I wanted to spend some time alone with my mother.

Not that I was *completely* sure it was Maggie. I had never seen a picture of her so young, had only ever seen the two photos Jack showed me, and had no memory of her at all from my infancy. Plus, as I've said, the quality of the snapshot was far from perfect. But the girl in the daring not-quite-a-dress looked *like me*. And besides, why would some total stranger have sent this mysterious package to me if the impossibly tall creature in the picture *wasn't* my mother?

On the assumption the girl was Maggie, I wanted us to have some quiet time.

I picked up the peacock feather again. It had undoubtedly come from that glorious headdress—because again, if it hadn't, why send it to me? Holding the feather, turning it slightly and seeing it glow in the light of my room, brought the girl in the photo to life, made her almost as real as if she had been standing there in front of me.

Growing up without a mother was . . . well, I can't exactly say it was hard, because it was all I ever knew. It was what it was. But what it was sucked. I'd like to tell you that Jack did a perfect job, that he took over and filled the roles of both father and mother with enough love and support for two parents, just like all those movie widower dads do. Only he didn't. He wasn't all that wonderfully qualified to be even one parent, much less two; by temperament, he was always much more of a Jack than a dad. If he was only fair to poor as a father, you can well imagine that as a mother, he was nonexistent.

I sat looking at the snapshot for a very long time. Hours. Finally I addressed my mother for the first time.

"I hope you die," I said.

Before you go thinking how harsh and awful that was, remember, it wasn't like I could bring bad luck on her. In fact, I was fully aware how stupid my statement was, given that she was already dead. It's a lot like the second time I saw *Love Story* at the Brattle Theatre. No sooner did Ali MacGraw start giving Ryan O'Neal that smart-ass poor girl superior attitude than I said, right out loud, "I hope you die." I swear, everyone in the theater turned around and stared at me like I was Satan or Bill Buckner. As if my saying it was going to kill her. But hello, people, *she was already dead*. She was dead the moment Erich Segal wrote her dead. And she stayed dead the first time I saw the movie. So I knew I wasn't doing her any harm by saying it. Not to mention that she was a fictional character.

Well, Maggie was already dead, too. And as far as I was concerned, she might as well have been a fictional character. Other than giving birth to me, and saddling me with her embarrassingly tall skinny genes, she had played no more real a role in my life than Jennifer Cavalleri. Which is the name of Ali MacGraw's character in *Love Story*.

Where was Maggie when my classmates tormented me for being not just the tallest girl, but the tallest kid, in the second grade? And the third, and fourth, and fifth?

Where was Maggie when I got my period at age twelve and Jack's only advice was to ask Bridget O'Reilly, the obnoxious fourteen-year-old who lived next door, and who told me I was going to bleed to death?

Where was Maggie when Miss Lynch kicked me out of dance class because I was too tall?

She was nowhere. Gone. As if she had never existed. Those times, and the million other times a girl needs her mother.

Over the years, I had wondered from time to time what she had been and done all those years before she inexplicably stumbled upon Jack in Prospect Hill Park in Somerville, Massachusetts, on a cold March day in 1979. I imagined she might have been a tall lonely manicurist. Or a tall lonely cafeteria worker. Or a tall lonely person who puts the paper wrappers around Crayola crayons. Perhaps she'd been assigned to Burnt Sienna and Raw Umber, which seemed like tall lonely colors to me. In any event, whatever she had done, I was always sure she'd been lonely. Because why else come to Somerville at age thirty-seven? And why, in a whole world full of men, pick Jack?

Now, suddenly, I was confronted with hard evidence that once upon a time she apparently lived some exotic, glamorous, *pretty* existence. Let's face it. Boring ordinary girls don't wear peacock headdresses, or gorgeous glittery stilettos, or decadent dresses made of rhinestones and feathers and almost nothing else. So she hadn't been ordinary after all. She hadn't wrapped crayons. She probably hadn't even been lonely.

Which made it all so much worse. She had actually figured out how to look like me and still lead a fabulous life—which is just the kind of critical information a very tall girl desperately needs to learn from her very tall mother. Instead she left me.

She should've found some way to stick around. She should've tried harder. *I* would've tried harder.

At some point, I dozed off. Being angry at your dead mother is exhausting, and it's hard to maintain intense anger for long stretches, especially when you've already been angry for your entire life.

When I opened my eyes, it was ten thirty. For a few seconds, I was afraid I might have crushed the feather or creased the photo in my sleep, but apparently before I nodded, I'd had the good sense to put them on my desk, out of harm's way.

I heard the toilet flush. The dog was smart, but not that smart, so I knew my dad was awake. I grabbed the two artifacts and headed for the kitchen.

Sure enough, there was Jack, in his boxers and ratty bathrobe. I've bought him new bathrobes but he won't wear them. I don't know why. I tell him that even if he doesn't care what he looks like, at least he could wear something decent out of respect for me and the dog. I guess he doesn't respect me and the dog, because he still wears that shredded holey mess.

I thrust the snapshot in front of his nose. "Who is this?"

I was blocking his view of the *Globe* sports page. He waited to see if I'd relent, but when I didn't budge, he put down the paper with a sigh that sounded more than a little like a belch. He pinched a corner of the photo between his thumb and index finger, drew the picture up close to his nose, then held it at arm's length, pulled it close again, pushed it away, until he found a distance somewhere in the middle at which his eyes would focus. He squinted. Sniffed. Huffed.

"Well?"

He handed the snapshot back. His expression looked pained. "Sure looks like Maggie, don't it?"

"I wouldn't know. I never met her."

"Sure you did. You just pretend you don't remember."

"I don't remember."

"Sure you do."

"Is that her?"

"Looks like her, don't it?"

"Aren't you sure?"

"Course not."

I very nearly hit him. "Why not?"

Again, he picked up the photo by its corner. He turned it over. "Yep. July 1960. She'd have been . . ."

"Eighteen." If I'd waited for Jack, we'd have sat there all day. Math is not his strong suit.

"Exactly. Eighteen. I didn't even meet her 'til she was thirty-seven. So between this picture and then was . . ."

"Nineteen years."

"Exactly. So is that Maggie or not, I'd just be guessing."

"Guess."

He looked at the image again. "I'm guessing it's her."

"What's she wearing?"

"Not much."

"I can see that. I mean why is she wearing it?"

"Beats me. I wasn't there."

"Didn't she ever say *anything* about her past that you never understood, only now that you see this picture, it finally makes sense?"

He didn't even hesitate. "Nope."

"What *did* she tell you about her past?"

"Nothin'."

Now Jack and I were back to our old useless Q-and-A.

"Didn't you ask?"

"Nope."

"Why not?"

"I assumed she lived a life all those years before she met me. If she wanted me to know, she'd have told me. She didn't tell. I didn't ask."

"But why?"

He shrugged and, I'm genuinely sorry to say, farted. The dog, who had been under Jack's chair, ran for cover. "I didn't care. I had her. She had me. What else did I need to know?"

I snatched the picture and the feather back and stomped away.

"Hey," Jack called after me.

I stopped. "What?"

"Sure looks like she had fun, don't it?"

showered, put on reasonably clean clothes, slipped the snapshot back into its envelope, jotted D. Belle's address on the envelope, sealed the envelope inside a Ziploc bag just in case the weather turned to rain, as the New England weather inevitably does, and headed out. My first stop was an easy jog, the public library on Highland Avenue. Even though I never went to college, I'm a big fan of libraries. I especially like sneaking into the fancy Harvard libraries; I've been doing it since I was ten years old. But the public library has free Internet access, so that's where I went.

Generally speaking, I have precious little use for the Internet. I don't see the allure of spending endless hours on MySpace convincing a hundred and fifty million people I've never met to call me their friend. I have better, more productive things to do with my time. Like, for instance, sleep. Drink. Pee. Pretty much anything seems more valuable. So, needless to say, I am not wired at home. Every so often, though, all those zeros and ones come in handy. The Internet let me confirm in only a few minutes that there is no such address as 7 Josephine Lane in Las Vegas, Nevada. There is no Josephine Lane at all. Nor is there a D. Belle. There are four Belles: two Ps, an R and a T. But no Ds.

Maybe I should've been discouraged. I wasn't, though. Because *someone* had sent me that package.

My next stop was the Kinko's in Harvard Square. The place was crammed with overwrought Harvard freshmen copying term papers, but Paul Favorino let me go ahead of them. I went to junior high school with Paul, who's the assistant manager at the Kinko's. As I recall, I let him feel me up when we were both fourteen. It was a much bigger deal for him than it was for me—although honestly, considering how flat-chested I was at fourteen, what he got out of it besides bragging rights, I'll never know. Be that as it may, Paul has always had a soft spot for me. When the bratty Harvards complained, Paul told them I was a Lifetime Priority Customer, and besides, if they didn't shut their whining, maybe he'd discover that that file on Chthonian Domination and Cross-Dressing in Aeschylus was hopelessly corrupted. Before some smartass could search Kinko's web site on his BlackBerry and discover there's no such thing as a Lifetime Priority Customer, Paul took my photo to a scanner, and in no time my three-by-three snapshot was a blurry ten-by-ten—which, miraculously, with a few taps on Paul's keyboard, sharpened before my eyes.

He printed out the enlarged and enhanced picture and waved it to dry. Before handing it to me, he looked at the image, then at my face. His brow furrowed. "This you?"

"Like I would wear *that*," I sneered.

"A man can dream," Paul said.

I pulled out the original snapshot and showed him the back. "Nineteen sixty."

He looked at the girl in the picture again, and shook his head. "Weird."

"Yeah." He handed me the enlargement. "What do I owe you?"

"On the house."

I'd been hoping he'd say that. "You're the best."

"You never got to find out."

I gave Paul a tiny little kiss on the lips. Not romantic or sexy; a thank-you kiss. "You're not my type," I told Paul, smiling.

"I guess not," he admitted. He probably figured I meant because I'm six inches taller than he is. More like because he's a nice guy who never lied to me, condescended to me, or cheated on me. Given how many guys I've picked who have done all three, I should be betting the trifecta at Suffolk Downs.

I jogged back to the public library. In the enlarged, sharpened photograph, I could make out details I had missed in the little snapshot. For example, in the corner of the photo, in the distance, there was an odd structure. It looked kind of like a big tall concrete tulip, out of the top of which was growing a smaller concrete tulip—and perched on top of the littler tulip was a sign. Most of the sign was cut off, but what I could see looked like TROP.

I got back on the Internet. Okay, I admit it. I may not need all those MySpace friends. Or any of them, for that matter. But for once technology came in handy. I Googled *Las Vegas* and *1960* and *TROP*, and I found it immediately. I was looking at the Tropicana Hotel and Casino. I clicked on a couple of the search results, and there it was. In the vintage nighttime images I found, the big bottom tulip glowed neon blue, the small upper tulip pulsed pink, and the TROPI-CANA sign radiated orange.

I ran another search, this time just *Tropicana* and *Las Vegas*. I found what I was looking for at tropicanalv.com. The big tulips are gone. But the Tropicana Hotel and Casino is alive and well.

Never mind that in my entire life I had never gone anywhere. In that instant, I decided. I clicked the Reservations link.

Vegas, baby.

$\mathcal{O}$kay, maybe the Internet isn't totally useless. Within ten minutes, I had booked my hotel *and* my flight. I was leaving that night.

If this all sounds terribly impetuous, consider:

Between Jack and Jack and my crappy sub-minimum wage jobs, I had nothing in particular to stick around for.

Plus, I hadn't taken a vacation in, well, ever.

Not to mention that the whole thing was costing me under five hundred dollars. The room rate schedule at the Tropicana is very peculiar. I booked myself five nights in a row at $39.95 a night, which wouldn't even buy you a cardboard box on the sidewalk in Cambridge— but a week later, the Tropicana rooms were going for $199.95. I don't know, maybe the porno convention was coming to town next week. But who could say no to $39.95? And my Delta nonstop was only $287 round-trip, which seemed pretty reasonable considering I was traveling tonight and flying almost all the way across the country.

Not that I spend five hundred dollars—to be precise, $486.75— lightly. In point of fact, I don't think I've ever spent that much, on anything. But notwithstanding that those bratty Harvards are world-class lousy tippers, I hardly ever buy anything for myself, or anyone else for that matter, so I had the money in the bank. Enough, and then some.

I ran home to pack. It took me all of ten minutes. Maybe eight. Jeans, T-shirts, a sweatshirt, running shorts, socks, panties and bras. The bras are 32B, in case you are morbidly curious. Personally I think I'm more of an A, but I found a particular Bali that fits me even though the tag swears it's a B. And let's face it, who wants to be an A when you can be a B?

I threw everything into my beat-up old backpack. Then I remembered the box with the peacock feather. Needless to say, I had to take that. I figured the easiest thing would be to shove it in the backpack and let it stick out the top. When I tried it, though, it didn't leave quite enough room for all my clothes in the backpack. I pondered for a few seconds, then headed for Jack's closet.

Up on the top shelf was his bowling bag. I took it down and removed the dry-cleaning plastic that covered it. The bag was a Brunswick, black-and-white leather, with two loop handles. It was very light, because there was no bowling ball in it. And it was perfectly clean and shiny, because it had never been used. Not once.

The bowling bag was the first gift Maggie ever gave Jack, shortly after they met, and before they got married. He had mentioned that he liked to bowl, so she bought him the bag. Wherever Maggie came from, it was clear she had never heard of candlepin bowling. They call it candlepin because the pins are tall and skinny like candles, and the balls are about the size of small grapefruits and weigh maybe two-and-a-half pounds. After your first ball, they just leave the pins lying wherever they fell, so you can use your second ball to hit those pins and knock down the rest. What with the skinny pins and the little balls, it's a lot harder than you'd think.

Skinny pin. Little balls. Harder than you'd think. Sounds like Ricky Jakes from twelfth grade.

Anyway, not everybody bowls candlepin in Massachusetts, and some alleys have candlepin and big ball, both. Maggie must've assumed Jack was a big ball bowler, because she bought him a big ball bag. According to Jack, when he explained to her about candlepin, they both looked at that big ball bag and had a pretty good laugh. She wanted to take the bag back, but Jack said no, he loved it. Just like he loved her. That's the first time he told her he loved her. They got married two weeks later.

Jack walked into the room and saw me putting my panties into his bowling bag. Incidentally, they are just plain white cotton panties, nothing fancy or sexy. What's the point of fancy and sexy? I mean, if you're going to have sex, the panties are coming off, right? And the sooner the better.

"Where you goin'?" Jack asked.

"Vegas, baby." That's from *Swingers*, in case you don't know.

"What for?"

"To find my mother."

The instant the words were out of my mouth, I stopped cold. I swore I was going to say *To find Maggie*. I always call her *Maggie*. Never *my mother*. Because, well, she never was. Don't ask me why I said that.

He nodded, like I'd just said something profound.

"Can I take your bag?" I hadn't intended to request permission, but now it seemed the right thing to do.

"Course," he said without hesitation. "She'd like that."

For some reason, that annoyed me. "I'm not doing it because she'd like it."

"I didn't say you was. I'm just saying she would. Anyways thirty years is long enough for that bag to collect dust. High time somebody used it."

"Twenty-eight years."

"Close enough."

Being the daughter of a trainman, naturally, I took the T to the airport. Because it's easy and fast: Red Line from Harvard Square to South Station in twelve minutes, transfer to the Silver Line and another fifteen minutes straight to terminal A at Logan Airport. Cheap, too: the fare is only $1.25. Not to mention that I still didn't have a car, or a license, for that matter.

When I was a teenager, sometimes I'd cut school and take the T out to the airport. The Silver Line didn't exist then, so you had to take the Red Line to the Green Line to the Blue Line to the airport shuttle bus. I didn't care; all those transfers helped pass the time. Then when I'd get to the airport, I'd tell security that my older brother was already inside, but he forgot his wallet. I don't have a brother, older or younger, or a sister either. Only me. I guess I was a good liar, because they always let me through—although I should mention that this was years before 9/11. I wouldn't try it now.

Inside the terminals, I used to pretend I had a flight to catch, and I was late. I'd run as fast as I could all the way to the farthest gate. Of course, I didn't really have a flight to catch, so the game always ended the same way: I missed my flight.

Now, for the first time, I was actually going somewhere.

10

*W*hen I checked in at the Delta counter, I handed my passport, which is the only photo ID I have, to the man behind the counter. I assume they're just supposed to look at it and confirm you're you, but he actually flipped through the pages—which, owing to the fact that I've never been anywhere, were all empty.

"World traveler," he said.

It didn't seem like a very service-oriented thing for him to say. Then again, he was a good six inches shorter than me, which probably explained his attitude. Anyway, for once in my life I kept my opinions to myself and just waited while he printed my boarding pass and directed me to security.

My backpack and the bowling bag were both small enough to carry on, although the screeners needed to discuss among themselves whether a bowling bag was the same as a purse or a briefcase.

One of them turned to me. "Bowling ball?"

"Panties."

That shut them up. I put my stuff on the conveyor, took off my running shoes, didn't set off the metal detector, picked up my stuff, and wiggled my New Balances back on my feet. Ah, the glamour of travel.

I looked at my boarding pass, then scanned the terminal for my gate. It was all the way down at the end. For a second, I thought about breaking into a dead run, the way I had in my teen years. This wasn't a game, though; I actually was going somewhere. Besides, I wasn't late. So, I strolled down to the gate.

Logan Airport is relentlessly Bostonian. The newsstands, gift shops and restaurants assault you with extreme Boston-ness. The Red Sox and Harvard and Boston Baked Beans seem to be everywhere.

My dad, Jack, is a big fan of Boston Baked Beans. I am not. I like the taste fine; I just don't care for the aftereffects.

When the flight boarded, I found my seat: 27E, which was stuck in between the lawyer-type in 27D and the purple-haired old lady in 27F. The old woman looked up at me as if I were a mile high. "Goodness, you're a tall one," she said. Yeah, thanks, I never noticed. Still, somehow, I managed a smile in response. The suit in 27D never even noticed me, yakking on his cell phone long past the announcement telling everyone to turn off phones and other electronic devices; he only put it away after a stern flight attendant who looked more like a gym teacher scowled at him.

This was my first time on an airplane, so you'd think I would find it exciting. Not hardly. Perhaps I had trouble getting past the fact that once the person in front of me reclined their seat, my knees spent the balance of the flight in my chest. Thank goodness for small boobs. Delta should take all of their executives who are over six feet tall and make them fly cross-country in coach. Just a thought.

The flight was almost six hours long. The novelty wore off after ten minutes. I closed my eyes and slept, which was easy given how late I'd been up the night before.

I dreamed. I don't always. At least, I don't always remember. Even this time, I didn't remember much. I was walking down a flight of stairs. There were lights: bright, and colored. And music. It wasn't very specific, but it felt quite real. Then we hit an air pocket, the plane bumped, I opened my eyes, and of course there were no stairs, no bright lights, no music. I closed my eyes and went back to sleep. If I dreamed after that, I don't recall.

Just like Logan Airport makes quite sure you know you're in Boston, McCarran International Airport fairly screams *YOU'RE IN*

LAS VEGAS! the instant you step off your plane. I wonder if any other airport anywhere has slot machines.

I followed the signs for Ground Transportation and found an information desk. They directed me to The Deuce, a double-decker bus that runs from the airport to The Strip. The driver of The Deuce told me the Tropicana was at the south end of The Strip, so it would be one of the first stops. I asked if it was close enough to walk. He looked at me like I was insane. I took that as a "No" and paid my two dollars.

The Deuce wound its way out of the airport. It made a right turn onto Las Vegas Boulevard. Which, the recorded announcement declared, was *The world-famous Las Vegas Strip!*

I guess people in Las Vegas don't walk. It wasn't a long ride. I could've walked.

After a first stop across the street from the enormous Mandalay Bay, The Deuce pulled up at the corner of Las Vegas Boulevard and Tropicana Avenue.

I had arrived.

11

This was my first impression:

I was in Hell.

Which, in my view, was not necessarily a bad thing.

I'm not a particularly religious person. But if there's anything to all that Heaven and Hell business, let's think about it. Sex? Check. Drugs? Not anymore, but check. Alcohol? Double check. Borrowing Toupee's Volvo for a ride that the Somerville P.D. considered Grand Theft Auto? Check check check. So let's face it, if I am going anywhere, it is clearly to Hell. As are most of the people I would care to spend any time with. The parties in Heaven must be wicked dull.

At night, which is when I arrived, the intersection of Las Vegas Boulevard and Tropicana Avenue assaults your eyes with what at first is just a blur of neon, a psychotic rainbow of colors that don't exist in the natural world. Then the blur resolves into specific images. Across the Boulevard are a giant pyramid and a castle. Diagonally across the intersection is a crammed New York City skyline. On the other side of Tropicana Avenue is a giant green lion, and peeking over the lion's back is the top of the Eiffel Tower. And all of them pulse in radioactive amethyst and emerald and topaz auras.

I would later learn that those were all hotel-casinos: the Luxor, Excalibur, New York New York, MGM Grand, and Paris Las Vegas. I prefer my first impression: Hell.

That impression was also bolstered by the fact that it was hot. It was the middle of May, and back home the nighttime temperatures were still dropping into the low fifties, but at eleven p.m. in Las Vegas it must've been ninety. And the air had a quality I'd never felt before: it was both hot and dry. Desert heat. Massachusetts gets hot in the summer, but it's a sticky wet heat. Las Vegas felt like brimstone.

I liked it.

Compared to the chaotic visual landscape on the other three corners, the Tropicana was almost calm, almost sane. But only almost. It had two huge wings, black glass and steel with a string of bright yellow lights across the top. The wings were flanked by enormous vertical signs spelling out TROPICANA in orange neon letters against a fuchsia neon background. Incongruously, at ground level, the architecture was a strange blend of Wild West and Victorian, with little pointy roofs and wooden fan moldings. And everything was outlined in a million tiny bright light bulbs that pulsed and danced. A big horizontal TROPICANA sign, this one rendered in turquoise neon, indicated the entrance.

When I stepped inside, the sensory assault shifted from visual to auditory. Never in my life had I heard such a cacophony of bells and buzzers and gongs and ding-ding-dings and ca-chings and rat-tat-tats.

I had expected a hotel. Silly me. I was in Las Vegas, after all. The hotel was secondary. The moneymaker was the casino. Mesmerized, I took a few steps inside—and instantly lost my bearings, notwithstanding that I have a better than average sense of direction. All around me were slots of every size, shape and color. Nickel slots. Dollar slots. *Thousand* dollar slots. Not to mention the roulette tables. Blackjack tables. Craps tables.

I looked up. The ceilings were mirrored, and there I was, looking down at me. My reflection looked overwhelmed.

I took a deep breath. I retraced my steps and discovered that in my distraction, I had walked right past the registration desk. The clerk looked at Jack's bowling bag. "Bowling?"

"Panties."

He didn't blink. "Credit card," he said. He took an imprint of my bank Visa, gave me a magnetic key card, and told me I was in the

Island Tower. "Up the escalators, past Pietro's and Legends, through the Trop Shops, over the pool, just beyond the Tropics Lounge, elevators are on your left. You can't miss it."

I wouldn't bet on that, but I was afraid if I asked him to repeat the directions, he'd say something different and then I'd be hopelessly confused. I braved the sea of slot machines. I made a wrong turn and found myself surrounded by Caribbean Stud Poker. Had I seen any Caribbean Studs I might have lingered, but I didn't, just a bunch of mostly older mostly balder mostly fatter men dressed like they were auditioning for World Poker Tour. After a few more wrong turns I found the escalator and cruised upstairs, where following the desk clerk's directions was surprisingly easy.

When I reached the Island Tower, just before the elevators I spotted a sign: HOSPITALITY DESK. Although the flash and din of Las Vegas had briefly distracted me, I remembered why I was here. I reach back and touched the long slender box protruding from the top of my knapsack, as if for a tangible reminder. I was looking for Maggie, my mother—for whatever strange, sparkling, nearly naked part of her past had occurred right here. And to find Maggie, I had to find the sender of the mysterious package, D. Belle.

I approached the Hospitality Desk, which was staffed by a young woman wearing a low-cut muumuu. "Excuse me," I said.

"Yes?"

The return address on the package was burned into memory.

"Where is 7 Josephine Lane?"

12

*I*t was eleven thirty at night. Despite having slept for most of my flight, I was exhausted. I was feeling more than a little overwhelmed. So what was I planning to do, find the address and go pound on a total stranger's door at midnight?

Whatever I was planning didn't matter. Beth—that was the name on her oval ID tag—said, "I'm sorry?"

Maybe she didn't hear me. Maybe, like Jack from the constant scream of subway wheels, Beth had progressive hearing loss from the unending din of the casino. "7 Josephine Lane," I repeated, quite loudly.

"You don't have to shout. I heard you the first time." Beth was almost a foot shorter than me, and I could see that it bothered her. To compensate, she thrust her boobs forward. She sure had me beat in that department. Without even meaning to, I looked down her cleavage. Lordy. I wondered how many hotel guests had gone searching for lost room keys down there. Hospitality, indeed.

"Where is it?" I asked.

"*What* is it?" she asked.

"It's a street."

"Where?"

"Around here."

"Where around here?"

"I don't know. That's why I'm asking you."

Beth and her cleavage ducked behind the desk for a second, then reemerged with a large map. She spread the map on the desk and bent over it, giving anybody who looked in her direction a prime view straight down her dress. I mean all the way down. The girl was not wearing any underwear, tops *or* bottoms.

"Could you stand up, please?"

She straightened and looked at me. "What?"

Whew. Show's over. "Nothing. Never mind."

"It's not on the map," she said.

"I know that."

"So why did you have me look?"

"I didn't. You did that on your own."

She gave me a distrustful look. "Are you messing with me?"

As much as I might have liked to just on principle, I wasn't. "No," I said, sounding as sincere as I could. It wasn't easy; sincerity is not a natural condition for me. "Somebody sent me a package. The return address said *7 Josephine Lane*. It came from around here."

"I bet the address is fake."

You mean like those boobs?

I didn't say that. I just said "Thanks anyway," rode the elevator up to the ninth floor, and found my room.

The centerpiece of the room was a queen-sized bed adorned with a heinous multicolored duvet cover that some man must have thought looked tropical. Definitely a man, and a straight one at that; no woman or gay man ever would have picked that comforter, much less bought drapes to match. There was a rattan loveseat upholstered— thankfully—in a different fabric, a matching rattan desk-dresser combination, and two rattan chairs with yet another pattern covering their seats. The décor wasn't much, although I suppose at $39.95 a night, I shouldn't complain. At least the room, and the bathroom, were very clean.

Oh, and there was a mirror over the bed. Actually, a mirrored headboard and matching ceiling mirror. I guess to be sure you can see every little detail of what happens in Vegas. Ugh.

I unpacked. It took two minutes. All of my clothes fit in one dresser drawer.

I peeled off my T-shirt and sniffed at it. Hmm. Maybe. I hung it in the closet, and did the same with my jeans. There was a plastic laundry bag, into which I put my bra and panties. I brushed my teeth, peed, washed my hands, and looked at myself in the bathroom mirror.

I don't know what I was expecting to see. A change? The glamorous creature in that old snapshot?

Nope. I saw the same old Linda Stone I had always been. Too tall. Too skinny. Boobs too small. Not pretty enough. Hell, not pretty, period.

I stepped out of the bathroom. The lights in the room were on, the drapes were open, and I was still stark naked. So what.

I walked up to the window. Outside, glowing and pulsating in the hot night, I could see the Tropicana's other tower, and, beyond, the casino-sized Empire State Building.

I spread my arms wide. *Here I am, Las Vegas! Take a good look!*

I don't know why I did that. I can't explain why I enjoyed doing it, either. And I really can't imagine what sort of response I was expecting.

Hearing no thunderous applause, I turned out the light, crawled into bed, and went to sleep.

woke up hungry.

It was hardly a surprise; I had barely eaten since receiving that package a day-and-a-half earlier. Sometimes I go days eating almost nothing, other times I chow down like Mo Vaughn. Neither seems to affect my weight. I've had other girls tell me I was lucky. Personally, I'd like a little more control over my life.

I showered and dressed. Since it had been so hot at eleven p.m., I assumed it'd be even hotter in daylight, so I opted for my running shorts instead of jeans. Heading out of the room, I noticed there was a full-length mirror behind the door. Too many mirrors, if you ask me. I glanced at myself and shrugged. At least my legs looked okay.

When the elevator opened, a man stepped out as I was stepping in. There was absolutely nothing memorable about him.

Except that as the doors closed, he whistled at me.

We were the only ones there. Believe me, I looked around, and there was nobody else in the elevator.

I've never been whistled at much. Just the occasional gross construction worker. Whereas this man was neither gross nor, by appearances, a construction worker.

Then again, maybe he was up all night drinking and gambling. He was probably so drunk he would've whistled at a potted plant.

Downstairs, I spotted the Island Buffet. There was a beautiful tropical garden, with waterfalls and palm trees and orchids. I was more attracted by the deal: all you can eat for $10.99. Trust me, I got my money's worth.

As I was finishing up, I spotted a gentleman of about sixty. I call him a gentleman even though that's not a term I use often, and despite the fact that he was bussing the tables after diners finished their meals. Watching him interact with the guests, his smile was brilliant, his manners were perfect, and he carried himself like, well, a gentleman. He seemed completely at home and completely confident in this environment, as if he had worked here his entire life.

"Excuse me, sir." I don't know what came over me. To my knowledge, I have *never* called anybody *sir* before. Ever.

"Yes, ma'am?" He looked at me, and then he *really* looked at me, the way you look at someone who looks oddly familiar.

"How long have you worked here?"

He stood up even straighter and smiled even wider. "Forty-one years next month."

Maybe my hunch was right. Maybe he knew. "I'm looking for 7 Josephine Lane."

I wandered through the shops, then headed outside and paced around the pool. I was just killing time until noon, the end of Gene's shift.

That was the gentleman's name: Gene. My hunch was right; he *did* know. First, though, he had questioned me. "Who told you about Josephine Lane?"

"A friend."

"Does your friend have a name?"

"Yes."

I've been to court enough times to know this: only answer *exactly* the questions they ask you.

"And what is that name?"

I hesitated. "D. Belle," I finally said.

"What does the D stand for?"

He had me there. "I don't know."

Gene winked. "But I do."

He told me I couldn't get there on my own; he'd have to direct me himself. From anyone else, I'd have suspected that was a creepy ploy—but after all the creepy ployers I've known, I've developed pretty good radar, and I trusted Gene.

At noon sharp, I was waiting at the entrance to the Island Buffet. Exactly one minute later, Gene emerged from a back room. He had changed out of his waiter's uniform and now wore a button-down short-sleeved white shirt and sharply creased tan slacks.

He bowed slightly when he saw me, and offered me his elbow as if he were escorting me to the prom. I slipped my hand through the crook of his arm. I looked right, then left. "Which way?"

"*This* way," he said, and, completely unexpectedly, he steered me straight into the door from which he had emerged.

The door opened into a wide concrete corridor. Waiters with room service carts sped past us in both directions. Maids carrying sheets and towels and pillows bustled by. Coming toward us was a handsome man wearing a black suit and blue shirt; at the end of the leash in his hands was an enormous snow white tiger.

"Hey, Dirk," Gene said nonchalantly to the man with the tiger.

"Hey, Gene," the man replied as he and the tiger passed us.

We kept walking. The corridor branched, then branched again, as if we were in a giant anthill populated by all the worker ants who made the Tropicana run.

"Where are we going?" I finally asked Gene.

He stopped abruptly in front of a door marked EMERGENCY EXIT. He leaned against it, and suddenly we were awash in hot dry desert sunlight.

"Welcome," he announced, "to Josephine Lane."

14

No wonder it wasn't on the map.

As far as I could see, Josephine Lane wasn't a lane at all. Or a street, or even an alley. It was just a space, maybe two hundred feet long and eighty feet wide, surrounded by walls on all sides. There was nothing in the space except an ancient, battered double-wide trailer down at the far end.

I looked at Gene, baffled. "What is this?"

"This is what you came to find."

"I'm looking for a street."

"You're looking for number seven Josephine Lane."

I looked again at the bare concrete space. It resembled the exercise yard of a prison. Not that I've ever been to prison, grand theft auto notwithstanding.

I turned back to Gene. "And . . . ?"

He pointed at the decrepit old trailer. "Number seven Josephine Lane."

"You're joking." I don't know why I bothered saying that. From the expression on his face—both sincere and helpful—I knew he wasn't joking. "What should I do?"

"Might try knocking."

"You mean there's somebody in there?" The trailer looked abandoned.

He shrugged. I swear his eyes twinkled. "Might be." He looked at his watch. "Got to run. I have an engagement with a lady." And before

I could say another word, he had vanished back through the emergency exit door.

I thought about following him. I didn't.

Instead, I made myself march across the space until I was facing the trailer door. Sure enough, a faded 7 was stenciled at eye level. I studied the flaking paint on the trailer walls. Gently, I shook the long box in my hands, and felt the quill of the peacock feather rattle inside.

I knocked on the door.

Nothing happened.

I looked around for assistance, but Gene was gone. I wondered what I would do if no one answered. Would I just pack up and slink back to my nothing life in nothing Somerville?

I knocked again, louder this time.

I was still knocking when the door was suddenly yanked open.

The yanker was a tall woman—not as tall as I am, but still tall—whose age I guessed as somewhere between sixty and seventy. She wore khaki capris and a floral print halter top, which despite her age was flattering to her figure, slender and small-busted. Her skin was fair. Her red hair, which appeared natural despite her age, peeked out from under a patterned silk scarf that she wore like a bandana. Her eyes, and in fact almost the entire upper half of her face, were covered by huge dark sunglasses. Her fingernails were long and manicured. She was holding an old-fashioned glass filled with what looked like a Bloody Mary.

Which she promptly dropped, splattering tomato juice all over my feet. At least the cup was plastic, so it didn't shatter.

"Sweet Jesus," she said. Even in two words there was no mistaking her Southern accent.

"Jesus Christ," I said, entirely irreligiously. I glared down at my New Balances. They used to be blue. Now they were blotched. I may not care much about what I wear, but they looked disgusting.

I turned my attention back to the woman. She was staring at me.

"Sweet Jesus," she said again.

"You said that already. How about you get me a towel?"

She shook herself, as if breaking a trance. "Aw, shit," she drawled. Not just from the South, but the *deep* South, by the sound of her.

Then she hugged me.

Not any old hug, either. You'd think we were best friends.

Finally she released me and stepped back. "Well, what are you waiting for? Kick those puppies off and get your skinny ass in here!"

I'm not generally big on taking orders, especially from total strangers, much less total strangers who ruin my running shoes. But she said it with such sheer force of personality that I did exactly what she instructed. I left the shoes outside. On my way in, the woman handed me a luxurious brown washcloth, already dampened. I wiped my ankles and stepped inside.

The trailer may have looked like a wreck on the outside, but that was clearly camouflage. The interior was small, but downright opulent. Glancing one way, I could see that the cabinets in the tiny kitchen appeared to be rosewood, and the miniature dining table ebony. The other way, at the far end, I saw satin sheets on the bed, which was unmade. Between me and the bed was the living room, furnished in dark leather. An enormous plasma screen TV dominated one wall, and a diminutive Bose sound system glowed in the corner.

The tall woman strode past me to a pint-sized bar. Over her shoulder, she asked, "What are you drinkin'?"

It wasn't yet 12:30. I don't object on principle to drinking in the afternoon, or in the morning, for that matter. Still, I thought I'd better get some answers before I started tanking up.

"Nothing."

"The hell," she said, and handed me a Bloody Mary.

"I don't drink Bloody Marys."

"You'll drink that one."

Who did she think she was? Still, there really was something terribly commanding about her. I sipped it.

"Good, huh." She was telling me, not asking.

She was right, though.

She made herself an identical drink, sat down in a leather armchair opposite me, drank down half of it, and shook her head. "Jesus, you look just like her."

"Who?"

"Don't be stupid, girl. *'Who.'* Maggie, that's who. Your mother."

"You knew her?"

She took another big pull at her drink. "You're worryin' me. Did you look at the picture?"

The snapshot. I opened the box, took it out and held it up.

"Can you take off your sunglasses?"

She did. She doffed her head scarf as well. I didn't really need her to remove them. Of course she was the other girl in the photo. But seeing her entire face confirmed it.

I took a big drink from my Bloody Mary. It was perfect.

"I'm Dixie," she said.

remembered the return address on the package, written in that flamboyant looping script. *D. Belle.*

Dixie Belle?

She had to be kidding. "Come on," I said. "Your name isn't Dixie Belle."

"Damn right it is."

"It sounds like a stripper."

That's when she slapped me.

Not criminally hard. But hard enough to get my attention.

"Don't you *ever* say that," she barked. She stood up to her full height. "I am a *showgirl.*" Then she leaned down over me. She was right in my face. "And if you learn only one thing from me, missy, you get this straight: *A showgirl is not a stripper.* Are we clear?"

Stunned, I nodded.

"Good." With that, the fire vanished from her eyes. She took my hands in hers, stood me up, kissed my stinging cheek maternally, and gave me another huge hug. "Now sit down." I did. "Course, that's not the name my momma gave me. That's my stage name. But after five or six years performing, I got so accustomed to it, I went to court and had it changed legal." She reached over her shoulder and snatched a Louis Vuitton wallet off a small lamp table. She removed a card from the wallet and thrust it at me.

It was her driver's license. As far as the State of Nevada was concerned, she really was Dixie Belle of 7 Josephine Lane.

A thought occurred to me. "How'd you get the trailer back here?" I tried to picture a helicopter lowering it into the enclosed concrete yard.

"Drove it here myself. Way back in 1969. In those days, this was a full-fledged alley. Since then, the casino's expanded. First they closed off one end. Then the other." She smiled. "At least I have my privacy."

"What about the address?"

"I made that up. Seven is, well, lucky seven, 'cause we're in Vegas. And Josephine Lane is for Josephine Baker."

I didn't know who that was. "Who?"

"Oh my girl, you have a lot to learn." She got up and plucked my drink glass out of my hand. I noticed that it was empty, as was hers. I watched her make the next round. You'd never know from the taste, but there was quite a lot of vodka in there. Maybe that's why I was starting to feel a warm little glow.

"Course, Maggie and I had a lot to learn, too, when we first got here. Dang, we was just a couple of kids. Eighteen, both of us. But we learned." She laughed a naughty laugh. "Oh, yes, we surely did."

In the hot wet summer of 1960, Dixie—née Blanche Smith—was just days out of high school when she scandalized her parents by announcing that she was going to Las Vegas as a graduation gift to herself. "Maybe if they'd named me Mary or somethin' plain to match Smith, I'd've had a more hometown attitude. Or maybe not. But you name a girl 'Blanche' and she's gonna get ideas, just like the gal in that Tennessee Williams play. Me, I got the idea I was supposed to be goin' places."

Her parents forbade the trip. Blanche went anyway, sneaking out and paying for her Greyhound ticket with savings from her waitressing at Bo's All Night. 'Course, I knew a big nothin' about Las Vegas. Just that Frank Sinatra and Dean Martin and Sammy Davis Jr. were there—and if they were there, what meat-eatin' girl didn't want to be there, too? Anyways, it sounded grown-up and dangerous, which is why my folks hated the idea, which is why I loved the idea. Not to mention it was way the hell far away from Mobile, Alabama, plus nobody I knew had ever been there.

"That damn bus ride took near two-and-a-half days, crammed in with cigar smokers and perverts and folks that just plain never heard of deodorant, bumpin' through Louisiana and Texas and New Mexico and Arizona in July with nothin' but open windows for air conditioning. Wasn't a whole lot of leg room for a girl built like you and me, neither. But it's good to be young. I swear, I laughed the whole way to Las Vegas.

"Got off that bus stinkin' of smoke and sweat and freedom. I walked over to the Golden Nugget, which was a block from the bus terminal. I just stood in that casino and gawked at all the good-lookin' folks dressed nice and drippin' money like it was tobacco juice. I swear, I wondered if I'd made a mistake and if my folks were right. I thought about turnin' around and gettin' back on the very next bus."

"Why didn't you?"

"All of a sudden I spotted another girl. She looked about my age, and if you can believe it, she was even taller than me."

In spite of myself, I felt my insides flutter. "Maggie?"

Dixie scrutinized me. "I swear, lookin' at you, it's like she was sittin' here herself. Only she was younger when I met her. Eighteen, like me. She was watching the roulette wheel, like she was tryin' to make up her mind. Finally she slaps a ten dollar bill down on red. Didn't even buy chips. Damndest thing. Ten bucks was money then—least it was to me. The wheel lands red, and ten bucks is twenty. She lets it ride. The wheel spins, that little ball bounces like a grasshopper in a frying pan—and it's red again! Forty bucks. Another spin, her money's still sittin' on red, then all of a sudden, quick, she slides it to black. The ball's about to drop, and crazy me, I drop a twenty on top of her forty. Croupier says *No more bets!* I looked at Maggie, Maggie looked at me, and I said, 'Sure hope you're right'."

Dixie got up to fix another drink. She took her time doing it. The suspense was killing me.

"What happened??" I finally blurted.

She smiled and handed me my third flawless Bloody Mary. "My new best friend and I picked up our hundred and twenty dollars and took us a taxi straight to the Sands." Then a shadow crossed her face. "The Sands ain't there anymore."

"Like Maggie."

"Yeah. Like Maggie." She raised her glass in tribute. I raised mine, too.

After we drank, I asked, "Why did you go to the Sands?"

"That's where Frankie was."

"Frankie?"

Dixie sighed. "I told you, darlin'. *Sinatra*. Lordy, you really don't know much of nothin'. We took us a room, got ourselves prettied up best we could, put on the sweetest dresses we had packed, and bought ourselves two tickets right up front to see Frankie and Dino that very night. Turns out Maggie'd just Greyhounded into town, too, only she came from Boston."

My mother—Maggie, I mean—was from Boston. Her childhood had occurred only miles from my own. I never knew that. Neither did my dad.

"So there we are, not a lick of sleep between the two of us, runnin' on adrenaline and hormones, they seat us at our front row table, and the first thing we do is order martinis. Neither of us had ever even tasted gin before, but playin' grown-up at the Sands in Las Vegas, there's nothin' else for a couple of girls to drink than martinis." Dixie made a face and shuddered. "To this day, I hate the taste of gin. Didn't stop us that night, though.

"Then things got *really* interesting."

16

*A*nd I thought things were already really interesting. Honestly, she had me on the edge of my seat. Considering the Bloody Marys, I had to be careful not to lean too far forward, or I'd fall off the chair.

"The show started. Frankie and Dino, they really used to work the audience. And there we were at the front table, two young things with legs that reached from here to Kentucky, and us already silly on that first martini, no sleep and no food. So Frankie starts buyin' us drinks."

No way. "You're asking me to believe Frank Sinatra bought my mother drinks." Damn. There's that *mother* word again.

"Believe it or not, makes me no nevermind. I'm just tellin' what happened. But that's not the interesting part."

"What's the interesting part?"

"They're up there singin', and Frankie starts makin' eyes at us. First we don't believe it. Cause neither one of us exactly grew up bein' the prettiest girl in town. Too dang tall, and titties too small." She raised her eyebrows at me. "Guess maybe you know what that's like."

I said nothing, because she already knew the answer.

"Anyways, after a while we start believin' it. Only Maggie said he's makin' eyes at you. Then I said no he's makin' eyes at you. Finally we both agreed he was makin' eyes at both of us. Cause he wasn't exactly keepin' it a secret. And if Frank Sinatra is gonna flirt with us, you just know we're gonna flirt right back. So maybe we smile, and maybe we wink, and maybe we hike up those skirts and show a little more leg than our mommas would've appreciated."

"My mother flirted with Frank Sinatra?"

"Shut up, girl, and let me get to the interesting part. After the show, the maitre d' comes and tells us that Mister Sinatra has invited us to visit him in his dressing room. Maggie and I look at each other, and we shriek and giggle like a couple of plastered teenagers, which we were, and backstage we go. There's Dean Martin, and like a perfect gentleman he says sorry ladies, he's gonna call it a night, kisses our hands and leaves. Frankie asks if we're hungry. Shit, I was so famished, I almost bit him then and there. So he instructs the maitre d' to call Pete and tell him to meet us at the Steer. Then he piles us into a limo and the three of us get chauffeured to the biggest steaks I ever ate." She raised her glass in another toast. "Frankie's gone, Maggie's gone, the Sands is gone, but the Golden Steer is still kickin'." We both drank. "Personally, I think the place looks like a cathouse, but they make a damn good porterhouse."

"The two of you had dinner with Frank Sinatra."

"Didn't I say shut up? Frankie takes us to his booth: big leather banquette as cushy as a couch, and a thick curtain for privacy. We order steaks, and wine, the waiter leaves, draws that curtain closed, and next thing you know Frankie starts pinchin' our skinny-ass butts. Before we can figure out what to do, all of a sudden somebody yanks that curtain open. We figure it's the waiter with the food, right? Except uh-uh. It's *Peter gorgeous Lawford*. He scoots into the booth, and the curtain closes. So there's the four of us: Peter bein' all British and witty and charming, Frankie bein' all New Jersey and brash and charming, and Maggie and me tryin' our best to be charming, but probably just bein' all young and giggly and drunk."

"Stop. I do not want to hear that you and my mother had sex with Frank Sinatra and Peter Lawford."

Dixie set down her empty drink. I was relieved to see that she didn't get up to fix another one. My head was starting to swim. Not to mention my bladder. "All right," she said, "you don't have to hear that."

She got up and sidled to the bathroom. After I heard her flush and the tap run, I traded places with her. The bathroom was closet-sized but gorgeous, with cool soapstone floor and marble walls and sleek nickel fixtures. When I was done, I stepped back into the little living room and sat down in my chair again.

"Well," I demanded, "did you?"

"Did we what?"

"Have sex with them?"

She chuckled. "I thought you didn't want to know."

"I don't. But I do. So tell me."

"No."

"No you won't tell me, or no you didn't?"

She waited before answering. Just to make me crazy, I think. She grinned wickedly. Finally, she said, "No . . . we didn't."

I was hugely relieved. And yet, simultaneously, a tiny bit disappointed.

"Don't mean we didn't mess around some."

"Dixie!"

"Let me tell you, girl, that Peter Lawford was a world-class kisser."

I did the math. "So Maggie kissed Sinatra?"

"Sure she did. And so did I."

"But you said you kissed Lawford."

"I did. And so did Maggie. We both kissed the both of them. Don't you go getting all prudy on me, neither. You ain't no angel, and don't tell me different. Besides, it was just kissin'. Once Frankie heard we was eighteen, he got spooked. Guess he thought maybe we wasn't even eighteen. He was up for a good time, but not for jail time. So after we ate those huge steaks and drank a bunch of wine and everybody kissed everybody for a while, Frankie put us back in the limo, we rode back to the Sands, and that, as they say, was that."

Dixie stood up, took my empty glass and hers, and rinsed them in her sink, then stuck them inside the smallest dishwasher I'd ever seen. Next, she handed me the box containing the peacock feather. I realized that, even though we had been speaking for hours, somehow the inexplicably appealing and appalling dress that Maggie wore in the snapshot had slipped my mind.

"I have to ask you something," I said.

"Not yet."

"But you don't even know what I'm going to ask."

"Of course I do. And you're not ready yet."

How could I not be ready? I was here, wasn't I?

"Trust me," she said. "After all, I'm the one who sent you that package in the first place. When it's time, I'll tell you."

I thought for a few seconds. "Okay," I concluded. "So now what?"

"You hungry?" she asked me.

"A little."

"Here's what you do. Go eat at any of the hotel's restaurants. Tell them you're Dixie's guest, and I said to charge the meal to me."

"I can't let you do that," I protested.

"That's okay. This place don't pay me near what I'm worth. But I eat free for life, and if I want a guest to eat free, too, so be it. Anyways, go have a snack, then you take a little nap. When you wake up, get yourself dressed all pretty and meet me outside the Tiffany Theatre at 8:15 sharp. Don't you dare be late, neither."

"What are we doing?"

"We," said Dixie as she escorted me out of her trailer and back into the maze of tunnels under the Tropicana, "are about to change your life."

t was just past four o'clock when I emerged from the maze and into the hotel. After the story Dixie had just told me, I was tempted to try Legends, the Tropicana's steak house, but it didn't open until five. I settled for a quick bite at Player's Deli, where the dishes all had names like The Gambler and Stacked Deck and Ace-High. Reading down the menu, I spotted Lady Luck. Sure, it was just chicken salad on a croissant, but if Dixie and I were about to change my life, whatever that meant, why not get a little extra help from Lady Luck?

I wolfed down the sandwich and a Coke and told the waitress to charge it to Dixie. I didn't feel too bad, because the whole thing was only eleven bucks. And that was with a twenty percent tip. I don't eat out in restaurants much, because who can afford it? But when I do, I try to tip decently, having gotten far too many cheapo B-School nickel-and-dime tips in my day.

Upstairs in my room, the bed had been made, and the duvet cover was as heinous as ever. I ordered a wake-up call for 7:30 and shut the light. Then I pulled the window shade closed, pulled the sheet and blanket down, pulled my clothes off and slid into bed. I've always liked the feel of bed sheets on my bare skin, and the fact that these sheets were actually clean, as opposed to the questionable state of my bed at home, was even better. I was asleep almost instantly.

The moment the phone rang, I was awake. For some people, forty-five minutes to prepare for a life-changing event wouldn't be remotely enough. I'm not one of those people. In fact, I was ready to go by eight. It would've been even sooner, except I decided to shave my legs—and having long legs means there's more to shave. I don't know why I bothered, since I was wearing jeans. I know Dixie told me to get dressed all pretty, but I hadn't packed anything pretty. Probably because I don't own anything pretty. I wore the dressiest clothes I brought, which consisted of black tall-boy Levi's, a black T-shirt and, in my big concession to fashion, a black bra and panties. I didn't put on makeup because I didn't pack any, because I don't own any. And fixing my hair consisted of brushing it.

I looked at my hopelessly stained New Balances and wished I had brought another pair of anything for my feet. Realizing I had time to spare, I ran downstairs, bought a pair of twelve dollar flip-flops at a sundries shop, zipped back upstairs and ditched the running shoes in my room.

At exactly 8:15, I arrived at the entrance to the Tiffany Theatre. There was a long line of people waiting behind a velvet cord. At the doorway to the theatre stood Dixie. She was wearing a different floral print halter top, and had traded her khaki capris for an ivory-colored skirt that rose well above the knee. She wasn't a young woman, but she sure had maintained her legs. Their shape was accentuated by her high-heeled sandals. In those heels, she was taller than I.

She waved me close, and gave me a quick appraising look up and down. "Well, don't you look nice?" she asked.

I was pleasantly surprised. "Really?"

She scowled. "No, not really. You look like crap. Thought I told you to wear your pretty clothes."

"These are my pretty clothes." I wasn't being a smartass. It was the truth.

"Lordy."

I looked at the line. "Do we have to wait?"

Dixie regarded me as if I were from another planet—which, considering the differences between Las Vegas and Slumerville, was about right. "Honey, I do *not* wait in line. And neither do you. Now remember that."

An usher opened the door for her and we stepped into a vast room. The walls and high ceiling glittered with thousands of lights like tiny stars. I didn't have time to examine the room, though, because Dixie was on the move. Don't ask me how she could walk so fast in those heels. She strode down the center aisle, down two small flights of stairs flanked by tables, then down more stairs with lush booths on either side, and at last down a final stairway. A huge stage with its heavy red curtain loomed in front of us. Dixie steered me into the first booth on the aisle. "Three oh one," she said. "This one's mine." She said it like she owned it. "Nine hundred and fifty seats, and these are the best two in the house."

So far, we were the only people in the place. A waiter scurried over to take our order. Dixie raised her eyebrows at me. "Magellan martini," I instructed. "Very dirty."

"Martinis it is," Dixie agreed. "Ketel One, with a twist." The waiter sped away. "Magellan?" she asked me.

"Sapphire gin. It's really blue. Not just the bottle, like that Bombay stuff."

"Expensive?"

"The most." Mind you, I never ordered one of these myself, but I have served a few in my time.

"That's my girl," she said. "You okay mixing vodka lunch and gin dinner?"

"I can handle it."

"Bet you can. So could your momma."

The drinks arrived. We were still the only ones in the house. I looked around. "Where is everybody?"

"They're holding the doors."

"How come?"

"'Cause I told them to." With that, it struck me that whatever was about to happen must be unusually important. "Anything you'd like to ask me?"

"What are we going to see?"

She almost fell off her seat. "Didn't you read the billboard in front of the hotel? The signs in the lobby?" The expression on my face told her I hadn't. "Don't you *know*?"

All I could do was shake my head, no.

For a moment, a look of hopelessness darkened Dixie's face. Then her eyes brightened. "What the hell," she said. "You're Maggie Archer's daughter. Whether you know it or not, it's in your damn blood."

I looked at Dixie. I felt suddenly weightless. "My mother's maiden name was Archer? I didn't know."

"Sweet Jesus," she whispered. "I found you just in time."

She stood up and waved toward the back of the room. Instantly, the doors opened, and the crowds flooded in. In seconds, tables and booths filled. In minutes, waiters and waitresses fetched a thousand drinks. Then the lights darkened. From the pit in front of us, the strains of an orchestra swelled out and filled the room. The curtain started to rise.

Dixie reached across the table and squeezed my hand. The way a mother would squeeze your hand. I knew that she did it because my mother had never lived to do it.

"Prepare yourself, little girl. You are about to witness . . ."

A chill ran through my body.

"The Folies Bergère!"

18

I am not a total ignoramus. I may not have gone to college, but I've read plenty of good books, and seen plenty of good movies. I can use words like *postmodernist* and *vacuous* without embarrassing myself. So it is with some embarrassment that I confess, when Dixie uttered those words, I had only the very vaguest idea of what the *Folies Bergère* was.

Vaguely, I thought it was a nudie show.

As in, naked women.

Instantly, I wondered: *Why is Dixie taking me to a nudie show?* For a split second, I was overwhelmed with doubts. All those drinks she poured into me this afternoon. The way she just squeezed my hand.

Then, just as instantaneously, the doubts vanished.

She had slapped me. *A showgirl is not a stripper. Are we clear?*

She had sent me the peacock feather. My mother's. And even more critically, that photograph of the two of them. Dixie and Maggie. My mother wearing her crown of feathers and sparkles, her glittering shoes, and most alluring of all, her dazzling, decadent, barely there dress. *Her showgirl's dress.*

My mother had been a showgirl.

Right here.

Not just any showgirl, either.

The curtain rose and confirmed what, in those few seconds, I had finally understood.

My mother—Maggie Stone, late of Somerville, Massachusetts, born Margaret Archer of Boston—was a member of the *Folies Bergère*.

For the next two hours, I was transported into a dream. Somebody else's dream, I suppose, because my own imagination was too limited to create such splendors.

The music. The colors. The glorious dancing—from hippie to hip-hop, from mambo to my childhood love, ballet. And of course the Cancan, which managed to be scandalous despite the fact that the girls were dressed from head to toe.

And oh, the costumes. It seemed as if every girl must have worn fifty different outfits. Sometimes they were fully, even heavily, clothed. Other times—often, in fact—they wore hardly anything more than feathers and a smile. My God, the feathers! Somewhere, there must be thousands of very naked peacocks and ostriches shivering in sacrifice to the plumed caps and headdresses, the downy scanties of the *Folies Bergère*. Feathers and sequins, rhinestones and G-strings, gloves and boots and capes and wings and, yes, skin, seemingly miles and miles of seductive skin.

There were singers, too, and comedians. But above all else, there were . . . *the showgirls*. Tall beautiful confident dreams of women, who cascaded down a beautifully illuminated staircase like a waterfall of angels, who wore everything and nothing with equal glamour, equal abandon, equal magnificence.

My mother had been a showgirl with the Folies Bergère.

When the show ended, the applause rang in my ears. I was mesmerized.

"Darlin'." It was Dixie. She pronounced the word very gently.

I looked at her. She was handing me something. It was a Kleenex.

I touched my face and my fingers came away damp. I looked at the table in front of me and saw where the droplets had spattered. I had been crying.

I never cry.

I looked around. The theater was empty. Everyone else had gone. Or had they really been there at all? I felt as if the entire glorious spectacle had been performed just for me. At that moment, I had only one question.

"Can we see it again?"

Not that night, we couldn't. It was Friday, and Dixie explained that the *Folies* performs only one show nightly on Tuesdays and Fridays. "Two shows on Monday Wednesday Thursday Saturday," she rattled off. "Seven-thirty, the girls are covered—no titties for the kiddies, we like to say. Ten o'clock is the same show you just saw; all bets are off."

We were seated on a leather sofa in the Havana Hideaway lounge. Soft jazz filled in the spaces in our conversation. It was the quietest place at the Tropicana I had found so far.

When the waiter took our orders, I asked for a Coke. Dixie smiled. "A girl's got to know her limits," I said.

"Smart girl," she said to me. "Vodka tonic," she instructed the waiter. "Hold the vodka."

"Sure thing, Dix," he said, and winked at her.

It seemed as if everyone who worked there knew Dixie. "Course they know me," she said. "I've been livin' here thirty-eight years."

"What do you do?"

"Hmm," she said, as if the question had never occurred to her. "It's a whole lot easier to tell you what I *don't* do. I'm not the choreographer or the dance captain. I'm not the costume mistress. I'm not the stage manager." She sipped at her tonic water. "You might say I'm the den mother. I spent thirty years on stage myself—first at the Flamingo, then the Desert Inn, then the Sands. Finally made it to the big time here in 1969. Showgirled the *Folies* 'til I was too old, then showgirled a couple more years 'cause I couldn't bring myself to give it up. Finally hung up my feathers in 1990. By then, though, you can bet I knew pretty much anything and everything about bein' in this show—and, more important, about how to be a showgirl in this show. There's thirty-two girls up on that stage: sixteen dancers and sixteen posers. That means on average, it's that time of the month for somebody every single day of the year. Girls fight over boyfriends, over girlfriends, over money, drugs, sex. Over who did or didn't steal whose titty makeup.

Over everything and nothing." She smiled. "Auntie Dixie keeps the peace."

I thought about what she had just said. "You didn't join the *Folies* until 1969?"

"That's right."

"But my mother . . ."

"Your mother was . . . somethin' special. If there's such a thing as a showgirl prodigy, that was Maggie Archer. The way she told it, all she had was some dance lessons as a kid. The thought of getting up on stage never occurred to her. Then the two of us went and saw the show at the Flamingo. Here we were, a couple of girls who up 'til the week before had spent our whole lives feeling like giraffes—us with our long legs and our little titties, lookin' down at all those curvy girly-girls who got all the dates. Only now, all of a sudden, here was this huge showcase stage filled with girls who looked *just like us*. It hit us like a bolt of lightning. We looked at those tall sparkly girls, I looked at Maggie and Maggie looked at me, and we said, *We could do that!* Couple of crazy kids. Anyways, that's when we decided we were here to stay. Got us a teeny little apartment and started cocktail waitressing to pay the bills. Nights off, we saw every showgirl show in town.

"Back then, the *Folies* was the hottest ticket around. The show was brand new—opened Christmas Eve, 1959. They brought the whole thing over from France. This wasn't the first topless show in town; Minsky's Follies at the Dunes took care of that back in 'fifty-seven. But word was that these Parisian girlies had Minsky's beat all to hell. Everybody said the show was *scandalous*—and Lord knows, everybody loves a scandal. Took us forever to get two tickets, but when we did, that's all she wrote. Maggie said, *That's the show for me.*

"She started waitressing here at the Trop just so she could be close by. Mornings she'd lay by the pool, and that's where she met some of the girls in the show. I guess she spoke a little high school French, which didn't hurt. Anyways, these French girls started teachin' her the routines on the side, just for fun.

"Then one night she came home, ready to bust. I'll never forget it. She said, *Gigi's pregnant!* Seems one of them girls from the original cast got knocked up by a high roller with a taste for French food. Maggie's buddies brought her in for an audition the next day. I guess they liked what they saw, 'cause they hired her on the spot." Dixie sighed.

"Were you jealous?"

"Hell yes! And hell no." She chuckled. "She'd spend all day learnin' parts of the show, then get up on stage that same night in the numbers she'd just learned—she was a total natural. She'd get home at two, then be up every morning to teach me every little thing they were teachin' her. I don't know when she slept. Anyways, she taught me to be a showgirl." Dixie looked me in the eye. "Best friend I ever had. And best damn showgirl I ever saw."

She drained her tonic water and stood up. "Well, darlin', tonight you saw the ecstasy. How 'bout tomorrow we show you the agony?"

19

The agony meant backstage.

Dixie showed me the stage door and told me to meet her there at six on Saturday evening. "You've seen the fun part," she said. "Let's see if you've got the stomach for the rest of it." She hugged me and headed back to Josephine Lane.

I went back to my room, hung the DO NOT DISTURB sign on my door, and proceeded to sleep for the next twelve hours. When I awoke at twelve-thirty the next afternoon, my energy was restored and my head was clear of alcohol. My brain was still buzzing, though. When I closed my eyes, I could still see the gorgeous, sparkling, near-naked pageantry of the night before playing over and over like a movie in my head.

I showered and dressed, then went downstairs and again gorged myself at the buffet. Then I did the strangest thing.

I went shopping.

I've always understood, intellectually, that girls tend to fall into two categories: those who like to shop, and those who *love* to shop. I didn't fit in either category—which was no great shock to me, as I didn't fit in much of anything or anywhere, whether it was the latest styles everybody else was wearing or the closed circles of friends who were wearing those latest styles. I just always assumed I wasn't meant to shop. So why was I suddenly drawn to the Trop Shops?

The answer was simple: I wanted to go to the pool.

Never mind that Las Vegas is in the middle of the desert, the

Tropicana uses a gazillion gallons of water, just like all the hotels and casinos apparently do. Everybody's got so many waterfalls and lagoons, you'd think you were in Hawaii. The pool at the Tropicana looks like a tropical oasis, and it was pretty inviting—especially since I had hours to kill and the day was blistering hot.

Needless to say, I had not packed a bathing suit. I hadn't planned on swimming. Not to mention that I don't own a bathing suit.

I found what I was looking for in the Necessities Boutique. How do I say this? It was . . . a bikini.

Although maybe *bikini* is too strong a word.

It was unquestionably a two-piece bathing suit. Black, with a little sparkle in the fabric. A top, and a bottom, revealing some expanse of skin in between. Given the modesty of both the top and the bottom, I suspect that on a normal-sized girl, that expanse of skin would've been at most an inch or two. Because I'm so long and tall, though, there was a full six or seven inches between the top of the bottom and the bottom of the top.

I can't remember when I've ever worn a two-piece bathing suit. First, because Somerville, Massachusetts, is not big bathing suit country. Second, because bathing suits are for girls who want to show off how pretty they are. And that was never me.

But then again . . .

Up until two days earlier, I had never even imagined myself wearing any such thing. But then that package arrived. And there was that snapshot. Of Maggie. My mother. In *that dress*.

And I confess. Since then, I had started to wonder . . . what would it be like to wear such a thing?

Not that I would, of course. But I did wonder.

Then seeing the *Folies Bergère* show the night before, with all those tall, leggy women wearing almost nothing. And do you know? Some of those showgirls weren't any bigger on top than I am. And trust me, I know what I'm talking about, because they weren't leaving anything to the imagination.

And they looked . . . amazing. Glamorous. Perfect.

Which is not to say that I looked amazing, glamorous, perfect, or anything close to any of those. Of course I didn't. But just maybe if I put on this bathing suit, I wouldn't look half bad. And that pool was awfully inviting.

When I tried the suit on and saw myself in the dressing room mirror, my first thought was, *Who is* that? Because I looked, well . . . okay. Maybe even a little better than okay. But then my second thought was, *Am I really prepared to wear this in front of people?*

I didn't wait around to figure out the answer. I bought it. Also a bottle of number forty-five sunscreen. I went up to my room, peeled off my clothes, slathered on half a bottle of Coppertone, and slid into the bathing suit. Then I headed for the pool.

The pool at the Tropicana is like a hallucination. It's a big lagoon, with waterfalls pouring off little cliffs, and palm trees all around. It occurred to me that when I got home to Somerville, I should recommend to the mayor's office that if they want to practice some really impressive Urban Revitalization, they should skip the dog parks and install one of *these*.

A handsome pool boy grabbed a couple of towels and set up a chaise for me, without my even asking him. "Are you in the show?" he asked.

I almost asked *Which show*—only then I knew he meant the *Folies*.

"No," I said. It was just one little word, but for some reason saying it made me sad.

"You should be," said Carl. That was his name. He asked if I needed anything else. I thanked him and said no. As he left, I swear I saw him turn around to look at me. It was probably my imagination. Or somebody behind me.

I laid on my back until my front felt so hot from the sun that I couldn't stand it. I jumped in the pool, cooled off, jumped out and laid on my stomach, until my back felt so hot I had to jump in the pool again. After about an hour, I'd had about as much public exposure as I felt my body could stand. At least nobody had booed, or laughed.

I flip-flopped back inside the hotel. My suit was still a little damp from my last immersion, and I stepped from the poolside inferno to the air-conditioned interior. As a result of the cold, and my damp bi-kini top, well . . .

All right, I'll just say it. My nipples stood up.

I didn't need to look down to confirm it. I could feel them push-ing against the thin fabric of the bathing suit.

At least I had picked a quiet moment to wait for the elevator. No one else was there to see.

After what seemed like forever, the elevator arrived. I rushed in-side.

And realized that my nipples and I weren't alone.

20

There was a man in the elevator. A good-looking man. Maybe thirty-five, very tan, wearing an ivory linen suit and a black T-shirt.

"Hi," he said.

"Hi." I pushed the button for my floor and looked away. Maybe he wouldn't notice my nipples, which were still standing at full attention.

As the door closed, I glanced sideways at the man. He was looking. At me. At my nipples.

"Very nice," he said.

I should have been outraged. I should have told him he was a pig. Three days ago, I would have done exactly that. "Thank you," I replied.

"You in the show?"

"Yes." Don't ask me why I said that. Or why I felt so good saying it.

"I thought so." The elevator stopped: his floor, not mine. He looked me in the eye, then looked down at my nipples again, and shook his head. In admiration, if I'm not mistaken. "*Very* nice." Still ogling, he stepped off the elevator. Then the doors closed and he was gone.

I looked down at my nipples, erect as ever. *Thanks a lot, girls.* When I said those words in my head, they sounded sarcastic. Then I thought again about that man, what he had said, and how I felt about it.

Instead of being mortified, I was . . . flattered. "Thanks a lot, girls," I said, this time out loud, and without a trace of sarcasm.

At six o'clock, I met Dixie at the stage door. "Well, look at you," she wondered.

I had shopped. Again. Twice in one day—something that had literally never happened. I was wearing tan canvas shorts and a halter top I bought in Tropicana Fashions. From a style point of view, I was fully aware that my choices resembled Dixie's wardrobe. The reason is simple: I've never cared much about style, never paid attention, so I had essentially no fashion sense of my own. I knew that Dixie was tall like me and that she looked good in shorts and halters, so I figured I couldn't go too far wrong.

She was smiling, so I guessed I had chosen wisely.

"I want you to prepare yourself," she advised, suddenly sounding like a schoolteacher. "Remember all that perfection you saw last night?" I nodded. *Perfection* was exactly the right word. "That is what we call theater. Illusion. What you are about to see is the bad-skinned, fat-assed, little-tittied reality."

She steered me through the stage door, down a short corridor and then through another door. Instantly, we were in Purgatory.

I say that not in a religious sense. At the Museum of Fine Arts in Boston, there's a painting called *Purgatory*. It's by this really twisted Dutch painter named Hieronymus Bosch. If you've ever seen one of his paintings, you'll remember: they're filled with weird naked half-animal people doing weird bestial sexual things.

Dixie had brought me to the main dressing room for the corps of the *Folies Bergère*. And although I didn't see anyone having sex with animals, the scene nonetheless bore an uncanny resemblance to Purgatory. The place was packed like the Red Line at rush hour—only instead of commuters in their work clothes, here the crowd was comprised of women in various stages of undress. Bra and panties. Panties only. Bra only. G-string only. Skin only. And true, although there were no animals in the crowded room, the abundance of feathers from costumes and headdresses, combined with all the naked flesh, made it feel as if everyone there was about to break out into one giant collective unnatural act.

And the din. The women were laughing, cursing, shrieking. There was joy, outrage, despair, jealousy, passion, all at the same time.

"Shut up, girls!" Dixie bellowed, and the decibel level dropped by half. "I'm showin' my niece around, so everybody play nice!"

I looked at her quizzically. She leaned close and whispered. "If they think you're family, you're safe. Otherwise they'd make you as a new recruit out to take steal their job, and soon as I turn my back they'd scratch your eyes out." Yikes.

Dixie moved me toward a corner of the room. "What should I do?" I asked.

"Just watch."

So I watched. It was fascinating. The first thing I noticed was how *different* everyone looked. On stage, the showgirls presented the image of uniformity; up close, though, they were all incredibly different. They ranged in age from late teens to the forties, at least. No one there was genuinely short, but there was probably at least a six-inch gap between the shortest girl and the tallest. Complexions were dark and pale, waxy and freckled . . . until the makeup went on, body and face, until they all looked the same.

What was most striking to me was how accurate Dixie had been. The on-stage perfection really was an illusion. When Dixie described *bad-skinned, fat-assed, little-tittied reality*, she wasn't kidding. The girls came in all sizes, all shapes, and there was not a perfect body among them.

At some point, I realized I was standing up taller.

After makeup and hair, they began to don costumes—and from this close up, some of the magician's secrets were revealed. The shorter girl wore taller heels and her shoes had a small platform. The feathered bottom for the J.Lo-butted girl had more plumes on each side to hide her ampleness in a downy haze. Costumes that appeared to consist of nothing but straps and rhinestones were engineering marvels of wire and elastic, lifting ten years off the older girls' breasts.

Watching one girl's boobs instantly perk as she shimmied into her costume's superstructure, I wondered about that dreamlike, alluring dress my mother had worn in the snapshot.

"Nope." It was Dixie, right behind me, and I jumped.

"'Nope' what?"

"I know what you was thinkin'," she said. "And nope, your momma didn't need one of them rigs. All that girl needed was what the good Lord gave her." She gave me a long look, and I thought she was about to say something else. Suddenly, though, a cacophony of screams erupted from the far corner of the dressing room. "'Scuse me while I go separate the cats." She plunged into the crowd.

A dark-eyed girl with huge hands sidled next to me. She leaned close enough that the feathers from her headdress tickled my nose. "'Niece' my ass," she hissed. "I know why you're here." Then the girl spotted Dixie working her way back toward us. "So glad you could make it," the girl bubbled, and walked away before Dixie arrived.

"Corinne's a bitch," Dixie announced, none too quietly.

"Yep."

"She only hates you 'cause she sees what I see."

Before I could ask what she meant, Dixie turned toward the center of the room and hollered, "Five minutes!" Then without another word she steered me to a stool in the wings, from where I watched first the seven-thirty "covered" show, meaning no bare boobs, and then the topless ten o'clock version. I sat there for five hours. Covered, topless, it didn't matter. I was utterly transfixed by all of it.

When it was over, Dixie came to retrieve me. "Stand up," she said. I did. "Turn around." Puzzled, I complied. "Now face me." She put two fingers under my chin and tilted my head up ever so slightly. After a long pause, she finally said, "Dang."

"What?"

"You've got it, too."

21

"It?"

"It."

"What's *it*?"

She just shook her head and walked away from me. I followed, and kept asking—practically pleading—but she wouldn't tell me. When I saw that she was adamant, I made a different request.

"Tell me about my mother."

Back in the cool coziness of 7 Josephine Lane, Dixie fixed herself a vodka and tonic. I watched her and wondered to myself if maybe she drank a little too much.

"Naw, darlin', not too much. Just enough."

Had I said it out loud?

"That's what you was thinkin'," Dixie explained. "It's all over your face." She handed me a tumbler. "Here's a tip. Stay away from the poker tables."

I sipped my drink. It was light on the vodka. Like she said, *just enough.*

"Anyways," she said apologetically, "don't know how much more there is to say. I've already told you most everything I know about Maggie."

"But you were best friends."

"We were indeed." She raised her glass in tribute, and we both drank. "For as long as it lasted. Didn't last long, though."

"What happened?"

"Maggie happened. She was just too dang good to stay here. Back then, sure, Vegas was Vegas, but Paris was the world. And she was as fine a showgirl as anybody ever saw. Those French folks runnin' the show back then, they knew what they had. Knew she was cut out for bigger things. So after about three months, they offered her a job. At the *real Folies*."

That took a minute to sink in. "In Paris?"

"You betcha."

"Did she go?"

"Your momma's daddy didn't raise him no fools. Course she went."

"To Paris?"

Briefly, Dixie scowled. "Am I talkin' too fast for you?"

"No. I just . . ."

"Never knew."

"Right." My mother. Was a Vegas showgirl. Who went to *Paris*. I wondered what else I didn't know. "Why didn't you go?"

"They didn't ask me."

"Oh." I realized suddenly that it was an insensitive question. "I'm sorry."

"Don't be. I wasn't good enough yet. It took me years to make the grade for the *Folies* here. Truth be told, good as I ever got, I'm not sure I was ever Paris material."

"But Maggie . . ."

"Was the best showgirl I ever saw. Ever. I told you that, and I meant it. A girl like that comes around once in. . . ." She thought. "Once. Period." Then an idea seemed to occur to her, and she amended her statement. "Or maybe twice."

"Who's the second one?"

"I'm not sure yet." She said it mysteriously, and with a sly smile. "Anyways, we were talkin' about your momma."

"That's right. So what happened?"

"She left."

"Just like that?"

"Course not just like that. I told you, we was best friends. She ago-
nized. She cried. We both cried. Then we laughed. Then we cried
some more. At the end of the day, though, she had to go. She knew it
and I knew it. I helped her pack her bags. I went with her to the airport. Gave her one more hug, then Mimi got on that plane and flew
away. And I never saw her again."

Mimi?

Again, Dixie read my expression. "That was Maggie's stage name.
Every showgirl needs a stage name. Helps keep the creeps from findin'
you. Plus it adds to the mystique. Every showgirl needs mystique." Her
eyelashes fluttered. "The French girls gave her that name when she
joined the company. I suspect that when she got on the airplane, your
momma left Maggie behind here in Las Vegas—and it was pure Mimi
who landed in Paris."

"What happened to her in Paris?"

There was a long silence. Finally, Dixie admitted, "I don't know."

"How could you not know?" It came out as an accusation, although I hadn't intended that. But Dixie was the only connection I
had to my mother's past. Now that connection was hanging by a
thread, and it seemed the thread was about to snap.

"It was a different world then. No such thing as e-mails. International phone calls cost a fortune—and I sure didn't have a fortune,
'specially since I went from payin' half the rent to payin' all of it overnight."

"What about letters?"

She shook her head. "I told Maggie I'd write, and she told me the
same thing. I guess neither one of us was any good at puttin' pen to
paper."

"You never wrote to her?"

Quietly, she admitted, "I never did."

"Were you jealous?"

Dixie flinched, ever so slightly. "Smart girl. I guess I was."

"Is that why you didn't write?"

"Maybe."

"Why didn't she write to you?"

She shrugged helplessly. "You'd have to ask Maggie." Dixie didn't say it to be mean. Just honest.

"So you never heard from her again."

"I didn't say that."

This time I was the one who flinched.

She stood up, walked to a dresser near her bed, and pulled open the top drawer. She removed something, closed the drawer, and returned to her seat close to me.

Dixie handed a white envelope toward me. "Here," she said. "I think you should have this."

22

*M*y hand shook as I reached for the envelope.

The paper was slightly yellowed with time. The envelope was small, about three inches by four—not nearly big enough to hold what I was looking for, which was the entire history of Maggie Archer's missing years.

It was addressed to Dixie c/o the Tropicana Hotel, Las Vegas, Nevada—no street address or zip code. I didn't recognize the handwriting, which was slanted and perfect, the type of script that appears only in penmanship primers. There was no return address. I looked at the stamp. It was an image of a stained glass window, the Madonna and Child. The bottom of the stamp said *Christmas USA 15c*. The postmark was blotchy but legible: BOSTON MA 021 PM 23 NOV 1980.

My heart beat faster. I opened the envelope.

In it was a one-sided card sized perfectly for the envelope. In the center of the paper was an image of a pink teddy bear. Above the bear, the card read:

Jack and Margaret A. Stone
Are Proud to Announce
the Birth of their Daughter
Linda Helene Stone

The inscription continued below the teddy:

I studied the card for a long time. Finally I slipped it back into its envelope and looked up at Dixie.

"Long and skinny from day one," she said with a quiet smile.

Here was another discovery, and in its own way, it was equally stunning to me as the snapshot of young Maggie in her decadent dress. *My mother had sent out birth announcements.* I was certain it was she who had done it; the thought would never have occurred to Jack. Maggie had announced my arrival to the world.

Proudly.

"When that card came," Dixie continued, "I almost threw it away. Never knew any *Margaret A. Stone.* Still, it was addressed to me, so I kept it and tried to figure out who it was from. Thought about it for days. Then one night in the middle of the ten o'clock topless show it hit me. Right in the middle of the Cancan. *Margaret A.* was Maggie Archer, back from France after all those years! I damn near high-kicked myself in the head. Soon as the performance was over I ran back here and got directory assistance on the phone. Asked for a Jack Stone in Boston, Massachusetts." Her voice rose in pitch, as if she were reliving the moment. Then her tone fell. "Nothin.' I tried John Stone. Margaret Stone. Maggie Stone. Maggie Archer." She shook her head apologetically. "All nothin.'"

"What did you do?"

Dixie drained her drink. I noticed that she didn't get up for a refill. "What could I do? I put the card away. I got me a box full of special things. Mostly love letters from good men I wasn't smart enough to marry. Anyways, I put that card in the box, and just kept hopin' Maggie would call me. She never did."

"She died," I said.

"I know that," Dixie said. "Lord have mercy."

I drained the rest of my vodka and tonic in one gulp.

"After a while, I confess, I forgot about it. I mean, it's been, what?"

"Twenty-six years."

Dixie gave a low whistle. "That long? Lordy. I really am gettin' old. See, that's how I found the card after all these years. Last week, I was feelin' old and lonely. Looked at myself in the mirror and wondered where that pretty young thing went. So I pulled out that box to read me some of them sweet letters. And there it was." She smiled. "The first time I tried to find her, all I had was directory assistance. All these years later, times have changed. Google did the rest. This time, when I went lookin' for Maggie, I found her." Dixie's voice got shaky. "Readin' a friend's obituary, that's a bad thing." She pulled herself together. "So I figured, if I couldn't reconnect with Maggie, maybe I could find her little girl. Ran me a search on Linda Helene Stone."

"Am I on the Internet?" The thought had never occurred to me.

"Oh yes you are." Dixie tried to frown, but as she spoke it morphed into a wry smile. "And you have been a bad girl, haven't you?"

I tried to remember how many times I had fought the law and the law won. How many of those episodes were online, memorialized forever like reruns of a bad sitcom? "Have I?" I tried my best to sound innocent.

Dixie laughed out loud. I guess I still don't do innocent very well.

"Okay, maybe a little," I admitted.

"Don't apologize to me, child. I've been a bad girl myself, and those were some of the best times I ever had. The important point is, I found you. Didn't exactly know how to start the conversation, though. Seein' as how you lost Maggie when you was so small, for all I knew, maybe your daddy got married again. Maybe you grew up with another momma. Maybe you wasn't curious."

"No," I said quietly.

"So I sent you that package, just to see what you would do. And you *were* curious. You came lookin'. And you found me."

"But I still haven't found *her*. Little pieces of her, yes. But not everything."

"I'm not sure anybody ever knows everything," Dixie opined. "Not even about themselves, much less somebody else."

"I still want to know more."

"Course you do. She was your momma. Poor child." She stood up.

Sitting there, looking up at Dixie, I wondered if this is what it would have felt like as a little girl, to have my own tall mother to look up to. I would never know.

"You already know I can't tell you everything. But I sure can give you one more piece. Would you like that?"

23

*D*ixie unlocked a tall cabinet over her bed. Inside the cabinet was a piece of luggage unlike any I'd ever seen. It resembled a hat box—but a hat box on steroids. It was a big cylinder, easily two feet high and a foot-and-a-half wide, with a large looping handle across the top.

"What is it?" My pulse raced. I thought—hoped—I already knew.

"After I rediscovered that card from Maggie, I took a ride out to our storage facility. The *Folies* have been running at the Trop nonstop since Christmas Eve 1959, and we hardly ever throw anything away. Everything gets catalogued and filed. Took me a while, but I finally found this."

As Dixie brought the box closer, I could see that the cylinder split in two, and there was a small lock holding it closed. Dixie retrieved a tiny key from a jewelry box on her dresser, inserted it into the lock, and the latch popped. She opened the box.

Inside was the headdress. Maggie's headdress. The gorgeous, sparkling, plumed crown my mother had worn in that ancient snapshot.

It was forty-seven years old, but it looked brand new. Up close, I could see details that were invisible in the photograph. The headpiece, which was shaped to fit close to the head like a swim cap, resembled a web spun by a magical spider, one whose silk was dotted with diamond-white rhinestones. From the crown of the cap rose an ornate silver stem out of which sprouted a small forest of luminescent ostrich plumes, each one perfectly placed to spread in a circular fan over the wearer's head. Under the halogen pinpoint spotlights in Dixie's ceiling, the whole thing glowed.

She pointed to a small hole at the top of the silver stem. "That's where I plucked that feather I sent you. Just pop it back in there and it'll be perfect." Dixie lifted the headdress out of the custom-made case and handed it toward me. "Take it," she said.

I hesitated, then accepted it from her. I almost expected to get an electric shock when I touched it, but I didn't. This wasn't a magical object after all; it was entirely real. In fact, for something that looked so delicate and ethereal, the headdress was surprisingly heavy—probably eight or nine pounds. The weight of the thing comforted me. To have worn such a thing, my mother must have been a real person.

"Aren't you going to put it on?"

I had been asking myself the same question, and yet hearing Dixie articulate it took me by surprise. I hesitated. "I don't know. Do you think I should?"

"Why not? It's yours."

"Mine?"

"Yours. To keep."

"You said the *Folies* never throw anything away."

"I said almost never. Besides, nobody's gone lookin' for this in almost half a century. They ain't about to start now."

Slowly, I approached the large mirror that hung over Dixie's dresser. Carefully, I lifted the headdress. For a few seconds I held it there, hovering just above my hair.

This must be what a queen feels like, just before her coronation.

I lowered the crown onto my head. It fit perfectly—just as, somehow, I had known it would.

I looked in the mirror, blinked, and blinked again. Because the girl I saw looking back at me was not Linda Stone dressed in her pretty new halter top and tan shorts. No—I saw Mimi Archer, showgirl extraordinaire, bejeweled and nearly bare, looking statuesque and seductive and nothing short of perfect in her oh-so-revealing, oh-so-enticing figment of a dress, in her coronet of feathers and gems, in her leg-lengthening sparkling strappy stilettos.

"Dang," Dixie whispered.

I turned to look at her, wondered if she saw it, too. When I turned back to the mirror, there I was—me, in my own clothes, in the present day.

Maybe there was some magic in the headdress after all.

I surprised myself with how hopefully I asked the next question.

"Do you have the dress and the shoes?"

24

*D*ixie laughed. It was a sweet laugh, and only a little sad.

"I'm sorry, darlin'. I looked everywhere. This was all I found."

My heart fell. "But you said . . ."

"I know." She shrugged. "I can't imagine they'd throw those things away. On account of you cannot believe how much one of them costumes cost. So all's I can figure is they sent Maggie's dress and shoes with her to Paris."

Then I have to go to Paris.

That was the first thought that popped into my head. My reasoning was very simple, and entirely logical. My mother's showgirl costume had given me a doorway to discovering . . . well, to discovering my mother. Up until only a few days ago, I hadn't known her at all. But it was worse than that. I had resented her. Even hated her. Here in Las Vegas, I had met her for the first time—and, in spite of all those angry years, I found myself wanting to know more about this total stranger who had brought me into existence. Maybe even . . . *liking* her. By following the ostrich feather of Maggie's plumed cap, I had already learned so many things. If only I could find her spangled shoes and her sliver of a dress, I thought—no, I *knew*—I could learn so much more about her.

Maybe a few things about me, too.

My reasoning may have been simple and logical, but it was not practical. I couldn't afford to go to Paris.

After I paid for my plane ticket and before I left for Las Vegas, I

had called Cambridge Trust and checked my balance. Since then, I'd
kept a running tab in my head. Charging all my meals to Dixie helped,
but still, subtracting out my Tropicana hotel bill and the uncharacter-
istic shopping I'd done, my checking account would have a whopping
three hundred and twenty dollars, give or take a few bucks. And don't
bother asking about my savings account. Savings accounts are for people with savings.

I must have looked crestfallen, because Dixie asked, "What's
wrong?"

"I can't afford to go to Paris."

Wait a second. I was in *Las Vegas*.

I stood up with a purpose.

"Sit down," commanded Dixie.

I sat down. She had that effect on me.

"I know what you're thinking," she warned.

"No, you don't."

"You're thinking you'll go get lucky at the casino and then you'll
have enough to run off to Paris and hunt down the rest of your momma's history."

Damn. She *did* know.

"You know what we call people who come to Vegas lookin' to
make money?"

"Stupid?"

"You're half right. Stupid *and* broke."

I was deflated. I *had* to get to Paris, somehow.

I looked around at the trailer's lovely interior. The furnishings, the
plasma TV, the audio components . . . everything was top of the line.

I have never borrowed money in my life. Ever. Not from anybody. Not five bucks for a late-night grinder at Three Aces on Mass
Ave. I don't believe in it.

But this was different. We were talking about my mother.

"Dixie . . . could you . . ."

"No."

Her answer sliced through me. She knew what I was asking, and
she wouldn't even let me finish the sentence.

Her face softened. She leaned close and took my hands in hers. "If I could, child, I would. But I don't have the money. Don't let this fancy place fool you. Sure, I live here for almost nothin'—but the trade-off is, they pay me almost nothin'. Took me nearly forty years to save enough to fix up the inside of this place. Take me another ten years to fix up the outside, if I live that long." She released my hands, stood up and walked to her jewelry box. She dug something out and held it up. It was a disk, about the size of a silver dollar, only it was yellow, with streaks of pink and purple. "Do you know what this is?"

She handed it to me. In the center of the disk was a round paper label. On the label was printed $1000. Without a word, I handed it back.

"Right now, this is my life savings."

"I'm sorry."

She laughed, which surprised me—and it was a real laugh, not at all rueful. "Don't be sorry for me, girl. I have lived a *life*, and I'm still doin' it. Better to enjoy it along the way, I say." She shrugged. "I just don't have money to lend. I wished I did."

Maybe I could go home and save up, she suggested. Maybe I could go to Paris in six months . . . or a year . . . or two . . .

"Yeah," I said. "Maybe."

I told Dixie I was going back to my room to get some sleep, and that I'd see her the next day. I didn't go to my room, though. I went straight to the ATM at the edge of the casino. The machine spat three hundred-dollar bills into my hand.

I thought about turning the bills into chips, but decided against it. Paper money had been good enough for Maggie.

Finding the roulette table was easy. Even over the bells and gongs and jingles of a thousand slot machines, the whirr of the wheel and the clatter of the bouncing silver ball called out to me.

I watched the game for a while. I was in no particular rush, because once I started, I knew I was going to win—or lose—quickly. I just wanted to wait until the moment felt right.

A fat woman in tight purple spandex put a tall stack of chips on black. She won, and the stack doubled. She picked up all the chips and moved them to double-zero. They were purple chips. Five hundred dollars each. The wheel spun. The ball bounced. Twenty-three. A loser. The croupier swept the chips away. The woman laughed.

Clearly, she didn't need that money. And clearly, she was not searching for her mother.

The fat lady walked away, still chortling. I took her spot.

"Bets," said the croupier.

I put my three hundred dollars—all of it—on red. The croupier looked at the bills, then at me. "I'm old-fashioned," I said.

He spun the wheel, then rolled the ball. The only sound in the world was that silver sphere racing around the wheel.

"No more bets," called the croupier.

The ball hopped, clattered, fell.

Fourteen. Red.

"Winner," smiled the croupier, and stacked three hundred-dollar chips on top of my bills. He looked at me expectantly, as if waiting for me to take my winnings and run. I didn't touch the money or the chips.

"Bets," said the croupier.

The wheel spun. The ball raced.

My heart raced, then stuttered as the ball fell.

"No more bets."

Three. Red.

"Winner."

In under a minute, my three hundred dollars had grown to six hundred, then twelve hundred.

I could quit. Maybe it was enough. Maybe it would pay for a flight to Paris.

But a hotel? Meals? And I had no idea how long I'd be there. Here in Las Vegas, I'd had a name and an address to start with—even if it was a stage name, and the address existed only in Dixie's fancy and on her driver's license. In Paris, I wouldn't even know where to begin.

"Bets," announced the croupier, spinning the wheel and releasing the ball.

I looked at my twelve hundred dollars sitting on red.

I watched the ball whirl around the wheel.

I recalled the story Dixie had told me about two young women, barely more than girls, about to start their lives.

Without giving myself time to think, quickly, I slid my winnings to black.

The ball slowed in its orbit. It was about to drop.

At that instant, a long arm reached over my shoulder. A woman's arm. In the woman's hand was a yellow disk with pink and purple markings.

Dixie slapped the thousand dollar chip on top of my stack.

The croupier declared, "No more bets!"

Dixie looked at me. I looked at her.

She smiled.

"Sure hope you're right," she said.

The ball fell.

25

*T*hree hundred dollars times two is six hundred dollars.

Six hundred dollars times two is twelve hundred dollars.

Twelve hundred dollars plus one thousand dollars is two thousand two hundred dollars.

Two thousand two hundred dollars times zero is zero.

But . . .

Two thousand two hundred dollars times two is *four thousand four hundred dollars.*

We won.

We won we won we won!

I instantly gave Dixie back her thousand dollar chip. As I said, I don't believe in borrowing money.

"Don't be ridiculous," she scolded.

"No," I said, "don't you be ridiculous." I thrust the chip at her. She wouldn't take it. I stuck it into the pocket of her shorts.

Four thousand four hundred dollars minus a thousand dollars is three thousand four hundred dollars.

I was going to Paris.

Dixie and I went back to her trailer. It was late, but both of us were too excited even to think about sleeping. The first thing she did was pull a bottle of champagne out of her tiny refrigerator, pop the cork, and pour us a couple of flutes. The second thing she did was turn on her computer.

"Go to Priceline.com," I instructed. I'm no Internet expert, but I do know that William Shatner, who plays Denny Crane on *Boston Legal*—which is an entertaining show despite the fact that it has absolutely nothing to do with Boston—is the Priceline spokesman. Priceline got me to Vegas for cheap, so I gave it a shot for Paris.

Continental Airlines. Departing the next day. Seven hundred and thirty-three dollars.

Leaving me with two thousand, six hundred and sixty-seven dollars.

Yes.

I gave myself two weeks. I wasn't sure what I was looking for, but I figured if I couldn't find it in two weeks, I wouldn't find it at all. Arbitrary, I know—but in the last few days my life had taken a very definite turn toward the arbitrary, and so far, it seemed to be working.

I did the math. I had $190.50 a day, which, according to the online currency converter, equaled 151.84 euros. That didn't sound like a lot. I needed to find the right hotel.

The Internet quickly told me that there are an awful lot of hotels in Paris.

Not knowing where to begin, I turned to Dixie for advice. "Where should I stay?"

"Beats me, girl. I only ever been two places: Mobile, Alabama, and Las Vegas, Nevada." She gave the matter some thought. "Why don't you stay close by where you're gonna be lookin'?"

"Where am I going to be looking?"

"Find the *Folies*. I mean the real *Folies Bergère*. Seems like that's as good a place to start as any."

It turns out that the web site for the real *Folies Bergère* is, wouldn't you know, www.foliesbergere.com. It was all in French. I learned a little French in high school, but the idea of trying to read a whole web site in a foreign language was daunting. Fortunately, it turns out that *Contacts* is the same in French as in English.

Les Folies Bergère
32, rue Richer—75009 Paris

That gave me a place to start. I narrowed my search to hotels in the immediate vicinity.

Hotel Peyris. Hotel du Leman. Hotel de Lausanne. Hotel Royal Medoc. Hotel du Centre. Hotel Acadia Opera. Hotel Aida Opera. All within one block of the *Folies*. So much for narrowing.

Those were three-star hotels. The prices ranged from about 90 to 130 euros a night for a single room. I looked again at my math: 151.84 euros a day, which had to include not just hotel, but meals and transportation and who knows what else. Three stars seemed like too many. Who needs stars, anyway? I went looking for one-star lodgings.

Hotel du Confort.

I was no French scholar, but even I knew that meant "Hotel of Comfort," which sounded, well, comfortable. There were no photos, but it was only three short blocks from the *Folies*. Better still, the rate was just 48 euros a night. Since I couldn't possibly spend more than a hundred euros a day on food, that would leave me plenty of money for other things, like . . . shopping.

Wait. *Shopping?* I never shop.

At least, not until I started following my mother's history and got to Las Vegas. Here, however, I had already bought a two-piece bathing suit, flip-flops, a halter top and nice shorts. Surely that was enough.

Then again, I was going to *Paris* . . . and it would be a real shame not to buy at least one or two pretty things while I was there . . .

Wait. *Pretty things?*

My head was spinning. It was as if someone else had, at least for a brief moment, taken up residence inside my skull. Whoever she was, I didn't recognize her. And she was distracting me. I kicked her out and went back to thinking like the practical hard-ass I've always been.

The simple fact was, sitting in Dixie's trailer in Las Vegas, I couldn't possibly know what unexpected expenses might arise in Paris. Maybe they have an entry tax on tall skinny girls. Since I was heading off into the unknown, spending less money on a hotel was better than spending more.

I made the reservation at Hotel du Confort.

I sat back and stared at the computer screen. I had my flight, my hotel, and money left to spend. It was nothing short of miraculous.

Dixie raised her champagne glass. "To Paris," she said.

"To Maggie," I said.

I was going to Paris. To find my mother.

$\mathscr{I}$ carried the bulky headdress case back to my room. As soon as I got there, I unlocked the lock, opened the case, and inserted the peacock feather back into its hole. For a second, I wondered if the feather was a magic key and its restoration would trigger a spell that would transform me into a princess.

There was that stranger in my head again. *Get lost, sappy girl.*

I locked the headdress case and slipped the little key onto my Red Sox keychain. Then I packed. My new acquisitions made packing a slightly longer process than when I had left for Las Vegas, although there was still ample room in my backpack.

With the feather restored to its home, I didn't need the long, un-wieldy box Dixie had used to send it to me. I picked up the box and held it over the trash.

My fingers refused to let it drop.

I've never been sentimental about a cardboard box before. Hell, I've never been sentimental about *anything* before. But receiving that package had changed me. I couldn't bring myself to throw the box away. I flattened it, folded it up, and slipped it into Jack's bowling bag.

I undressed, ordered a wake-up call, turned out the light, and went to sleep.

No sooner had I closed my eyes than the phone rang. At least, that's how it felt. But the room was full of daylight, and the clock radio confirmed that I had slept and it was morning.

After showering, I dressed in my old skinny-boy jeans, an ancient

Aerosmith T-shirt, and my hopelessly stained running shoes. With a long trip ahead of me, I figured comfort was more important than fashion . . . although I winced at the sight of the New Balances.

Briefly, I considered phoning my dad and telling him I was going to Paris. Quickly, though, I dismissed the notion. I'd only be gone for two weeks. I've disappeared for lots longer than that before, and Jack has barely noticed I was gone, much less worried. He doesn't worry about much, and certainly not about me.

I was about to head downstairs for breakfast when there was a knock on the door.

"Yes?"

"Room service."

I hadn't ordered room service. I looked through the peephole, and indeed, there was a tropical-shirted waiter with a tray. I opened the door.

"With our compliments," he announced, as he swept into the room with a flourish and set the tray on the desk. Instead of handing me a check, he never stopped moving, and swept out of the room before the door had even closed.

On the tray were scrambled eggs, French toast, pancakes, bacon, sausages, fresh fruit, pastries, coffee, tea, orange juice and grapefruit juice. It was more food than any one person could possibly eat, although I made a pretty good dent.

As I was finishing, out of the corner of my eye, I noticed a piece of paper slide under my door. I picked it up. It was my room bill. I scanned the charges, which matched my expectations, until I reached the bottom. The last line stated: *Balance due $0.00*. Someone had paid my bill.

There was another knock on the door. I opened it, and there was Dixie.

"You paid my bill," I said.

"Did I?" She handed me several brightly colored notes. "Here," she said. "Pocket money." They were euros, pink tens and blue twenties. A hundred euros in all. "Just to get you into town. Anyways, Lester in Accounting says never change money at the airport or at your hotel."

For an instant, I thought I would cry. I didn't, though. I'm not the crying type. Still, I gave her a hug. A long hug. The type of hug someone my age would give her mother, if her mother was still alive. I think Dixie knew she was a stand-in. I think she was happy to do it.

"Come on," she said. "Your cab's waiting."

"I can't afford a cab."

"I can."

She helped me carry my bags downstairs, where a taxi was waiting. Once everything was stowed in the trunk, she handed the driver money. Then she gave me another big hug, and kissed my cheek. When she pulled back, her eyes were moist. "So long, Lindy."

"Lindy?" Nobody had ever called me that.

"That's right," she said. "No more Linda. Now you're Lindy. Lucky Lindy, flyin' off all alone to Paris." Through her tears, she winked at me. "Good stage name for a showgirl, too."

She closed the car door, waved, and the cab pulled away from the Tropicana. Soon she was out of sight.

At the airport, I was more than a little nervous about checking my mother's headdress. It was too big for carry-on, though, so I had no choice. They marked the case with a FRAGILE tag and assured me it would be safe.

At security, the screener eyed Jack's bowling bag and asked, "Bowling ball?"

"Panties," I replied. I wondered if these guys worked off a script.

The less said about my flights, the better. First I flew from Las Vegas to Houston, Texas, in a seat with sufficient leg room for a six-year-old child. Not a tall six-year-old, either. Then I transferred to a larger plane for the flight from Houston to Paris. There was more leg room this time. At least enough for an eight-year-old.

The flight departed at around seven p.m. and was scheduled to last over nine hours. Mercifully, because I hadn't slept much the night before, I was so tired that I was able to sleep despite the cramped quarters.

Somewhere over the Atlantic, I dreamed. Even though I was asleep, and it felt entirely real and not like a dream at all, I recognized it as the same reverie I'd had on my way to Las Vegas. Once again, I was walking down a flight of stairs. There were lights: bright, colored. And music. The dream was more specific this time, though: the staircase was steep, although I had no trouble descending. Among the lights was a spotlight that followed me as I moved. I felt the rush of air against my skin. My bare skin.

I woke up, and the round nozzle of the air vent over my head was blowing cold air. I twisted it until the stream of air hissed to a stop. Then I closed my eyes.

Before I dozed again, a thought occurred to me: perhaps it wasn't a dream at all. Perhaps it was my mother. *This is what it was like.* I can't even remember the sound of her voice, but I could almost hear her saying those words.

Of course, I don't believe in such things. Clearly, it was all part of the dream.

Clearly.

I went back to sleep.

And awoke in France.

27

*T*he bump and squeal of landing gear on tarmac woke me.

I retrieved Jack's bowling bag from the overhead bin and hobbled down the aisle and off the plane. Fortunately, by the time I reached passport control, the blood was flowing to my legs again and I was walking more normally.

I dug my passport out of my pocket. Maybe Dixie was right. Maybe I was Lucky Lindy. Maybe things really did happen for a reason. After all, if I hadn't borrowed Toupee's Volvo and had my license lifted, I never would've gotten a passport—in which case I wouldn't be here, in France, on the hunt for my mother's tantalizing past.

Lindy.

I liked the sound of it. Then I remembered what Dixie had said. *Good stage name for a showgirl.*

A showgirl? Me?

At that moment, I arrived at the head of the line. A stern woman wearing a uniform and sitting in a little glass booth reached through a tiny opening in the window. *"Passeport,"* she said, sounding very officious and very French.

I handed her my passport and smiled.

She looked at my passport. At me. At my passport. At me. She did not smile.

Finally, she asked, *"C'est toi?" This is you?* I didn't love the fact that she called me *"toi"* instead of *"vous"*—they both mean *you*, but *"toi"* is the word you use when speaking to children or people you know really well. Or when you're trying to be condescending.

Still, I wanted to make a good impression. I smiled again. *"Oui, c'est moi."* Yes, it's me.

She looked again at my passport. At me. And frowned. *"C'est pas toi."* This is not you.

What was she talking about? Of course it was me. Who else would it be? *"Vraiment, c'est moi."* Really, it's me. I hoped she would see the light soon, before my high school French ran out.

She continued to look skeptical. *"C'est toi?"*

I tried to remember my passport photo. I had been pretty grumpy when it was taken, fresh from losing my driver's license. In fact, Riley at Quick Photo in Somerville had said that my picture made me look even crankier than usual—and since Riley has known me and annoyed me since kindergarten, that was going quite a ways.

Suddenly I realized my problem.

I quit smiling. Instead, I scowled. I downright glowered at the petty power broker who was still deciding whether or not to allow me into her country.

The woman studied my glower. Perused my photo. Then, at long last, her face twisted into something almost resembling a grin. *"Ah, oui, c'est toi."* She stamped my passport and handed it back to me. I had arrived.

My luck held at baggage claim. The precious headdress case was one of the first bags to roll up the conveyor belt, and there was not a scratch on it. My backpack followed a few minutes later, and I was ready to go.

I stepped out into the bustle of a terminal that made Logan Airport look organized, which means that the mayhem at Terminal A of Charles de Gaulle Airport is truly world-class. There were people in African multicolored robes who were shoving businessmen in perfectly tailored suits who were shoving women in full Muslim veils who were shoving pierced rockers in leather and chains. Everyone was shoving someone, but no one seemed to know where they were going or what they were looking for.

That added to my confidence, because at least I did know what I was looking for. In a moment I spotted it: a sign that said PARIS PAR TRAIN. I exited that door and boarded a shuttle bus to a station marked RER. I got off the bus, walked to the station, paid eight euros for a ticket, and in less than ten minutes was comfortably aboard a train rumbling its way to Paris.

If that sounds too easy, remember, as Jack Stone's daughter, the T was my playground, and mass transit is in my blood. Before boarding the train, I glanced at a map posted in the station. Paris has more subway lines than Boston does, but a subway is a subway. And one airport shuttle bus to the train is pretty much like the next, regardless of what language they use to announce the stops.

In about half an hour, the train stopped at Gare du Nord, and I exited. *Gare du Nord* means *"North Station."* I took the fact that Boston has its own North Station, on the Green Line, as another good omen. Unlike Boston's North Station, though, which is pretty generic as train stations go, the Gare du Nord was striking, with its enormous peaked roof a hundred feet high supported by elegantly sculpted green metal columns, light pouring in through huge arched windows, and platform after platform occupied by sleek bullet trains just arrived or raring to depart.

I had expected to change trains, but I found a street map and was delighted to see that my hotel was only five blocks away. I wrestled my bags through the crowds, down the stairs and out of the station. After one block on Boulevard de Denain, I turned right on Rue la Fayette. Cars honked, pedestrians jostled, bicyclists made obscene gestures . . . *just like at home*. I don't know what fundamental differences I had expected, but the fact that Paris looked like a real city—crowded, worn at the edges, and with more than a little genuine rudeness—was very reassuring to me. If I had stepped out of the train station and into a fairytale land, I wouldn't have had a clue how to behave. A crowded, worn, rude city I could handle.

Still, I was acutely aware that my mother might well have walked down these very same streets, and the thought made my heart beat faster. Of course, I grew up in a house where my mother had lived, and that had never affected my pulse. But that was back when all I knew about Maggie was that she had died and deserted me. Now I had begun to learn about her unimagined, unimaginable past, and I wondered if I might literally be retracing her footsteps.

After two longish blocks on Rue la Fayette, I turned left on Rue du Faubourg Poissonnière, which is where my hotel was located. As best I can translate it, Rue du Faubourg Poissonnière means *Street of the Fishmonger Suburb*. Putting aside that that doesn't make any sense, now that I think about it, it also doesn't seem to bode very well as the address of a hotel. Still, I was paying only forty-eight euros a night. Plus, so far, my luck had been very, very good.

Two blocks down, I spotted my hotel. It had a modest façade most accurately described as nondescript. Next to the doorway, a large pot held a small tree. The tree's leaves obscured the Ministry of Tourism sign that bore the hotel's single star.

I stepped inside the Hotel du Confort.

And that is when my luck ran out.

28

The lobby of the Hotel du Confort was about the size of an SUV. Not a Suburban, either; more like a RAV4. The far end of the SUV was occupied by a counter that was surfaced in three different patterns of linoleum, none of them matching. Behind the counter was a young man wearing a black wool Nike cap and opaque wraparound shades. He had a half-hearted goatee, and was bopping to gangsta rap that I could hear distinctly from his iPod's earbuds. I considered warning him about the risks of hearing loss, but decided at least to check in first.

"Excuse me."

Actually, I said "*Excusez-moi*." But if I continue to describe everything I said in French and then give the translation, that will prove embarrassing, given the poor quality of my French, not to mention tiresome. So from now on I will stick to the English translations.

"*Excuse me!*" Not only did I shout, but I had to wave my hand in front of his sunglasses to get his attention. Even then, he said not a word, only looked at me inscrutably. "*I have a reservation!*"

"Name?" His voice was surprisingly high-pitched, and I wondered momentarily if he might be a she, although the goatee suggested otherwise.

"Lindy Stone." It just popped out. "Linda."

"Credit card."

I handed him my Visa ATM card. He looked at the card, looked at something on a computer screen, and handed the card back to me. "No."

"No? What do you mean, *No?*"

"The reservation is for Stone Linda. The card is for Linda Stone."

At an earlier, less mature time in my life, I might have smacked him. Like, say, last week. Instead, speaking slowly and using small words, I explained to him that *Stone Linda* and *Linda Stone* were the same person. Finally he seemed to understand; either that, or he just got tired of my presence and wanted to get back to Snoop Dogg. "You have room seven. It is a very good one." He handed me an old-fashioned metal key attached to a doorknob that felt like it was made of lead.

"What is this?"

"Your room key."

"Not the key, this." I held up the doorknob.

"A doorknob."

"I can't carry a doorknob around Paris."

"No, you can't."

"What?"

"When you leave the room, you leave the key with me. When you come back, I give you the key."

"What if you're not here?" I've been known to stay out late.

"I am always here."

Why did that not reassure me?

"Where's room seven?"

"On the fourth floor."

"Where's the elevator?"

He pointed to a door on my left. I opened the door.

"Those are stairs."

"For three stars, you get an elevator. Maybe two stars. For one star, that is the elevator."

The stairway was exceedingly narrow, and, with the backpack on my shoulders, Maggie's headdress case in my right hand and Jack's bowling bag in my left, I could barely maneuver. If this was the main stairway, I wondered what the fire stairs must be like.

At the third floor landing, I passed a sign: FIRE STAIRS.

I reached the fourth floor. There were two doors, one marked 7 and the other, inexplicably, 12. I opened the door to my room.

If the lobby was the size of an SUV, room 7 was more like a MINI Cooper. Not one of the nice new ones, either, but the old, *really* small ones. I set the headdress case and bowling bag on the floor next to the single bed. Once I removed my backpack and put it down, there was a patch of empty space about a foot-and-a-half by three feet for me to stand in.

Hotel du Confort, indeed.

I looked around for the bathroom.

There was no bathroom.

I locked the room and ran down to the lobby. "*There's no bathroom*," I shouted at the pale gangsta behind the desk.

His sunglasses stared at me, expressionless. "Of course there is. There are two."

"Two? I don't even have one."

"Of course you do. It is on the fifth floor."

"Why is my bathroom on the fifth floor when my room is on the fourth floor?"

"So that everyone on the fifth and sixth floors can use it, too."

"Are you telling me I'm sharing a bathroom with five other rooms?"

"Six. There are three rooms on the sixth floor."

"Can't I get a private bath?"

"For two stars, you get a private bath."

I'm not spoiled. Not remotely. I've lived my life with pretty much a whole lot of nothing. And our little house back in Somerville has exactly one bathroom, so I've always shared with Jack—who is not the world's best person to share a bathroom with, from an olfactory point of view. But I was appalled at the idea of sharing a bathroom with six roomfuls of total strangers.

Still, I really had to pee. I cut the discussion short and ran up to the fifth floor.

And immediately ran back down.

"There's no lock."

The sunglasses just stared at me.

"There's no lock on the bathroom door."

"Of course not." Had he said *For two stars, you get a lock on the bathroom door*, I would have punched him. Lucky for him he stopped after *Of course not.*

"If there's no lock, what's to stop anybody from just walking in on me?"

"We use the honor system."

By that point, I *really* needed to pee. I abandoned the discussion and ran back up to the fifth floor. At least the toilet was clean, and there was paper.

I'm not a huge believer in the honor system. Perhaps because I myself haven't always been so honorable. In any event, the toilet was close to the bathroom door, and I have very long legs. So I sat on the toilet, stretched one leg out to hold the door closed with my foot, and peed.

Don't try this at home.

When I finished, I looked around. There was a sink, which I used, but no shower.

Back in the lobby, I demanded of iPod boy, "Where's the shower?"

"On the second floor."

"It doesn't have a lock either, does it?"

"Of course not."

On the theory that there is no honor among thieves or the guests of one-star hotels, I was done. *Finis. Terminé.* I walked back upstairs to my MINI room, retrieved my belongings, and marched back downstairs. After a brief discussion with the clerk in which I informed him that both Stone Linda and Linda Stone were leaving, and in which there might possibly have been the threat of physical force to ensure that neither of their credit cards would be charged for the privilege of using the toilet in an unlocked bathroom, I left.

I was enormously relieved to be out the door. *Hotel du Confort?* So much for truth in advertising. No wonder they used that little tree to hide their single star.

In seconds, however, my relief turned to panic. Yes, I was in Paris.

But I had no place to stay.

erhaps *panic* is too strong a word. I already knew there were plenty of three-star hotels nearby, and surely one of them would have a single room available. I didn't want to spend the money for three stars, though—particularly because it sounded like two stars would suffice to get me a private bath, a shower, an elevator, and a room key sans doorknob with which I could come and go at any hour I pleased. The trick was finding a two-star hotel that was not only close by but also had a single room available for the next two weeks at a rate I could afford. I had no idea if that was possible or not.

I started to walk. I was only a few short blocks from the *Folies Bergère*, which is located on Rue Richer. Instead of going that way, though, I headed west on Rue Bleue back to Rue la Fayette, then turned left onto Rue Cadet. After a block, I found myself at the corner of Rue Cadet and Rue Richer. Down the street, fully two blocks away, I could just barely make out a long vertical white sign with red letters that spelled out FOLIES BERGERE. Seeing that the theater was a safe distance away, I breathed a sigh of relief.

Why was I relieved? Wasn't this what I had come to Paris to find?

Well, yes, exactly. This was it. This was *everything*. I had come thousands of miles, looking for secrets that could only be unlocked at the *Folies Bergère*—and now there it was, a mere two blocks away. I had circled it cautiously, as if the whole area were radioactive with history and meaning. I needed to be ready, intellectually and emotionally, before I entered that charged territory. And I wasn't ready. Not quite yet.

I turned my attention back to finding my perfect two-star hotel. And, wondrously, there it was: right across the street, practically staring me in the face.

The sign above the darkened square window read

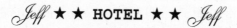

and painted on the window was the legend

HOTEL ★ ★

Jeff

whereas the gold lettering on the black awning over the doorway said

After my misadventure with Hotel du Confort, maybe I should have been wary about hotel names in general. But I looked at it differently. Hotel du Confort had been quite certain what its name was—yet the name most certainly did not accurately represent the hotel. The fact that this little two-star establishment couldn't seem to make up its mind whether it was Jeff Hotel or Hotel Jeff seemed, I don't know, charming. Not to mention that compared with all the terribly French names of all those three-stars in the vicinity, Jeff Hotel Jeff sounded so absurdly American. *Jeff.* I could absolutely picture myself staying at a hotel named Jeff.

The outside looked perfectly presentable. Like most of the buildings in the neighborhood—in fact, like most of the buildings I had seen in Paris so far—Jeff Hotel Jeff was six stories high, counting the street level and the gabled top floor. The façade was a stone the color of parchment, which seemed to be the principal building material in

Paris, just as red brick dominates Boston and its environs. The windows on the middle stories were floor-to-ceiling, and opened onto tiny wrought-iron Juliet balconies. In short, the building was quite attractive, bordering on lovely.

I strode across the street and into the lobby. It wasn't fancy, but for starters, I took as a good sign that it was at least eight times the size of the Confort's SUV. Plus, the downstairs was divided into two sections, a reception area and a small breakfast room with several tables neatly set below a trio of gilt-framed mirrors. The gentleman behind the front desk was an actual adult, and his immaculate dress and charming manner suggested that he took the hotel business seriously. The fact that sixty-eight euros a night got me a single room with my own toilet, shower, sink, closet, room safe, TV, phone, and magnetic card room key, *and* that I rode up to my third-floor room in an elevator, albeit a small one, sealed the deal.

The room was cozy, but huge compared to the MINI Cooper at the Hotel du Confort. The full-sized bed was covered with a royal blue bedspread that matched the curtains and coordinated beautifully with the rich-looking patterned carpet. The walls were painted a soothing cream color, and the ceiling was white. The desk, dresser, night table and lamps looked like antiques. The closet and dresser were on the tiny side, but considering that I wasn't a big packer, I had plenty of room.

The bathroom was a little odd, with no shower curtain and only a narrow glass panel to keep the water from the hand nozzle from spraying the room. Still, the towels were clean and thick, there was a lock on the door, and, best of all, the whole thing was my very own.

Honor system, my ass.

I opened the large window in the bedroom and stepped onto the tiny balcony. Everywhere I looked I saw lovely stone-faced buildings, white and ivory and tan and all shades in between, their roofs and chimneys all different and yet soothingly all the same. At street level, the storefronts reflected this year, today, this minute, but the view from my window was timeless.

My mother had met my father in 1979. Assuming she had gone

straight from the *Folies Bergère* to Somerville—a transition so bizarre I still couldn't get my brain around it—she would have left France twenty-eight years ago. In a city as old as Paris, twenty-eight years was the blink of an eye. The city Maggie waved good-bye to before I was born would have looked quite the same as the city I was discovering now. That thought sent a shiver up my back and then down again.

After I unpacked, I showered, then put on fresh clothes. Although the day was very comfortable, Paris was a far cry from the desert heat of Las Vegas, so my new halter and shorts wouldn't do. With a pang of regret, I pulled on a clean pair of jeans and a T-shirt. Back home I wore these clothes without a second thought. Here in Paris, though, they seemed inadequate. I vowed to buy something more appropriate to my surroundings.

I literally could not bring myself to wear my splotched running shoes. I opted for the flip-flops instead; at least they looked nice. For the few blocks to the *Folies*, they would suffice, although if I was going to walk any distance I would have to buy shoes that were more substantial. And pretty, too.

Pretty shoes?

I dismissed the thought. My confrontation with history was approaching. I wondered if I was truly ready to meet my mother's past.

I left my room, rode the little elevator downstairs, and headed for the *Folies Bergère*.

s my foot hit the pavement on Rue Richer in front of Jeff Hotel Jeff, I trembled. Maybe this is what Moses felt like as he approached the burning bush.

Despite my strong sense that I was walking on hallowed ground, the physical reality did very little to support that impression. I'm not sure what, if anything, I expected the street on which the *Folies Bergère* was located to look like, but Rue Richer wasn't it. My hotel was wedged between a pharmacy and a car rental company. As I edged closer to my destination, I passed a pizzeria, a dry cleaners, a Century 21 realty office, a Tandoori Indian restaurant, an Italian restaurant, a Jewish book store, a photo shop, a medical laboratory, and a kosher butcher. Parked cars and vans crowded the street, and clunky green recycling cans cluttered the sidewalk. Despite the looming theater sign that grew larger with every step I took, the surrounding neighborhood seemed to pay no heed whatsoever to its renowned attraction.

I was only a block away. I stopped for a moment. Without a doubt, my mother had trod this very same path, perhaps hundreds, even thousands, of times. I hoped no one was watching me, because I was shaking as I walked.

Now even the street acknowledged its star. Here was *Le Royal Folies* bar and brasserie. There the *Aux Folies du Livre et de la Plume* newsstand.

A few steps more and I had arrived.

The façade was stunning, overwhelming, as it loomed up over me.

At its center was sculpted in dark green bas relief a huge stylized depiction of a woman, the ultimate *Folies* dancer: her small breasts and long legs bare, her body lithe and coiled in movement, waves and swirls suggesting veils and feathers that only emphasized her naked vitality. On her left and right, graceful archways depicted the universal symbols of theater, the masks of comedy and tragedy. Above her, in dark green streamlined Art Deco letters, FOLIES BERGERE. Below her feet, the marquee of the theater, capped by red neon letters again proclaiming the establishment's birthright, FOLIES BERGERE, and below, directly over the theater's many doors, its claim to fame: LE PLUS CELE-BRE MUSIC-HALL DU MONDE.

The most celebrated music-hall in the world.

It was closed.

I don't mean it was closed because it was only midafternoon, and the doors wouldn't open until hours later.

It was closed. Shuttered. Out of business. Defunct.

I started to cry.

Yes, the Deco dancer was spectacular . . . but she was also in desperate need of repair. Her come-hither gaze was untarnished, but her arms and chest were scarred white where the dark green paint had flaked off. Her thighs, although still eternally toned, were cracked and peeling in the architectural equivalent of varicose veins. The finish on the entire façade was crackled with age, and on the border to the dancer's right a huge patch of dark green had broken away completely.

Below the marquee, the doors were papered over with layer after layer of handbills, all announcing something other than the latest *Folies* extravaganza.

I had come to discover my mother's life. Instead, I felt as if I were witnessing a funeral.

I wallowed in despair for about thirty seconds. Maybe a minute. Then I shook it off.

So the *Folies Bergère* was closed. So the magnificent Deco dancer was in desperate need of architectural BOTOX. So I had run full speed into a historical brick wall. So I was facing total abject disaster.

So what.

I hadn't come all this way for nothing. I wasn't going down without a fight.

Besides, I had enough money to stay for two whole weeks. And who cared if I didn't know where to look? What better time to start looking than right away?

I crossed the street and stood directly under the marquee. Rather than confronting those morbid handbills, I turned around to face the street. If the theater was open, and someone was exiting, this was the view they would see.

Two streets, Rue Geoffroy Marie and Rue de la Boule Rouge, came together like an arrowhead, pointing straight into the *Folies*. A third street, Rue de Trevisse, intersected Rue Richer only a few yards east. Thus, everywhere I looked was another street corner leading to endless possibilities of people who might still remember the tall slender American dancer—the one with the black hair, the pale skin, the petite breasts and endlessly long legs. My mother.

I had brought with me Dixie's snapshot. I wasn't sure if people in the neighborhood would recognize Maggie in her showgirl costume, but it was the only photograph I had.

At the Josse Boulanger, most of the staff was under the age of thirty, so by definition no one recognized the dazzling girl in the photo. Once they understood that I was the dazzling girl's daughter, though, they were wonderfully sympathetic, and wouldn't let me leave without sampling their *pain aux chocolat* and espresso. The pastry was flaky and light and crunchy and the chocolate deliriously bittersweet. Sorry, Au Bon Pain, but you've got nothing on the French. To add to the perfection, they refused to let me pay, and everyone there, even the other customers, kissed me on both cheeks before I walked out the door.

Buoyed by the chocolate and caffeine, I ventured across the street to *Le Royal Folies Bar Brasserie*. From the outside, it had the look of an establishment ever-present and untouched by time, and I hoped it might be filled with waiters, waitresses and patrons in their sixties and seventies. Once inside, however, I was disappointed to find that the place had been converted to a young, hip venue. Posters near the door advertised coming concerts. A promising locale if I had come to Paris to meet men. I hadn't, though. I was looking for my mother, and this was not the place to find her.

The next corner was occupied by the Dizengoff Café, a kosher pizzeria. I was detecting a trend. Apparently, the *Folies Bergère* was located in the heart of a Jewish neighborhood. I had already passed kosher burger joints, kosher butcher shops, kosher steak houses, and now kosher pizza parlors. I have a soft spot for Jewish men; David Klein from Brandeis was one of the sweetest, smartest boys I ever slept with, not to mention surprisingly well-hung, and if he hadn't started fretting on our second date about what religion the children would be, he might have made it to the fourth date. The point is, I have nothing against kosher establishments. I simply thought the possibility that anyone there would have known my tall gentile half-naked mother was remote, so I skipped the Dizengoff Café and kept searching.

Up and down Rue Richer, I made inquiries in my halting French and showed the precious photograph. At L'Echevin Bar Brasserie. *Non*. At Pressing Retro-cherie. *Non*. At La Foire du Livre, Folie Cuir, Pharmacie Richer. *Non, non, non*. Even at La Sellerie Clare, though who could guess what a saddle-maker was doing here, with not a horse in sight. *Désolé, mais non*.

Hours of fruitless searching were taking a toll, on my flip-flopped feet and my resolve. Plus, the sugar and coffee jolt from the Boulanger had long since worn off. As I scuffed my way back toward Jeff Hotel Jeff, I neared the Dizengoff Café. Its exterior was a pleasant yellow decorated with gray stone accents. The windows advertised an odd assortment of foods: pizza, of course, but also crepes, bagels and cappuccino. There was a take-out window, and a sign promised that both English and Spanish were spoken within. I was dubious, but then the door opened and I caught a whiff of pizza hot out of the oven. The smell made me realize how hungry I was. Besides, pizza is a cheap dinner anywhere, which would help me stretch my budget. My brain yielded to my stomach, and I stepped inside.

Although there were plenty of tables, I sat down at the counter.

An old waitress, tall, and wide across the middle, had her back to me as she worked the espresso machine. The coffee cup was tiny, but she took her sweet time filling it. When she finally turned around, instead of delivering the cup to a table, she leaned one hip against the counter, sipped the coffee herself, and sighed.

I hoped she made a good cup of coffee, because she wasn't much of a waitress. Remember, I have plenty of experience doing a poor impersonation of a waitress, but compared to this woman, I was a speed demon.

She finished her coffee, turned, and refilled the cup. The entire time, she still had not looked in my direction. Hungry or not, I thought about leaving.

The old woman turned around. This time she couldn't possibly miss me, as we were barely three feet apart and she was staring right at me.

Suddenly I realized: She was *staring. Right at me.*

At that moment, she dropped her cup, splattering coffee all over me.

31

"*W*hy do you people keep doing that to me?"

The words burst out of my mouth before I could even think. Then my synapses caught up to my lips. I knew exactly why she had spilled her coffee. It was the same reason Dixie had ruined my New Balances with her Bloody Mary. The shock of recognition will do that.

This woman recognized me.

Correction: she recognized Maggie.

"You knew my mother."

I don't know if I whispered or shouted. It didn't matter, because the waitress was obviously not one of the people who spoke English. Probably not Spanish, either. I repeated my statement, only this time in French.

The woman's complexion had been ruddy only a moment ago, but now she was pale. At first, she just nodded. Then, quietly, she said, "Oui."

I needed to be sure. Holding my breath, I showed her the snapshot.

She gasped, as if that old image had rocketed her back forty-seven years in an instant. I swear, the lines on her face smoothed, and for a moment I could see the tall slender girl this big heavy old woman had once been. "Ah, *chere* Mimi," she said. *Dear Mimi.* My mother's stage name. At that instant, I knew: this old waitress had not only known Maggie; the two of them had been showgirls together.

· · ·

Claudine—that was her name—told a bald man half a head shorter than herself that she was taking a break. The place was nearly empty, so he just shrugged. Without asking permission, Claudine grabbed a bottle and two glasses, and steered us to a table. The label on the bottle read SLJIVOVICA. The liqueur that poured out was crystal clear. *"Lechayim,"* Claudine said, and waited until I clinked her glass before drinking.

I've toted enough shots in my time to know that Slivovitz is plum brandy, and if you think that makes it a sweet girly drink, prepare to get knocked on your dumb ass. It burned going down. The fire inside of me had been fading after hours of fruitless searching, but now the alcohol was fresh fuel for my curiosity.

Before I could ask a single question, though, Claudine poured another drink for us both. Then she stood up, raised her glass in the direction of the *Folies Bergère,* and fervently intoned, *"La Gazelle."*

I didn't know what *La Gazelle* was. I mean, sure, I could guess that *Gazelle* in French was the same as *Gazelle* in English. But what did it *mean*?

Either Claudine didn't know that I didn't know, or she didn't care. She was waiting for me. Somehow I divined what she wanted. I, too, stood and lifted my glass toward the faded theater. *"La Gazelle,"* I repeated, and we both drank.

Then we sat. Apparently sensing my hunger, the bald man fetched me a pizza. It wasn't great, but I was hungry, so it was good enough. I wolfed it down.

While I wolfed, Claudine told me about my mother.

"Everyone loved her," Claudine explained. "Or hated her. And for the same reasons. She was so young. So fresh. So American. And . . . so talented. She had had very little training. Almost none, in fact. And so many of us had studied the dance our entire lives. But whatever she saw, she learned almost instantly. Instinctively." Claudine looked solemnly at me. "I was one of the ones who hated her."

"But—"

"Only at first, though. I was jealous, you see. So many of us were jealous. Here, we had worked so long and so hard, and here came this girl, this child with her very bad French." Claudine smiled wryly. "You speak the French as badly as she did."

"Thanks."

"You are interrupting. She came along and it was plain to anyone with two eyes and half a brain that she was going to dance right past us as if we were standing still. Which is exactly what she did."

"How?"

"You are again interrupting." She poured herself another drink. I had barely touched my first, so I held my hand over the top of my glass. Claudine frowned, thinking me a lightweight, and put the bottle down. "It is very simple. She was the most natural creature on stage that anyone had ever seen. She made us all look like performers." She saw I was going to ask a question, and cut me off with a stare. "Weren't we supposed to be performers? That is what you want to know?" I nodded. "Yes. But no. On the stage, everything is illusion. Especially at *Les Folies Bergère.* What we did was intensely difficult, and entirely artificial. Yet the audience should never see the difficulty or the sham." Subtly, subconsciously, she shifted to the present tense, as if she were still a young showgirl talking about her next performance. "Because if they do, they remain always on the outside, always remembering they are watching a show. Instead, we wish to draw them in, to take them along, to transport them. To do that, what we do must appear as effortless and as natural as the warm breeze in spring." She tilted her glass back and took a big swallow. "Mimi Archer was the warm breeze. And we were not. So of course, many of us hated her."

Claudine pointed through the café's window to the sidewalk, where people walked by, this way and that, without so much as glancing at one another. "Even though *Les Folies Bergère* are very special, in many ways, they are like the whole world. The world is full of people who have no face, whose name no one ever knows. To join *Les Folies,* one must be very very special—and yet, after one joins, she can spend a whole lifetime without a name. Many girls spent years and years, but never rose above being one of *Les Mannequins,* who simply posed and looked beautiful, or *Les Nus,* who were simply nude and looked beautiful. Even *Les Danseuses,* the ones like me, who danced so beautifully—in the programme for the shows, we were never names, never faces. It was as if we had no identity beyond the group: *Les Danseuses*.

"When Mimi arrived, even with her lack of training, she went straight into the ranks of *Les Danseuses*. But then very soon, word spread among the girls. *The new American, she is going to get a name*." I must have looked puzzled. "In the programme. She is going to get *billing*. In this number, in that routine, she is promoted, she is made the soloist, the lead dancer. And sure enough, soon she has her name in print, for all the world to see. First in the small plain print. Then the small bold print. Then the bigger bold print. I swear to you, she rose so fast, I thought that many of the girls would kill themselves. Or her." Claudine smiled. "But no one died." Then she paused, and I could tell that this time, she was waiting for me to interrupt.

"Why not?"

"Because. Because Mimi Archer really was the warm spring. Because she was not mean, or lordly, or bitchy—and most girls with even a quarter of her talent were all three. Do you know what she did?"

Of course I don't know what she did, I wanted to say, *I never knew her. You did, but I didn't*. I just shook my head no.

Claudine lowered her voice to a whisper, as if she were about to say something truly scandalous. "She baked *cookies*. Oatmeal. And chocolate chip. Not at all like the French patisserie. Such wonderful *American* cookies. And just in case anybody might think she was trying to get us all fat, she would redeem herself by eating more cookies than anyone else.

"And most impressive of all," Claudine intoned reverently, "she studied French. She improved. Many of the girls were British, and spoke only a little French, and spoke with those awful accents, and never tried to get better. But Mimi learned. She took classes. By the time her name was in the bigger bold print, she spoke it quite beautifully." Claudine sighed, remembering. "She was very endearing."

I had seen Maggie's photograph. I had watched the *Folies* performances in Las Vegas and imagined her there on stage. I had even
worn her magnificent headdress on my own head. Now more than
ever before, though, listening to Claudine, sitting in a café just across
the street from the theater where she had performed, now the reality
really sank in.

"Wow," I said.

"Wow?"

"Wow. My mother. *My mother was a showgirl.*"

Claudine slapped me.

32

*O*kay, listen up, everybody. The spilling was bad enough.

But the slapping absolutely has got to stop.

"What was that for?" I asked, rubbing my cheek.

"Your mother was no *showgirl*. I was a showgirl. The rest of us—nameless, faceless—we were showgirls." Claudine stood up, and again raised her glass toward the old theater. "Your mother was . . . *a headliner*."

Claudine then launched into a very earnest history of the *Folies Bergère*. I won't tell you the whole thing, because it was long, I'm sure I missed a lot of the details, and some of it was not entirely fascinating. But the bottom line was this: in all those decades, there were a few stars who rose above everyone else. There was Colette. Then an American, *La Baker*—Josephine Baker, the namesake of Dixie's Josephine Lane back behind the Tropicana, whose notorious dance with a costume made of bananas and little else set Paris aflame with desire. Then Mistinguett, with her fabulous legs insured for a million dollars, in an era when a million dollars meant something. After that, for years, even decades, many leading ladies, Claudine said, many big names, but not true stars.

And then, she said. Then came . . . *La Gazelle*.

The act that made her famous came about almost by accident, as remarkable discoveries often do. Maggie was backstage before a show: stretching, perhaps, or simply fooling around. Whatever she was doing, it bore no resemblance to any of the traditional *Folies* acts in which she performed so spectacularly. Her movements were a study in contradictions: raw but refined, demure but sensual. The choreographer, Billy Petsch, watched her for a while. Then he took her aside. *If you will arrive early*, he said, *and stay late, and work with me very hard, then perhaps we can make something special.*

So Mimi the American, already with her name in the bigger bold print, arrived early and stayed late, and worked with Monsieur Petsch. She must indeed have worked very hard. Because when they were done, they had not merely made something special.

They had created a star.

La Gazelle.

Monsieur Petsch did not create the name. Nor did my mother. Nor the legendary Michel Gyarmathy, who staged the *Folies* revues for forty years, nor Monsieur and Madame Derval, who owned *Les Folies Bergère*. No, the name was coined by a theatergoer who was blessed to be in the audience for the new work's debut performance. With the stage shrouded in a dry-ice mist, and the mythical, mystical strains of Debussy's *Prélude à L'après-Midi d'un Faune* swirling up from the orchestra pit like the tendrils of an erotic vine, Mimi Archer took the stage, barefoot and wearing, well, more than nothing, but apparently not much more. She tiptoed . . . she glided . . . she stalked, and pranced, and preened. Then her eyes widened at the discovery of the stimulation she could generate simply by the arch of her back, the flex of her thigh. Each moment that passed, she seemed to take greater raw animal pleasure from the sheer power of her own movements, her every motion awesomely feminine. And as the music neared its climax, her own excitement in the long-legged perfection of her body grew . . . built . . . pulsed . . . throbbed . . .

finally *exploded* with a sexual shock wave that rolled over the audience and left sixteen hundred breathless voyeurs silent and spent.

Silent, that is, until one man in the center of the orchestra section rose slowly, as if in a trance, and announced in an awed voice,

"Voilà—La Gazelle!"

The name stuck. Overnight, those two words were on the lips of virtually every Parisian man, woman and child: *La Gazelle.*

It was not the first time that Paris had been scandalized, and seduced, by a dance performance—and by this very same music, no less.
In 1912, it was Nijinsky's faun whose masculine erotic release at the
composition's finish had rocked the *Théâtre du Châtelet*. Fifty years
later, the sexual creature was female, and the location the *Folies
Bergère*—which drew an audience predisposed to titillation. Yet no
one had ever seen anything like Mimi Archer. The next day, *Le Monde*
labeled her performance high art, *Le Figaro* derided it as pornography,
and on the streets of Paris, it was called everything in between. It was
a huge badge of honor to have been present for its premiere—so much
so that over time, enough people to populate a football stadium would
claim to have been one of the 1,600 who filled the *Folies* that night.

Throughout its history, the shows at the *Folies Bergère* had routinely been sellouts. But this was a phenomenon. Soon there was not a
seat to be had a month in advance . . . six months . . . a year. All because of La Gazelle.

And La Gazelle was . . . my mother.

Just listening to Claudine's description left me winded. I did my
best to slow my pulse as I tried to wrap my brain around everything
she had told me.

"Now wait just a second." It was starting to sink in. "Are you saying that my mother had an orgasm on the stage of the *Folies Bergère*
in front of 1,600 people?"

It's a good thing for me that *orgasme* is the French word for *orgasm*. As I said, Claudine didn't speak any English, and I wasn't about
to ask the total strangers in the café to translate that.

Claudine's eyes shone, and not just because she had already
knocked down three glasses of the brandy. "That was the question.
The mystery. The secret all of Paris wanted to know. La Gazelle never
told, though." She refilled her tumbler. She neglected even to offer me
more, which was fine; if I had to hear this, I was better off sober. Claudine leaned close to me and lowered her voice. "Let me say this: I was
there. And if it was not real, she was our greatest actress."

Up until that moment, I had been chasing my mother's history
with a single-minded devotion. Now, suddenly, everything was so

much more complicated. Mind you, I'm no prude. Ha! With my past, far from it. But this new live-sex-show aspect of my mother's past was appalling. Mortifying.

And yet . . .

Still alluring. Fascinating. Even . . . inviting?

For the thousandth time since I had received that fateful package only a week ago—or was it a hundred years?—I asked myself: who *was* this woman? This divine creature, this beast, this inexplicable contradiction who had given me life?

"What happened the next night?"

"The line for tickets extended three times around the block."

"I mean, what happened when she didn't . . . you know."

Claudine looked puzzled. Then her brow unfurrowed. "Oh, but you are wrong. She *did*."

I figured maybe the first time had been an accident. You know, caught up in the moment. "You mean she did it again?"

"Again, and again."

"How many times?"

"Six nights a week."

"Six?"

"No shows on Mondays."

"For how long?"

"Fifteen years."

Six nights a week for fifteen years.

Wow.

Talk about your multiple orgasms.

started to calculate in my head. I'm no math whiz, but even I could tell that we were talking about a career of over four thousand consecutive on-stage orgasms. Lou Gehrig and Cal Ripken had nothing on my mother.

My head was swimming, and not from the brandy. I decided to shift the conversation to less provocative territory. "Let's forget about *La Gazelle* for a minute."

Claudine eyed me suspiciously. "No one can forget *La Gazelle*."

"That's not what I mean. I don't want to talk about her stage act. I want to talk about Mimi Archer. As a person. What was she like?"

"She was *La Gazelle*."

"I know. But besides that."

"Besides that?"

"Exactly."

"Besides that." Claudine looked briefly puzzled, as if the thought had never occurred to her. Then she brightened. "She baked cookies."

"You said that."

"Oatmeal and chocolate chip."

"I want to know what kind of person she was."

"The chocolate chip were my favorite."

"So you said. What did she do for fun?"

"She was *La Gazelle*."

"We've established that. I don't mean that kind of fun."

"There were all the men."

All the men? I didn't exactly love the sound of that either. It sounded like we were heading straight for more stories concerning sexual gratification, possibly on a grand scale. Mind you, I'm totally in favor of sexual gratification, especially my own. But let's remember that we're talking about my *mother* here. Did she have sex? Undoubtedly—I'm living proof. Did she have orgasms? Apparently— over and over and over again, live and on stage, no less. Did she have countless lovers? At this particular moment, already overwhelmed with a classic case of Too Much Information, I really didn't want to know.

"Forget about the men."

"How can you forget about the men?"

"I mean, just for right now. Did she have . . . girlfriends?"

"No, all of her lovers were men."

I guess I had translated wrong. I tried again. "No—did she have friends—who were just friends—who were girls?"

She thought about that for a while. "I don't know," she finally admitted.

"Were you her friend?" As soon as I asked the question, I regretted it. If she had been, Claudine already would have said so.

She didn't take it as a slight, though. "Here is what I remember of your mother. She was kind, and polite, and not at all arrogant. She would always say hello. From the very first day she arrived, when she was no one, to when she was the biggest star in the land, she was sweet and said hello. But once she became *La Gazelle*, she had her own special dressing room, far away from the rest of us. We saw very little of her. She came to the theater alone, prepared for her act alone, performed alone, and left alone." Claudine sighed. "So, sadly, no. I would have liked to be her friend. But I was not."

"Where can I find other people from the show who knew her?"

Her shrug conveyed futility. "Who knows? Maybe they have moved to Miami. Maybe they are dead. Or maybe they are walking around Paris. In those days, you could not mistake us—we were tall and slender and beautiful. But now"—she wrapped her arms around her girth—"Now we are old and fat. Perhaps you could ride the Metro and ask all the old fat ladies if they were in *Les Folies*." She chuckled at her own joke.

I was hoping for something with better odds than getting on the subway and questioning random overweight senior citizens.

Having come so far, the notion of running into a dead end in my search for my mother was unsettling. But if I couldn't find someone who really knew her, maybe I could locate something more tangible, the thing that had launched me on this quest: her showgirl costume. "When did the theater close?" I asked.

Claudine narrowed her eyes to think. The subject seemed to pain her. "Nineteen ninety . . . three."

Fourteen years was an awfully long time. What were the chances that the costumes were still around? "When it closed, what happened to the costumes?"

She shrugged. "Who knows? I was already retired for many years." She waved a fleshy hand around the Café Dizengoff. "Now this is my stage. Isn't it glamorous?" I tried my best to smile. "When the last revue closed, everyone acted as if there would be just a pause while they raised the funds to mount the next show. The spectacles are fabulously expensive to produce: so many girls, so many costumes, so many musicians, so many stagehands. For a while, everyone waited. Then they started leasing the theater. Sometimes to a musical from Broadway. Sometimes to a naughty gay show. But never *Les Folies*. Years have passed. Now it is just a dream."

I brought her back to my question. "And the costumes?"

"On the street, one heard many rumors. Everything was in storage for the next show—which never came. Everything was sold to pay debts. Everything was auctioned on eBay. Everything was bought by the competition."

The competition?

"Who's the competition?"

Claudine shook her head at my ignorance. *"Le Moulin Rouge, Le Lido, Le Crazy Horse."* She snorted disdainfully. "Although what *Le Crazy Horse* would do with costumes, I don't know."

Le Moulin Rouge. Le Lido. Le Crazy Horse. I committed the names to memory. Right now, they were my only leads.

Suddenly, Claudine gasped. She stood up like a shot, banging her big hip against our table and knocking her brandy glass on its side. The clear liquid spilled out, but at least this time I was able to dodge out of the splatter zone. Practice, I guess.

"I must tell Madame Renard," Claudine announced.

Without another word, she ran out of the café.

Leaving me alone.

$\mathcal{J}$ looked at the bottle of Slivovitz, now almost half empty. Then I glanced at the bald man who appeared to be the boss. I wondered if he would expect me to pay for all those drinks. In any event, I owed him for the pizza.

He grinned, rolled his eyes, and waved his hand in a universal gesture: *It's on the house.* I wondered how many brandies he had written off on Claudine's behalf over the years.

"Thank you," I said, and headed back to Jeff Hotel Jeff.

When I got back to my room, I was exhausted. Undoubtedly, jet lag had a lot to do with it. The revelations about my mother's unique place in French theatrical history had probably also taken their toll.

I peeled off my clothes and put them, together with my other dirty things, into the plastic bag the hotel had thoughtfully provided. Then I examined my shrinking selection of clean garments. Either I was going to have to do laundry or go shopping, and soon.

I climbed between my clean sheets and turned off the light. *I bet shopping will be more fun than laundry,* I thought. And with that in mind, and a smile on my face, I fell asleep.

When I awoke, it was almost noon. I hurried to shower and dress, because I didn't want to waste my time in Paris. I had a busy day ahead of me.

I had missed the hotel's breakfast, so I scoured Rue Richer for a likely spot. I found what I was looking for, but it was far more un-likely than likely.

Only a few doors east beyond the *Folies* was a row of restaurants: l'Echevin (a brasserie), Chez Mimi (kosher), Toyama (Japanese), and then, I kid you not, Restaurant Montana Americain. I took a quick look at Montana's menu, which was posted in the window. They had scrambled eggs and bacon, and I knew I was home.

Inside, the place looked not the slightest bit like Montana. Granted, I've never been to Montana, but trust me, it doesn't look like this restaurant, which looked, well, French. I expected a burly guy named Bo in a greasy apron slinging hash onto chipped plates, mis-matched yard-sale tables and chairs, and butcher-paper tablecloths. Instead the place was tidy, the chairs all matched, and neatly rolled burgundy cloth napkins protruded from the wineglasses that spar-kled on each clean tabletop.

"*Bonjour*," said the dapper young man with long sideburns who escorted me to a table, held the chair for me, and handed me a menu. "*Je suis* Tex." *I am Tex.* He didn't look like a *Tex*. I wondered if he knew that Texas and Montana aren't even close to one another.

I scanned the menu. The scrambled eggs, fried eggs, bacon, hash browns and toast all seemed distinctly *American*—but they were listed right next to Eggs Benedict, Eggs Norwegian and Eggs Floren-tine. There were pancakes and maple syrup, but those were listed under *Desserts*.

Tex returned. "You have chosen?"

"Fried eggs, over hard. Bacon, crispy. And a huge cup of coffee."

It took a few minutes for Tex to comprehend *over hard* and *crispy*, and a while longer for him to find a coffee cup that wasn't munchkin-sized. When the food arrived, though, it was fabulous. Don't ask me how anybody can make something special out of fried eggs, but the French can. Even a Frenchman named Tex.

The bill was seven euros. I left nine. I know that's almost a thirty percent tip, but I've depended on tips long enough to feel that a one-euro gratuity wasn't enough.

I was almost out the door when Tex came scurrying after me. "Mademoiselle!"

I stopped and turned. "Yes?"

He handed me two euros. "It is too much," he said.

"It's for you."

"No, it's too much."

For the record, I have never told anybody the tip they left me was too much. Ever.

Tex sat me down and explained tipping in France. The tip is built in to the bill. If you think the service was really special, you leave a little bit more—maybe an extra two or three percent.

"Okay," I said, and put a one-euro coin on the table.

"It's still too much," he protested.

"That's not a tip," I explained. "That's for the lesson."

"Oh," he said seriously. He thought about it for a few seconds, then bowed to the inevitable. "Then I am very grateful."

If restaurants and waiters in the United States were like this, I'd eat out a whole lot more.

Next I headed to Boulevard Haussmann, which the desk clerk at Jeff Hotel Jeff had told me was the location of not one but two of Paris's most fabulous department stores, Galeries Lafayette and Printemps. Think Filenes, only older, prettier, and *way* more fashionable.

I reached Galeries Lafayette first, so that is where I shopped. It was daunting. Mind you, I've had very little experience shopping; my usual fare consists of overstocks and factory seconds. Here, there were several whole floors devoted to women's fashions, and I had no idea where to start. I began to hyperventilate.

Just then, an extremely pretty girl walked past me. Galeries Lafayette was filled with extremely pretty girls, but I noticed this one because she was very tall, perhaps only an inch shorter than I, and because she was walking a very tiny poodle at the end of a very long leash. The dog looked completely at home in the store. In fact, judging from the glittering collar around the poodle's neck, I suspected the dog might have its own Galeries Lafayette credit card.

The tall girl was wearing a killer outfit. On the one hand, it was just an off-white T-shirt with a black jacket and dark gray pants. On the other hand, it was totally devastating. The T-shirt's low neckline and bottom hem looked unfinished, but in a flawless way; the jacket was purposely too small to close, with edges of crumpled silk that provided a perfect border for the T-shirt; and the pants appeared as if they had been tailor-made for the hippest paratrooper on the planet. She looked fabulous.

And, incredibly, so did I. First, of course, I had to chase her down, avoid stepping on the poodle, and find out that the clothes were all by a label called IKKS. Once I found the IKKS boutique, and after I got over my sticker shock, I bought the very same outfit. Also another one, with a wicked patterned T-shirt, tailored waistcoat, and long slender skirt with a crumpled silk hem, all in black. I rationalized away the price by reminding myself that my stay in Las Vegas had been free.

Then, of course, I had to buy shoes. Shoes and boots, actually, because both outfits simply cried out for boots, plus I needed more practical shoes for walking. A little budgetary warning light flashed in my head, but I decided I could fill up on the huge seven-euro breakfasts at Restaurant Montana Americain and skip lunches altogether. Over two weeks, those savings might cover the shoes and the boots. Or at least the shoes.

I walked out of Galeries Lafayette having spent more on clothes in an hour than I had probably done in the past two years.

And for possibly the very first time in my life, the thought occurred to me:

I was worth it.

$\mathcal{B}$ack at my hotel, I asked the desk clerk, whose name was Claude, about tickets for *Le Moulin Rouge, Le Lido, and Le Crazy Horse.* I suppose I could have made inquiries about my mother at those places without seeing the shows, but I was curious. Sure, I had seen the Las Vegas version of *Les Folies Bergère*—but now I was in Paris. This was the real thing. Having been told my mother's legend, I hoped that seeing a show here would make it feel that much more real.

Claude checked his computer screen and then rattled off prices. When I heard them, my first thought was, *Maybe I'd better go return these new clothes.* My second thought was, *I love the clothes too much— maybe I'll skip the shows.* The cheapest ticket at the Moulin Rouge was eighty-seven euros. Over a hundred dollars. And that didn't include dinner. "But it comes with a half-bottle of champagne," Claude offered helpfully.

"Next."

"Eighty euros at the Lido," he suggested. "Also the half-bottle of champagne."

"Next."

"Ah," he said, and smiled. "At the Crazy Horse, if you sit at the bar, the show is only 35 euros."

"With a half-bottle of champagne?"

"Sadly, no. One drink. With two drinks is fifty euros."

At fifteen euros a drink, almost nineteen bucks, one was plenty, thanks.

There were two shows, at eight-thirty and eleven P.M., and no reservation needed to sit at the bar. I opted for the earlier show, just in case jet lag clobbered me again.

"The Crazy Horse is a little more naughty," Claude warned.

"I think I can handle it."

After I stashed my purchases upstairs, I realized that shopping had made me hungry. I ran back to Restaurant Montana, where Tex was happy to see me. The dinner menu was as idiosyncratic as breakfast. Sure, you could order a Bacon Cheeseburger, BBQ Pork Ribs and Chili—but those American staples rubbed elbows with Beef Tartare, Chicken Tandoory, and Breast of Duck with Pepper Sauce.

"So, where in Texas are you from?" I asked Tex.

"Aix-en-Provence." He said it with a totally straight face, so I forced myself not to laugh.

He may not have been from Texas or Montana, but boy, could he cook a cheeseburger. And I don't know how anyone can make fries special, but he did—although they are *French* fries, after all, so maybe the French know something we don't. Anyway, my French American meal, washed down with good old American Coca-Cola, was terrific, and cost me about fifteen dollars. It was lots more than I'd spend at home, but for a burger and fries that taste like Tex's, I'd pay that much anywhere.

Back in my hotel room I showered and shaved my legs. I felt like I was preparing for a date, even though I was going out alone. *A date with destiny?* The phrase just popped into my head. I have very little tolerance for cheesy catchphrases, though, so I popped it right back out.

I opted for the funky white T-shirt, black jacket, paratrooper pants and boots. As I dressed, it occurred to me that this was probably the fanciest outfit I had ever worn.

Claude told me the Crazy Horse was about five kilometers away. Once I ascertained that was three miles, I was ready to start walking. Then I remembered I was wearing brand new boots. I'd never worn dress boots before, so even though they were flats, I thought perhaps I should minimize my mileage until they were broken in. Claude suggested a taxi, but I had already blown way past my budget for the day, and I didn't want to make matters worse with cab fare. "What about the subway?"

Claude unfolded a Metro map and showed me the closest stations for the hotel and the Crazy Horse. I determined my route immediately: the 7 line to the 9 line. I told you, mass transit is in my blood; give me a subway map and I can get anywhere.

At the Cadet station, my ticket was only 1.40 euros. I fed it into the turnstile, which swallowed the little card and then spat it back at me. Once I took it, the gate opened and I entered. It was easy to figure where I was going, because on the wall of each platform was a list of all the stations you would get to if you headed that way. In minutes, the train rolled in. I had to push a button to get the door to open, which was new to me, but other than that, a subway is a subway. The transfer to the next train was just as easy, and before I knew it, I was exiting at the Alma-Marceau station. From there, it was just one long block to my destination.

I don't know what I had expected the neighborhood to look like. Since I was going to a show comprised entirely of women in various advanced stages of undress, maybe I assumed I was heading to Paris's version of Boston's Combat Zone, which is packed with adult bookstores and scuzzy little theaters advertising live sex acts.

Instead, it was as if I had stepped into Back Bay or Beacon Hill. Those are two of Boston's wealthiest neighborhoods, all centuries-old brownstone town houses worth a gazillion dollars. On Avenue George V, where the Crazy Horse was located, the buildings were made of white stone, not brown—but there was no mistaking that I was in an extremely high-end district. In fact, I wondered briefly if Claude had given me the wrong address. I kept walking, though, and there it was.

The Crazy Horse was plugged incongruously into the ground floor of one of the most elegant residential buildings I've seen: immaculate white stone with elaborate black iron balconies gracing the floor-to-ceiling windows on each story. If you were looking up as you were walking, you could easily miss the theater altogether. A small oval CRAZY HORSE sign extended from the side of the building just below the second floor. The theater itself was marked by black glass doors topped by three modest white awnings, over which the words *le Crazy Horse de Paris* and *Saloon Bar Theatre* glowed quietly in white neon.

I guess I was early; as I stood there, a gentleman dressed all in black set up a maroon velvet rope between brass stanchions for the line that, presumably, was about to materialize. I walked inside, found the ticket desk and paid my 35 euros. To my surprise, instead of directing me to the line outside, they escorted me downstairs to the bar. I suppose I shouldn't have been surprised; at 15 euros a cocktail, they wanted me drinking early and often. I was sorry to disappoint them, but I knew how to pace myself. When the handsome bartender asked to take my order, I thanked him and said I'd wait a while.

He eyed me up and down. He reminded me of a hungry dog, albeit a good-looking one.

"You are very nice," he said in English.

"How would you know?" I asked. "We've only just met." I've had plenty of experience handling horny bartenders.

"I mean you are very beautiful," he continued.

I shrugged—nonchalantly, I hoped. It must have been the new clothes. Still, even though it was a blatant come-on, his choice of words surprised me. Back home, all those lame horndogs trying to get over will say things like *You're so hot* or *Hey baby let me rock your world* or the perennial *Wanna fuck?*—but honestly, I couldn't remember anybody starting out by telling me I was beautiful. This charming European hound may not have been subtle, but he hadn't alienated me, either.

"I am Giancarlo," he said, although he said it with a French accent, not Italian. "And you are . . . ?" He extended his hand.

"Lindy." We shook hands. I think I surprised him with my grip—not hard, but firm enough to let any man know he couldn't push me around.

"So, beautiful Lindy, what are you drinking?"

"I told you, I'm waiting."

He shook his head. "No no no. This is not the one drink you are paying for. You buy that later. This is the one drink *Giancarlo* is paying for."

Never turn down a free drink from a bartender. First, it's rude. Second, it's free. "Martini. Very dirty."

"Very dirty indeed," he said with a lascivious smirk. I noticed that he made my drink with Boodles gin off the top shelf. He didn't need to do that. "Cheers," he said as he handed it over.

As I sipped my martini, which was quite perfect, the audience for the show began to filter in from the stairway, and the small room filled quickly.

The temperature seemed to rise. I drained my drink. I could feel my heart beating faster.

The room went black.

Then the show began.

36

I had never seen anything like it.

Picture twelve perfect women. All the same height, the same shape. All bedecked in identical silver wigs. All wearing nothing but stockings, or a few black leather straps that only emphasized their nakedness. Or nothing at all, other than a shaved, perfectly painted black triangle that concealed everything and nothing.

Twenty-four perfect natural breasts. Twenty-four perfect buttocks. Twenty-four perfectly shaped legs, their perfect calves emphasized by black stiletto heels. Every motion of every head, hand, every foot executed in exquisite, perfect unity.

And then the lights. Yes, there were twelve perfect bodies on the tiny stage—but they were more than just bodies, they were canvasses for the ever-changing artworks of patterned light and darkness that played over their arched backs, their pointed nipples, their taut thighs. Endless quilts of squares, flowers, triangles and diamonds marched brazenly across all that bare skin, making the women seem unreal and yet simultaneously human and vulnerable.

The lights pulsed and throbbed, rose and fell with the music, which vibrated through every inch of me. At some point during the show, Giancarlo handed me my second drink. I was grateful for it.

One of the women, perhaps the most perfect one of all—although I had previously formed that opinion about several of the other dancers, maybe all of them—floated magically, mysteriously suspended in the darkness, encircled by the glowing orbit of a giant hoop. Slowly she swept her legs back until her whole naked body formed one glorious balletic arch.

At that instant, I realized I was arching my own back, drawing back my own elbows, thrusting my own small breasts forward in emulation of the ethereal being floating there so exposed above the stage. Embarrassed, I looked around, but of course nobody was watching me; all eyes were transfixed on the dancer. I resumed watching the show.

I couldn't lose the feeling, though. I had liked the tension in my muscles. The momentary sense of complete abandon.

I wondered what it would feel like—what *I* would feel like—to be up there, entirely exposed, bare to the world except for a wig and makeup and body paint. I felt myself flush, and I shuddered slightly.

For that brief moment, I thought perhaps I knew what *La Gazelle*— my mother—had felt onstage with the eyes of all Paris upon her.

I tried to capture the feeling, define it, save it . . . but it was gone. The music changed and the woman in the hoop vanished. Soon all twelve dancers had resumed their places, and, as the music built to a crescendo, they undulated through their perfect finale.

Then it was over.

The room went completely black again, and when the lights came up, the dancers were gone—if such perfect beings had ever existed in the first place.

Giancarlo turned his attention back to me. "You are excited," he observed.

"No," I said. It was a dumb thing to say. The man had eyes.

"You like the girls?"

"Yes. I mean, no. But yes." That wasn't a very clear answer, but he hadn't asked a very clear question. If he meant, did I like them *sexually*, well, no. They hadn't excited me because I wanted to be with them.

They had excited me because I wanted to *be* them.

"You will audition for the show?"

I looked at Giancarlo. At first I assumed he was mocking me— but there was not the slightest bit of irony on his face. He seemed entirely serious.

"That is why you are here, yes? To see if you like the show? If you would like to be in it?" He sounded hopeful.

Instead of denying it, I found myself saying, "I think I'm too tall." I sounded sad when I said it.

Giancarlo frowned, then nodded morosely. "I think you are too tall, too. But it is a great shame. You should not go to the Moulin Rouge or the Lido. They have too many girls. They will lose you in the crowd. You need the spotlight."

Let me tell you, this guy's lines were absolutely world-class. "Thank you."

"You have a phone number?"

"Yes."

"Ah. Yes. You will *give* me your phone number?"

"No."

"Ah." He shrugged. Brightening, he asked, "You will come back to the Crazy Horse?"

"Maybe."

"Maybe!" He proclaimed it like a triumph, and grinned broadly. He was still grinning as I climbed the stairs and he vanished from sight.

37

*U*pon reaching the street-level exit, I found myself reluctant to leave. Even as I kept walking, I turned to face the theater's entrance, as if inviting its power to draw me back in. So I wasn't watching where I was going.

Neither, apparently, was the man who walked right into me. Or I walked right into him. Anyway we walked right into one another. *Bang.*

I picked myself up off the floor, and he did the same. I was about to berate him for being a careless asshole.

Then he looked at me.

For an instant, I could have sworn I was looking at Louis Jourdan. Not the old Louis Jourdan who played smarmy over-the-top villains in movies like *Octopussy* and *Swamp Thing*, but the younger, incredibly gorgeous, sophisticated French leading man who fell hopelessly in love with Leslie Caron in *Gigi*. The man who had plowed into me bore an uncanny resemblance, in his suave dark good looks and his immaculate dress. He was wearing a slim gray suit that had undoubtedly been custom made and must've cost three thousand bucks, easy, and beneath it a crisp white shirt and a rich burgundy tie. He had broad shoulders and narrow hips, jet black hair and soulful dark eyes. In short, he was everything a smoldering Frenchman should be.

He was mad. Probably didn't like having his perfect suit mussed. He drew himself up to his full height and got right in my face.

He was an inch shorter than me. Which, as I've told you, gives some men terrible inadequacy issues that can have some really unfortunate consequences.

I bet he *has no trouble maintaining an erection.*

Sorry, but I swear, that thought occurred to me as the gorgeous smolderer was about to holler.

Maybe he read my mind. Or maybe he just looked at me for the first time. Either way, after he opened his mouth but before he started to bellow, his entire demeanor changed. I had tensed to receive his verbal onslaught, so he threw me entirely off balance when he smiled rakishly. "You sure are tall," he said. In English. Perfect English. American English.

Wait a second. My Frenchman was an American.

Wait another second. How had he instantaneously become *my* Frenchman?

Wait a third second. Up until this moment, I'd spent my entire life hearing the word *tall* as the ultimate insult. So why did it now sound like a compliment, and a yummy one at that, coming out of this total stranger's mouth?

Incidentally, he had lovely teeth.

The better to bite you with, my dear.

Honestly, the things that this man was filling my head with. The nerve of him.

He took my hand—quite uninvited—and kissed it, just brushing his lips over my skin. I shivered slightly. I hoped he didn't notice. "*Enchanté*," he said with a lovely French accent. *Charmed.* "Are you in the show?"

I finally regained the power of speech. "The show?"

He indicated the theater with a nod of his head. Oh, yeah. The *show*. My fateful collision had, in a matter of seconds, completely obliterated my memory of the spectacle which, only moments before, had totally captivated me.

"The show? Me?" I wasn't sure if I should be offended or flattered. I looked into his lovely dark eyes and picked flattered. "No. But thank you."

"Pity."

Was I wrong, or did he really sound disappointed? Was that his way of saying he wanted to see me naked? Wasn't that a little crass for a guy wearing a three thousand dollar suit?

"Did you enjoy it?" he asked.

The kiss on the hand? Oh, yes. "It?"

"The show."

"Oh. Yes. Very much." I think I blushed.

"Has anyone told you lately that you're perfect?"

I'm not making this up. Those are the words that his lips uttered. Lovely full lips.

What was happening to me? Sure, I was wearing the nicest outfit of my entire life, but in one evening I had vaulted from invisible to Giancarlo's *beautiful* to my stranger's *perfect*.

"No."

"You're adventurous enough to come to the Crazy Horse alone. Confident enough to admit to a man you've just met how much you enjoyed the show. Genuine enough to blush. Perfect," he repeated. This man was leaving Giancarlo in the dust. If this was a line, it was the best I'd ever heard.

I struggled to find something to say. Something adventurous. Confident. Witty.

"Do you come here often?"

Lame.

He laughed. Charmingly. "Never. Nude shows aren't exactly my fare."

Did he sound . . . disapproving? Regardless of how expensive his clothes were, he did look awfully buttoned down. "Then why—"

"Business," he said, anticipating my question. He indicated three men wearing dark business suits standing in line behind the velvet rope. "My clients. Mr. Wang from Macau. Mr. Lai and Mr. Issen from Hong Kong. It was their idea."

"Clients?"

"Investment banking. My firm is underwriting their new casino venture."

Oh, no. He was an *investment banker*. Sadly, I've known several.

Cambridge, Massachusetts crawls with them, expensive suits representing venture capitalists looking to bankroll MIT and Harvard techie geeks who're all trying to become the next Bill Gates. Good dressers, sure, but conservative to the core. I even dated one once. Twice, actually. On the second date, we went to see *9 1/2 Weeks* at the Brattle Theatre. My suggestion, obviously, not his. In retrospect, it was a pretty bold choice, but he'd been very handsome, too. Watching Kim Basinger get herself off, he started to squirm. I misread his body language and began to unzip his fly. He broke up with me on the spot. Buttoned-down over-educated prude. Biff Hardly. I kid you not, that was his name.

"I'm Eddie Atkinson," said the handsome stranger.

"No you're not," I said, because the name *Biff Hardly* had just popped into my head.

He smiled a puzzled smile. "Yes, I am."

I blushed again. Massively, I think. "Of course you are." I shook his hand. It was cool and dry, and his grip met mine perfectly.

"And you are . . . ?"

"Lindy," I said. "Lindy Archer." I hadn't planned to give my mother's maiden name, but that's what came out of my mouth, and I wasn't about to correct myself and then try to explain it.

"Lindy," Eddie said. "That's nice. Different. I've never known a Lindy."

"I've known lots of Eddies." Blunt, but true.

"Not like me, you haven't."

At that moment, the theater doors opened, and the line started to move.

"Your business," I said.

He looked over his shoulder and frowned as Wang, Lai and Issen shuffled toward the entrance. Turning back to me, he said, "I've got the tickets."

"Then you'd better go."

"I guess I'd better."

He didn't move. That was unlike an investment banker. Business is first, second, third and last for them.

"Can I call you?" he asked.

"No."

"Why not?"

I tried to think of an answer. *Because you're an investment banker and Biff Hardly broke up with me when I unzipped his fly* hardly seemed appropriate. "I don't know the number at my hotel." It was the best I could come up with on short notice.

"But you do know your hotel's name."

"Yes."

"And . . . ?"

Eddie's clients had reached the doors. They were letting people go ahead while they waited for their host. They looked impatient. I didn't want to get him in trouble. I'm sure that's why I told him.

"Jeff."

"Your hotel is named Jeff?"

"You asked."

I don't think he believed me.

"On Rue Richer," I said. Maybe that last fact convinced him I was telling the truth. Or maybe business simply couldn't wait any longer.

"Bye," he said. In seconds, he had rejoined his party, and the four of them disappeared into the dark interior of the Crazy Horse.

Leaving me alone, wondering what I had just gotten myself into.

kept wondering, all the way back to Jeff Hotel Jeff.

It was a lovely evening, not too cool and not too warm. Perfect, I thought—just like Eddie Atkinson. Then I corrected myself. He would have been perfect, if he hadn't turned out to be a buttoned-down investment banker.

I walked up Avenue George V. Across the street, I saw fashionable names I knew, but of course had never worn. Givenchy. Yves St. Laurent. Armani Collezioni. Louis Vuitton. I resisted an unprecedented urge to cross the street and window-shop.

At the intersection of George V and the Avenue des Champs-Élysées, I glanced to my left. There, only a few blocks away, beautifully spotlit, was the Arc de Triomphe. It looked so . . . Parisian. So . . . romantic.

I have never thought of myself as a romantic person. For example, I do not cry at cinematic love stories. What's more, as you know, I typically root for the doomed heroine to die. And yet . . .

I wondered if Eddie would call.

Who was I kidding? Of course he wouldn't.

But he might.

I crossed the Champs-Élysées and continued up Rue Washington until it reached Boulevard Haussmann. I turned right on the broad street. I strolled past parks and theaters, churches and museums. Everything was closed because of the late hour, but even in the dark, they all looked lovely and inviting.

The windows of the magnificent department stores, Printemps and Galeries Lafayette, beckoned me desperately to return during business hours. I knew I didn't have the budget for more shopping, but I was tempted nonetheless. I was particularly drawn to one display, a stunning mannequin provocatively posed, barely covered by an outfit that a small sign identified as by Jean-Paul Gaultier. I could picture myself wearing it—or, to be more precise, barely wearing it. Then I noticed a placard in the window. It listed the prices. The aerated blouse and tiny skirt cost 1,400 euros. Lead us not into temptation.

Across the street was the opera house. I recognized it from *Phantom of the Opera*, which is arguably the second worst movie I have ever seen. No matter how bad the movie was, in real life, the monumental opera house was magnificent.

I turned onto Rue la Fayette, and in only a few blocks I had reached Rue Richer and my hotel. Claude was still at the front desk.

"Don't you ever leave?"

He looked up and smiled. "Almost never. Did you enjoy the show?"

"Very much." I'm pretty sure that this time, I did not blush.

"Excellent. It is very Parisian."

I remembered how, for that brief moment at the Crazy Horse, I had imagined myself into the spectacle. *It is very Parisian.*

In that instant, I grasped a new fact about my mother. It was no wonder she had stayed in France all those years. She felt very much at home—in the city, and on its stage. *Very Parisian.*

I wondered if I might ever feel at home here, too.

The next day, after another extremely *Americain* breakfast with Tex, I followed directions Claude had given me and headed up Rue du Faubourg Montmartre. I do mean *up*. It's all uphill. I climbed past comedy clubs and antique shops and luthiers. Finally I reached the Boulevard de Clichy. Across the street, there it was.

The red windmill was just as odd, and just as ugly, as in the movie. *Le Moulin Rouge.*

If *Phantom of the Opera* is arguably the second worst movie I've ever seen, *Moulin Rouge* is inarguably the worst. It is a dizzying, disorienting, self-important train wreck of a film. That has always been my opinion of the movie.

All seventeen times I've seen it.

Literally. I don't know why I watch it again and again. I despise it, over and over.

Especially Nicole Kidman. Every time she makes her first appearance, I hope she dies, right out loud. And of course, by the end of the movie, obligingly, she does.

In the film, the windmill looks decadent, and mysterious. In real life, stuck between two perfectly lovely white stone examples of classic Parisian architecture, it just looked weird.

If the neighborhood surrounding the all-nude Crazy Horse show was inexplicably elegant, the environs of the *Moulin Rouge* were almost stereotypically decadent. Both sides of the Boulevard de Clichy were lined with sex. Supermarche Erotique. Love Shop Librairie DVD Gadgets. Musee de l'Erotisme. Sex Machine Projections 1€. Porno Shop. Sexy Store. Pigal's Peep Show Sex Shop. Sex sex sex sex sex.

I have nothing against sex—but this was really too much of a good thing.

I walked past the gaudy multicolored neon marquee of a small theater called L'X O! A poster with pursed pink lips promised *LIVE SHOW*. Two women lolled in the open doorway. They were both unnaturally blonde and unnaturally busty. Their ages could have been twenty, or fifty, or anywhere in between. They worked hard for the money.

One of them spotted me. "Hey, you want to fuck me?"

The physical impossibility of the request threw me off balance. "No," I finally said.

"You want a job?" the other one asked.

"No," I repeated, and kept walking.

"Snooty bitch."

Ouch. They were a couple of anonymous sex workers. So why did that sting?

Maybe it hadn't been a snide remark. Maybe she really was asking me if I wanted a job, doing what she did for a living. Maybe it was a compliment.

I stopped, then retraced my steps back to the theater. "I'm sorry," I said. "Thank you. But no thank you."

The second woman smiled. "You're welcome."

"You sure you don't want to fuck me?" her friend asked amiably.

"I'm sure," I said. "But thank you, too."

She beamed. "You're welcome, too."

Well, I thought, *if my money runs out and I want to stay on in Paris, at least I know where I can find work.*

I smiled at my new friends, waved, and walked away. It might have been fun to stay and chat. But I had more pressing business.

The *Moulin Rouge* awaited.

39

*D*on't let the ugly old red windmill fool you. It sits atop a lovely, glittering modern theater, where a huge banner proclaimed the current show: *FÉERIE: LA REVUE DU MOULIN ROUGE*. On one side of the bright lobby were the ticket windows. The other side was dominated by the gift shop, where official *Moulin Rouge* ashtrays, baseball caps, key chains, perfume, playing cards, posters, T-shirts and umbrellas awaited unsuspecting tourists. I opted for the ticket windows.

"Which show?"

"I don't want to see the show." Actually, I did—but not at 87 euros.

The woman in the window looked at me, then nodded knowingly. "You want a job?" I wondered if my buddy at L'X O! sex theater was spreading the word.

Yes. Yes, of course I want a job.

What?

I didn't say that. Really, nothing had come out of my mouth.

"No. I'm . . . looking for someone."

"Who?"

"An old friend. Of my mother's. I'm sorry, I don't remember her name. But she's an old woman."

It was a total shot in the dark. I had no idea if anyone there had ever known my mother. But if Claudine was right, at least some of the people put out of work when the *Folies Bergère* closed would have joined the competition, including the *Moulin Rouge*. If my mother were still alive, she'd be 65 years old. If her contemporaries were still working, they'd be that old as well, possibly older. It was worth a try.

The lady in the ticket window pondered the matter. "There is Marie," she finally said. "She works in costumes."

My heart beat faster. "May I see her?"

She shrugged. "Who knows? Marie is unpredictable. I will call her." She lifted her telephone, then hung it up again. "You are sure you don't want a job?"

"I'm sure." In fact, I wasn't at all sure, but that was what I said anyway.

"It's too bad. I think you are very good for the show."

I waited in the lobby. Finally, after minutes that seemed like hours, a woman came to take me into the inner realm of the theater. I was disappointed. She certainly wasn't 65; she probably wasn't even half that age. She was petite and delicate, maybe five foot two, and I towered over her.

"I am not Marie," the woman said, shaking my hand. She escorted me through a door and up a stairwell. "I am Marie-Rose. Marie is my mother. Celeste at the box office said your mother and my mother were friends."

"Maybe."

Marie-Rose stopped climbing the stairs. "Celeste did not say *maybe*. My mother does not enjoy talking to strangers."

"If they were friends, then I'm not exactly a stranger."

"How will she even know who your mother was unless she talks to you?"

"She'll know."

Marie-Rose swayed slightly, as if weighing the issue first with one hand and then the other.

"You say she will know even without talking to you?"

"Yes."

Based on my experiences with Dixie and then Claudine, I figured that if Marie dropped her drink or slapped me, or both, that would mean she recognized me—that is, recognized my resemblance to my mother.

"All right, then."

We kept climbing. The stairwell narrowed as we rose. At the fifth floor landing, Marie-Rose turned the knob of a narrow door. It opened into a long room that, at first glance, resembled the exotic bird exhibition at a zoo. There were feathers everywhere, of all kinds and colors. At the far end of the room was a large sewing table. Seated at the sewing table was a tiny little woman. Although she was sitting down, I could tell that, standing up, she would not top five feet.

I walked the length of the room until I was directly in front of the little woman. The light was behind me, so my shadow fell across her face and I couldn't read her expression.

There was a cup of coffee on the sewing table. The woman did not spill it. It was the first time in my life I was disappointed *not* to be splattered.

After a long moment, Marie stood up. She was even smaller than I anticipated. As she arose out of my shadow, I finally saw her face. Her eyes were very pale blue, and they were wide and round. She raised her right hand and crooked her index finger in a universal *come here* gesture. I bent down.

She got up on her tiptoes and kissed my cheeks, first the right, then the left. After the kisses, she indicated another chair at the sewing table. I sat down.

Marie looked at her daughter and nodded. Marie-Rose leaned close to her mother, and the older woman whispered in her daughter's ear. "She was your mother's costumer," Marie-Rose said.

"Tell me about her," I said to Marie.

Marie looked solemn. She whispered again to Marie-Rose. "She cannot," the younger woman apologized.

"Why not?"

"Because she promised your mother to keep her secrets."

"But she was my mother."

Whisper whisper whisper. "If your mother had wanted you to know, she would have told you."

"She died."

That fact hung motionless in the air. Not even the feathers dared to move.

Finally Marie resumed her silent conversation with her daughter. "She is sorry," Marie-Rose said. "But a promise is a promise."

I wanted to cry. All this woman would tell me was that my mother had secrets.

No shit.

I couldn't, wouldn't let myself believe that I had found this woman only to learn nothing. I tried a different subject. I took out the old snapshot Dixie had sent me and placed it on the table in front of Marie. "I'm looking for this dress. And the shoes."

This time, Marie said nothing. Instead, she stood up and noiselessly walked out of the room.

I looked at Marie-Rose questioningly. "Wait," she said.

After several minutes, the little old woman returned. Without a hint of a smile, she handed me a piece of paper. I looked at it. It was a business card. It said:

> FRANÇOISE MALRAUX, EXPERT

Below the name there was simply a street address on Rue de l'Échaudé. Nothing else.

The older woman whispered to the younger. "She does not know where these clothes are," Marie-Rose said. "When *Les Folies* closed, everything went everywhere. But this is the finest vintage shop in Paris. This person may know."

I waited. Neither woman said anything further.

I looked into Marie's eyes. "Is there anything you can tell me? Anything at all?"

There was a long silence. Finally, Marie whispered again to Marie-Rose. "She misses your mother," Marie-Rose said.

The conversation was over. I could tell. I had gotten almost nothing. Then I looked down at the business card clutched in my hand. Maybe something after all.

"Thank you," I said. I stood up and walked slowly away from the two women.

I reached the exit. My hand touched the doorknob.

"She liked to sing."

I turned, wondering if I had really heard it, or if it had been my imagination. The voice was lower and smoother than Marie-Rose's, as if worn down with age like a stone on the beach. Up to that moment, I hadn't been sure if Marie could speak at all.

"She was not such a good singer," Marie continued. "But she liked to sing. Bobby Darin. Paul Anka, not so much. And Elvis Presley. 'Are You Lonesome Tonight?' That was her favorite song."

"I thought . . ."

"That I could not tell you her secrets? I cannot." She chuckled. "But she used to sing out loud. Very loud. And very bad. So I guess the singing was not a secret."

I waited, but there was nothing more. I slipped out the door and closed it behind me. As the latch clicked in the doorframe, I heard—or perhaps only thought I heard—two last words. Maybe they weren't even directed at me. If they were, I hoped they weren't said sarcastically.

"Good luck."

$\mathcal{A}$s I headed downhill and back toward my hotel, a terrible thought occurred to me.

I had told Eddie Atkinson that my name was Lindy Archer.

There was no *Lindy Archer* registered at Jeff Hotel Jeff. The hotel's guest was named Linda Stone. If he actually came looking, he wouldn't find me. He'd be convinced that I had lied to avoid him.

I wondered if maybe, subconsciously, that was exactly what I had done.

I shook it off. First, I hadn't lied. The name had just come out, unbidden. Second, none of it mattered. Because who was I kidding?—he wasn't coming. Let's face it: guys like that don't come looking for girls like me.

When I got back to the hotel, remarkably, Claude wasn't working at the front desk. In his place was a neatly dressed blonde woman.

"Has anyone come looking for me?" I held my breath.

"No one has come looking for anyone," said the blonde woman.

Okay, exhale. Now inhale. What did I expect?

Back in my room, I considered my day thus far. I had found a woman who had known my mother, been close to her, shared her secrets—and who would tell me almost nothing. And the gorgeous stranger who had so disturbed my equilibrium the night before had apparently lost what little interest he'd had in me.

I was so depressed, there was only one thing to do:

Laundry.

I don't mean to suggest that doing laundry cheers me up, or that I find the mindless folding of undergarments to confer a Zenlike calm. On the contrary. First, I don't fold undergarments; wadding works just as well. Second, I hate doing laundry. Despise it. As a result, I try to wash my clothes only when I'm already depressed. That way, the only direction to go is up, and once the last T-shirt is out of the dryer, my mood inevitably improves almost immediately.

I was running dangerously low on clean attire, and I was in a foul mood. So, laundry it was.

"Is there anyplace around here where I can wash my clothes?" I asked the blonde woman at the front desk.

"We will be happy to wash them for you."

"You will?" Things were looking up already. "That's awfully nice of you. I hope it's not too much trouble."

"It is no trouble at all." She handed me a plastic bag and a printed form. "Just fill this out, and put a copy of it in the bag with your things."

I looked at the form. It was a price list.

They wanted twelve euros to wash a pair of jeans. That's fifteen dollars. Three euros to wash panties—almost four bucks. For one pair.

"How about a Laundromat?"

The woman took it all in stride. She directed me to a place on one of the side streets almost directly across from the *Folies Bergère*. I hurried upstairs and gathered my soiled things. I briefly considered tossing my Bloody Mary-spattered New Balances into the trash, but shoved them in the laundry bag instead.

The local laundry was called Lav'Club, and I'm happy to say that from one country to the next, a Laundromat is a Laundromat is a Laundromat. Soon I was watching my clothes swirl in soapsudded waters.

One of the things I don't like about doing laundry is the boredom. Once I had loaded everything into the dryers, the spinning rhythm and the heat from the machines, coupled with a little leftover jetlag, started to take their toll. My eyelids began to droop.

Suddenly the reverie was broken. The door swung inward with a bang, and the doorway was filling with the silhouette of an imposing figure. I blinked myself awake. The shadowy outline belonged to a rotund woman dressed all in black. Her hair was stark white, but her eyebrows were as black as her dress. My best guess was that she was nearly eighty years old, but somehow her age only added to her fearsome aspect.

The old woman scanned the place. There were three customers: an olive-skinned young man wearing an orange T-shirt, black jeans and unusually ugly green sneakers, a blue-haired teenage girl, and me.

I could feel the woman's intense gaze fix on me. "So," she intoned, "it is true."

That didn't seem to demand a response. I said nothing.

"You cannot be here," she continued.

That called for an answer. "I beg your pardon?"

She looked around at the interior of the Lav'Club. "It is not acceptable. You must not stay in this place. Not a moment longer."

I wondered if the French were doing an adequate job of security at their mental health institutions.

Without another word, she marched up to my dryers. Never mind that the cycles weren't finished, she opened the machines and lifted out the lumps of my still-damp clothes.

"Wait a second. You can't take my clothes."

I tried to stare her down. She was half a head shorter than I, but what she lacked in height, she made up for in intensity. "I can," she declared. "And I will. Come."

She headed out the door. I followed her. What else could I do? She had my clothes.

"Where are we going?"

The old woman turned. Her expression suggested that I, not she, was the one who was crazy.

She answered with only a single word.

"Home."

41

*D*espite her apparent insanity, I followed the black-clad woman. If my recent adventures had taught me anything, it was that when eccentric old women behaved strangely in my vicinity, inevitably, there was a connection to my mother. That possibility made my heart beat faster.

We stepped out onto Rue Geoffroy-Marie and followed its angled path toward the *Folies Bergère.* My enthusiasm waned. Maybe the lady *was* nuts, leading me "home" to the shuttered site of Mimi Archer's triumphs.

On Rue Richer, though, she turned right. We weren't heading to the theater after all.

We walked only half a block before she crossed the narrow street. For an instant, it appeared as if she were taking me to Restaurant Montana Americain. With all due respect to Tex, no matter how good the food was and how much I enjoyed eating there, it certainly wasn't my home.

The old woman didn't go to the Montana, or to its neighbor, Restaurant Japonais Toyama. Instead, she walked straight into a passageway between the two eateries. Despite having repeatedly dined only a few feet away, somehow, I had never noticed the passageway. It was paved in soothing gray stones laid out in a diamond pattern. Pretty old round lanterns hung overhead. On the right was a large bank of mailboxes so ugly they must have been installed in the 1960s.

The short tunnel opened into the courtyard of a small apartment complex. By Paris standards the buildings looked relatively new, which means they were probably only a hundred years old. Straight ahead and to my right, double doors painted forest green led to stairwells wainscoted in dark wood. Like the surrounding neighborhood, the buildings were faced in white stone, but they were in need of a good washing. Plants and ivy were placed strategically around the courtyard in an attempt to make it more attractive and, perhaps, to conceal unrepaired wear and tear.

"This way," instructed the stern woman, pushing through the doors on my right. As I followed her, I noticed that the floor was tiled in an old mosaic pattern that appeared vaguely Moroccan to me. At least, it reminded me of the Casa B restaurant in Harvard Square, which is supposed to look vaguely like Casablanca, which is in Morocco. It was lovely detailing. I bet the whole apartment complex, although modest, had been quite attractive in years gone by.

The black-dressed lady may have been old, but she climbed stairs like a mountain goat. I kept up with her, but barely. She did not stop until we had mounted six flights and reached the top landing. With a nod of her head, she indicated a heavy door, its oak surface veneered with time, its identity marked with a tarnished letter *A*.

"In my pocket," she directed.

I don't typically go reaching into total strangers' pockets. Who knows what might be in there? But she was very commanding, I had come this far, and I still had the unshakable feeling that this had to do with my mother.

I slipped my hand into the pocket of her dress. It was a long pocket, and I had to bend down to reach the bottom. Fortunately, I didn't have to guess, because there was only one thing in there: an old-fashioned iron key.

"Home," she said again. Before I could ask any of the million questions bouncing inside my head, she started down the stairs without even glancing at me. "I must finish the laundry," she announced to the stairwell.

I was alone.

Me. The door. The key.

Home?

Had I been back in Somerville, or even Las Vegas, I'm pretty sure I wouldn't have opened the door. After all, who knew what might be in there? I certainly didn't want to end up on the five o'clock news, the pathetically trusting victim of some psycho killer, *qu'est ce que c'est*, fa fa fa fa.

That's the Talking Heads. Barenaked Ladies, too. Stay with me here.

But I wasn't in Somerville, or Las Vegas. I was in Paris, France. Somehow, I suspected they didn't even have a five o'clock news, much less the tawdry grotesqueries that we Americans invent to fill such broadcasts.

Not only was I in Paris, I was learning my mother's history, following her path. And she wouldn't let anything happen to me.

My mother was watching out for me. It was a revelation, stunning because such a thought had never before entered my mind. Ever.

The cold iron key seemed to grow warm in my palm.

I slipped the key into the lock and turned it.

42

The old lady had been right. There was only one word for this place.

Home.

Not my home, though. My mother's home.

The instant I stepped across the threshold, I knew I was standing in the Parisian home of Margaret Archer, known as Maggie, then Mimi, renowned across France as *La Gazelle*, wife of Jack Stone, mother of Linda, born 1942, died 1982.

She had always been purely theoretical to me. At first, I had tried to remember—really tried. Probably until I was eight years old. I was encouraged to do so by thoughtless aunts: *How could she not remember her mother?* Jack, my highly imperfect father, had answered perfectly: *Give the poor kid a break. She was too little.* Of course, I didn't listen to him, just as I spent all the years that followed not listening to him. Instead, I worked, struggled, fought to remember. And lost.

Once I realized my little brain held no record of her, I wrote Maggie off as if she'd never existed—never mind that my own life was the best evidence to the contrary. Jack made my mother's nonexistence easier, never talking about her and rarely displaying the only two photos he possessed. All my life, it was as if she were fiction: a novel written by a forgotten author that I'd never read, but only been told about by someone who claimed to have read it but couldn't remember the story.

Then Dixie's photograph and that peacock feather had arrived, and suddenly I couldn't ignore the signs that, at least for a time, Mag-

gie had been startlingly real. Since then, the evidence had continued
to build: brandy-fortified Claudine, next silent Marie. Now there was
the still-nameless iron-faced old woman with the black dress and the
white hair, who had found me as if by magic, plucked me out of a
Parisian Laundromat, and brought me to my mother's home.

The apartment was modest in size, a simple one-bedroom with
living room, full bath, a little dressing alcove, and a tiny kitchen. The
furnishings were sumptuous, though. The curtains on the windows
were heavy brocade and the rugs on the floor were huge Persians.
The furniture was very feminine and very French. None of the pieces
matched, and yet everything belonged.

I peered into the bedroom, which was dominated by a four-poster
upon which floated a multicolored array of billowy duvet covers and
plump pillows, like the rich, lavish decorations on a pastry from the
finest patisserie in Paris. Given what I knew so far about my mother's
past, I wasn't sure I was ready to confront her bedroom; I closed that
door and returned to the living room.

A divan, loveseat and club chair formed a grouping around the
marble fireplace that dominated the far wall. The mantelpiece was
filled with framed photographs. Other photos were displayed atop
two delicate lamp tables, illuminated by a soft silk-shaded glow. Every
flat surface seemed to have pictures. It was a stunning counterpoint to
the home in which I'd grown up, where the virtual absence of photographs had for so many years lent credence to the notion that my
mother not only was gone, but had never existed.

I began to inspect the framed images. At first, I almost expected
to see pictures of Maggie with Jack, and even with myself in infant
form—as if such photos had existed all along, but were spirited out of
our home and transported here. Of course, I saw no such thing. These
reflected my mother's reality long before she met my father, when I
could not even have been a glimmer in her imagination. Still, I was
stunned to see who *was* in the photographs.

There were several of Maggie alone—Mimi, I suppose, since these
were taken during her Paris years. Some were posed portraits, other
were charming candids. She was clad in everything from gowns to

sundresses to furs. In none of them did she wear anything that might have been a costume from *Les Folies Bergère*. In all of them, her resemblance to me—or, more correctly, my resemblance to her—was quite striking. I would have bet money that at least two of the photos were taken when she was twenty-six, the exact same age as me.

If I looked so much like her, how could I explain that she was so . . . beautiful?

The pictures that really floored me, though, were the couples: my mother and a man. All of the men looked devastatingly handsome, or rich, and often both. A few of the men I recognized: here was my mother and Jean-Paul Belmondo; there, my mother and Gérard Depardieu. Every one of the men looked completely enraptured.

I'm not sure any man ever looked so entirely taken with me, much less world-famous movie stars and sex symbols.

For an instant, my mind composed a snapshot of me, dressed glamorously, and Eddie Atkinson, perfectly suited, gazing at me with total adoring dedication.

The image was too farfetched, the fiction too preposterous. My brain snapped back to my present situation, which, however unlikely it seemed, was undeniably real.

The photographs told the tale: Those men had adored Mimi Archer. Dated her. Maybe even—

All right, that's quite enough. This is my *mother* we're talking about here.

Overwhelmed, I sat down.

At that moment, there was a knock. A few seconds later, the apartment door opened. It was the severe old woman.

"You did not lock the door," she said.

"Sorry."

"I would not enter if the door were locked."

"Okay."

"I am the soul of discretion."

"Okay."

The woman turned and retrieved a basket from the landing. She carried it into the living room and set it down on the floor in front of me. Curious, I opened it. There was my laundry. Everything was not only dry, but pressed. The clothes looked like new. Better than new.

"You didn't have to do that," I said.

"Oh, but I did." She retreated to the landing again, and returned carrying my New Balances. She held them at arm's length, as if they'd had an unfortunate run-in with a skunk. "These are very ugly," she observed.

They were, although I was pleased to see that much of the staining had washed out. "Kinda."

"Shall I throw them away?"

Jesus. They were still a little splattered, but who throws away a perfectly good pair of running shoes? "No. No, thank you."

She looked at me dubiously. "Very well," she said. "Perhaps I will try to wash them again. Only properly, this time."

"You don't have to do that."

"Oh, but I do."

Before I could ask why, she had disappeared into the landing again. When she returned a moment later, she was carrying my backpack, Jack's bowling bag, and the case for my mother's headdress.

"Where did you get those?!"

"From the hotel."

"Why did they give them to you?"

"Because I checked you out."

What? That was my *hotel*. "Who said you could do that?"

"The daughter of *La Gazelle* cannot stay in a two-star hotel. In fact, the daughter of *La Gazelle* cannot stay in a hotel at all."

I wasn't sure why the old lady was referring to me in the third person. I didn't care. "Where am I supposed to stay?"

For the very first time, the old lady smiled. "Here."

I felt like I had just fallen into an episode of *The Twilight Zone*. One of the good old Rod Serling ones. "Who the hell *are* you?"

She straightened herself and, with enormous dignity, intoned,

"I . . . am Madame Renard."

adame Renard. Why did that sound familiar?

Then I remembered. Café Dizengoff. Claudine's last tipsy words, just before she had abandoned me: *I must tell Madame Renard.*

That explained how the old woman found me. Claudine had alerted her to my presence. Presumably, she, and maybe both of them, had scoured the neighborhood until Madame Renard found me in the Lav'Club.

But who was Madame Renard?

"Who *are* you?"

"May I sit?" She asked the question as if genuinely requesting my permission.

"Of course."

She sat down on the edge of the divan. "I . . . was your mother's . . . landlady."

I waited. Surely there was something more revelatory than that. But there wasn't.

"Okay. So?"

Madame Renard sighed. "You do not understand. When your mother first rented this apartment, she was simply one of *les danseuses.* Then she became Mimi Archer. And then she became . . . *La Gazelle.*" The woman's tone was reverent, almost patriotic. "She could have lived at *le Ritz, la Plaza Athénée*—anywhere. But she was loyal. This was her home, and she remained here until the day she left Paris. Such loyalty is rare; it is a great gift, and it must be rewarded. Only what can

I give *La Gazelle* that she does not already possess?" She leaned closer to me. "All I have are the things that money cannot buy, and that time will not fade. Devotion. And discretion. Those, I gave to her. She was very grateful. She told me that she could expect those things from no one but me. That is why I have kept this place, even after she was gone. That is why I now give it to you."

I looked around the apartment. Everything was spotless. There was not a mote of dust. Somehow, I knew that Madame Renard had not suddenly brought out the dust mop only upon hearing that I was in town. My mother had left Paris in 1979. Her landlady had kept this place perfect, immaculate, for twenty-eight years—with no reward except for the memory of her famous tenant's loyalty. On the one hand, that sounded crazy. On the other hand . . .

Once again, I saw my mother in a new light. How extraordinary must she have been to inspire such lifelong dedication?

In that instant, I knew I had to stay here. To leave would insult Madame Renard, and I couldn't possibly do that. And if I stayed, I knew I would learn even more about my mother.

Just as instantly, though, I realized it was impossible for me to stay.

"I can't pay the rent."

Madame Renard's expression softened. "There was no rent for *La Gazelle*. There is no rent for her daughter, either." She stood up. "I will cook for you, and clean for you, as I did for your mother. And you may rely upon my discretion as surely as she could." The old lady reached up and stroked my cheek with her callused fingertips. It was a gesture that I can only call motherly. I wondered how many times she had stroked my mother's cheek just the same way. "Welcome home."

After Madame Renard left, I spent some more time exploring the apartment. I still felt a bit like an intruder. I assumed that feeling would pass eventually, although I wondered whether I'd be able to bring myself to sleep in my mother's bed.

I peered into her closets. They were crammed with full-length fabric garment bags. I wondered what was inside. Considering how fabulously she was dressed in all the photographs, I had no doubt that the bags concealed treasures. I began to imagine myself wearing one beautiful vintage dress after another.

I wondered which of those timeless fashions Eddie Atkinson would find most appealing.

Oh, no.

Eddie.

I had told him that I was staying at the Jeff on Rue Richer. That was the only place he knew to look for me, and I had no idea whatsoever where or how to find him. I had to leave word at the hotel so that he could find me if he came looking.

I realized then just how badly I wanted him to come looking.

I locked the apartment door behind me and hurried down the six flights of stairs, then through the courtyard to Rue Richer. The street was crowded with people and vehicles. I squeezed my way toward Jeff Hotel Jeff. Finally I crossed the street. I reached to open the door to the hotel.

"She's not there," said a man's voice.

I turned. There was Eddie. He was wearing another flawless custom suit, navy pinstripe this time, another perfectly crisp white shirt, and a striking red tie.

I was so happy to see him, I hugged him. Practically jumped on him. Through his suit, I could feel the muscles of his back.

What was I doing? I let go and scurried back. Eddie looked surprised. And uncomfortable? I wasn't sure.

"I'm sorry," I said. "I was happy to see you."

"Apparently."

"You came looking for me."

"Didn't I say I would?"

"I'm not sure."

"You don't mind."

"No."

He examined the awning and the window. "This hotel is undoubtedly named Jeff." He looked at me searchingly. "But you're not staying here."

"I checked out."

"Actually, you were never staying here. Because you're Lindy Archer. And they've never had a guest by that name. They *have* had a guest matching your description and named Linda Stone. So which is it?"

"Both."

"I see." He nodded, as if he often met women who introduced themselves using aliases. "In any event, Linda Stone checked out. Or, to be more precise, some old lady checked her out. Where did you go?"

The short answer was, *My mother's apartment.* But that would inevitably lead to questions. *Who was your mother?* and *Why did she have an apartment here?*

How would I answer those? Let's see. *My mother was a famous exotic dancer who had four thousand consecutive orgasms onstage at the* Folies Bergère.

I'm not sure I've ever known a man who could hear that introduction and stick around for the rest of the story. How much less tolerant of Maggie's outrageous past would Eddie Atkinson be—Eddie the investment banker, buttoned-down, white-shirted, conservative Eddie? I couldn't tell him. Not if I wanted a chance to get to know him. Not yet. Maybe not ever.

"Someplace else," I responded. Uninformative, but true.

"Obviously. Anyplace you'd care to tell me about?"

"No."

"No." He pondered that for a bit. "Someplace else with a man?"

His directness took my by surprise. "No!" I had already blurted out the truthful answer before I had time to be insulted. "Not that it's any of your business."

"Of course it's my business. I came here to invite you to dinner. But if you're someplace else with another man, I'm pretty sure dinner is not such a good idea."

He was inviting me to dinner. "No. No other man. And yes. I'd love to have dinner." Again, the words rushed out of my mouth before my brain could catch up. I probably sounded overanxious. Hell, I *was* overanxious.

"Great." He looked at his watch. It was about five thirty. "I'll pick you up at eight thirty. Where are you staying?"

I wondered if he was trying to trick me into revealing it. "Someplace else."

"Right. Someplace else. We established that. So I'll meet you . . ."

"Here."

"Here. In front of the hotel named Jeff, where you're not staying any more."

"Exactly."

Eddie gave me a long puzzled look. I think he was trying to decide whether I would actually be here at eight thirty, or maybe whether he would.

"Bye," he finally said. He turned and, without a glance back at me, he ran to the corner, hailed a taxi, and in seconds was gone.

had three hours to fill. I realized I was hungry, not having had lunch, and I wouldn't eat dinner until at least nine. I was sure Madame Renard would've gladly fixed me a feast, but I only wanted something to tide me over. Besides, although I was confident she really was the soul of discretion, I had just met her, and I didn't want to feel obliged to explain my plans with Eddie. It was much easier to stop in at Montana and have a quick bowl of the *soupe du jour*, a hearty vegetable concoction yummier than any soup I could remember ever having eaten. I thanked Tex, left the restaurant, and turned directly into the passageway next door.

When I returned to my mother's apartment—my apartment—the first thing I did was look for the second outfit I had bought at Galeries Lafayette: the black patterned T-shirt, tailored waistcoat, and long narrow skirt with the crumpled silk hem. I'd already decided that was what I would wear for my dinner with Eddie. It was funkier than his traditional business attire, but neither so far out nor so provocative as to send him running.

I looked in my backpack, but the outfit wasn't there. I started to panic. Then a thought occurred to me, and I checked the little dressing alcove.

Sure enough, someone had pressed the clothes and hung them out for me. Undoubtedly, Madame Renard. It was as if she had waited almost thirty years to perform such services for a preferred tenant, and now wanted to do everything she possibly could all at once. She was good, too—in pressing the skirt, she'd been careful to leave the silk hem crumpled, just as the designer had intended.

It occurred to me that for someone whose idea of high fashion a week ago was to wear matching bra and panties, I was rapidly developing extremely refined taste.

Was it only a week ago? I thought back. Seven days earlier, I had been home in Somerville, Massachusetts, when the fateful package arrived. Since then, my life had spun wildly, launching me back in history nearly fifty years and propelling me across time zones in my quest for my mother's past. First to Las Vegas, and now Paris.

Paris . . . where I was, somehow, home.

I stepped into the bathroom. A black silk robe hung on a hook. The thickest towels I had ever touched, deep purple in color, were draped over ceramic bars. On the vanity was a bottle filled with pink crystals. Under the bottle was a note: *These bath salts were your mother's favorite.*

The far side of the bathroom was dominated by a long, deep tub crafted of hammered copper, which rested on claw feet of dark bronze. I turned on the tap and adjusted the temperature. I shook some of the pink crystals into the flow. When the tub was half full, I climbed in.

The hot water rose past my waist, above my knees, until it reached my breasts. A fine dew of perspiration formed on my face. I tilted my head back and let the water soak my hair. The bath salts released a delicate aroma of vanilla and spice and tropical breezes. I've never been to Tahiti, but I imagine that's what it smells like.

I couldn't remember the last time I had taken a bath. Probably when I was a little girl. What had I been waiting for?

I closed my eyes and stretched out my legs. The tub was huge: big enough for two. Instead of dwelling on who might have shared this space with my mother, I substituted an image with which I was much more comfortable, picturing Eddie here with me. I imagined us facing each other, arms and legs wrapped around one another, fitting together like puzzle pieces forming a single whole.

The picture in my mind was enormously exciting. The surface of the bathwater lapped at my nipples. I realized that, unconsciously,

I had begun to flex my pelvis in time with the beating of my heart. I had to will myself to stop moving, to hold myself back.

I'm going to speak candidly here about orgasms. I understand that some women have trouble with them. Achieving them, I mean. For the record: I am not one of those women. In fact, in the grand scheme of things, I guess you could say that I come rather easily. Assuming such things are hereditary, it added some credence to Claudine's description of my mother's legendary act.

I don't mean to suggest that I finish every single time. Things still have to be right: the man, the environment, the mood. Sometimes I just don't. And I am proud to say that I've never faked it. Not once. I'm not about to put my credibility on the line just to assuage some little-dicked loser's ego. If you want to feel good about yourself, buddy, then get the job done.

There in the tub, I was on the verge. It would have been so easy to let go and ride those waves until I drifted ashore, spent. Instead, I pulled myself back. The evening was just beginning, and I didn't want to reach its climax, as it were, before I'd even set foot out the door. Besides, despite my misgivings about his buttoned-down investment banker nature, Eddie intrigued me; I couldn't recall the last time a man had gotten me this excited before he'd even so much as kissed me. I didn't want to fantasize about Eddie. I wanted the real thing.

I dried myself with the luxurious towels, then I dressed slowly, carefully. Why hadn't I ever before appreciated the feel of fine garments against my skin? I thought again about the fashion mysteries that awaited me in my mother's closets. Soon. Not yet, but soon.

I did venture so far as to examine her shoes. For one thing, I hoped against hope that I might discover the pair of bejeweled heeled sandals Maggie had worn in the snapshot of her showgirl costume. No such luck. The good news, though, was that the many pairs of shoes arranged neatly in their own little cubbies were in flawless condition. The shoes were all size 43, which was a mystery to me—but when I picked a sample pair to try on, black Bally pumps with a two-inch heel, they fit me perfectly.

Briefly, I considered wearing a pair of Maggie's shoes to my dinner with Eddie. I vetoed the idea because nearly all of her shoes had heels. I've never worn heels, and this didn't seem the time to start learning how. Besides, although he seemed quite secure in his self-confidence, I didn't want to push my luck by taking my one-inch height advantage and trebling it. I stuck with the black shoes I'd bought at Galeries Lafayette: low, comfortable, pretty, and still a little sexy.

I looked at myself in the mirror. My mother looked back at me. At least, the woman whose reflection I saw was pretty enough to be my mother.

At eight twenty-five, I locked the apartment door and headed out for my date with Eddie. Or was it my date with destiny?

There was only one way to find out.

45

*B*y eight thirty-five, I was standing in front of Jeff Hotel Jeff. Eddie was nowhere to be seen.

I wondered if he had arrived at eight thirty sharp, given me three minutes' leeway, then left. Guys in business suits can be like that.

I waited. I wasn't sure if I was waiting for him to arrive by foot, by cab, or driving a car. Consequently, I paid no mind to the muscular BMW motorcycle that roared to a stop only a few feet away. I barely noticed that the helmeted rider was wearing a business suit. Navy pinstripes. Perfect.

Just as the man started to remove his helmet, it struck me.

Eddie drove a motorcycle.

How did that fit together with his crisp white shirts and expensive neckties?

"Hop on," he said.

I looked down at my long narrow skirt. Obviously, I hadn't planned on riding a motorcycle when I selected my outfit. Then again, riding bitch behind Eddie meant I could legitimately wrap my arms around him and press my thighs against his sides while 1200 ccs of power roared between my legs.

Oh, baby.

I hiked the skirt up—way up—and climbed on.

"Nice," he said over his shoulder. I couldn't tell if he meant my outfit or my legs. "Helmet?" He offered it to me.

"No thanks." I know, from a safety point of view, I should've worn the helmet. But with the stimulation from Eddie and the bike, I was already at risk of getting seriously overheated on the ride. I didn't want to arrive at a nice restaurant sweating like a pig in heat.

"Risk-taker," he said. I couldn't tell if he thought that was a good or bad thing. He slipped the helmet back over his head and we roared off.

He sure didn't drive like an investment banker.

The Parisian streets were crowded with cars, but we never slowed down. Eddie raced through the narrow spaces between the traffic and parked vehicles. When we approached a red light, instead of stopping, he roared the bike up onto the sidewalk and veered us in a new and seemingly unplanned direction. When our route was blocked by a large truck, he swung the big BMW around and sped for two blocks the wrong way down a one way street.

My sexual excitement was quickly replaced—by fear, yes, but by a different physical thrill, the thrill of danger and exposure, the rush of risking everything.

We burst out of the traffic and there in front of us was the Seine. We hurtled across first one wide stone bridge and then another, crossed a broad street that paralleled the river bank, then Eddie executed a sharp left turn and drove the motorcycle across the sidewalk, barely missing a uniformed footman who stood attentively in front of an elegant doorway. He braked abruptly and the bike squealed to a stop. I looked over my shoulder. There was a trail of burnt rubber across the pavement. The footman, who had dodged for cover, was brushing himself off and glowering in our direction.

"We're here," Eddie said, making absolutely no reference to his acrobatic driving. I hoped we weren't dining at the corner restaurant that employed the poor footman. I hopped off the motorcycle and let my skirt slide down to its proper position. Eddie lowered the kickstand and left the bike parked right there in the middle of the sidewalk.

He hooked his hand under my arm and steered us away from the corner. A few doors down, an awning lettered in gold script identified our restaurant as *La Table de Fabrice*. The glass entryway was framed in wood, and the entry rose two stories high, with the second story comprised of a large arched window. Eddie pointed up at the arch. "That's where we're going. Best table in the house."

We were greeted by a very pretty young woman who kissed Eddie on both cheeks. The woman looked at me. To Eddie, she said, "She is very brave to ride with you." Then she led us up a flight of stairs to the long narrow dining room. The walls were old rough stones and the ceiling was crossed by ancient wooden beams. It was absolutely charming.

As Eddie had promised, we were seated at the end table, by the semicircular window. The view was lovely: the river, and the stone bridge we'd just driven across. The bridge was prettier now that we weren't moving a hundred miles an hour. What's more, at that moment, a row of lights across the bridge's span began to glow, painting the stone a warm honey color.

The hostess brought us two glasses of champagne. She was really *very* pretty. I remembered her remark to Eddie. Had he taken her on a similar adventure?

"Who's that woman?" I asked him, as soon as she had stepped away.

"That's Brigitte. She's married to Fabrice." He picked up the menu and waved it at me. "As in, *La Table de Fabrice.*" He smiled. "You're not the jealous type, are you?"

"Of course not." I'm not. At least, I've never been before.

Dinner was lovely. A waitress brought up two tiny soups that were incredibly flavorful, and that, sorry Tex, left Montana's vegetable soup in the dust. After the champagne, Eddie ordered a bottle of wine, a Rhone called Saint-Pierre. He sipped it and smiled. "It's my favorite," he explained. "It'll keep changing all the way through dinner. Just when you think you know what it is, the next time you taste it, it's something different, and better."

We ordered appetizers: Eddie, a crab millefeuille, and I, crispy warm morsels of goat cheese tanged with balsamic vinegar. At Eddie's insistence, we both ordered the same main course, a special written on the small chalkboard that Brigitte displayed to us: risotto with summer truffles. "Fabrice's risotto is famous. He gets only the best truffles. Of course, the black truffles are even better."

"Of course." I know what a truffle is, but I'd never tasted one before, much less known they came in different colors.

"But you can only get those in the winter."

The appetizers were amazing. Then the risotto arrived, its surface covered with a layer of thin slices of truffle. Before I'd even put the first forkful in my mouth, I could taste it; the aroma was that good. The flavor was even better. I moaned. Literally.

"How could the winter truffles be better than this?"

Eddie shrugged and took a drink of his wine. "They just are. Too bad you won't be here in the winter to find out."

I looked at him. Focused on his dark eyes. "I might be."

His eyes locked on mine. "Really."

"Really." His gaze was intense. I felt like an electric current was flowing between us, and somebody was turning up the voltage. I blinked. "Maybe."

"Maybe. Hmm." He reached across the table and took my left hand in his right. "So tell me: what are you doing in Paris?"

"Looking for someone." I hadn't meant to tell him, but I was distracted, what with him holding my hand.

"A man?"

"No."

"A woman?"

"It it's not a man, then it has to be a woman, doesn't it?"

"You've obviously never been in the Bois du Boulogne on a Saturday night." He chuckled until he saw that I didn't get the joke. "Old or young?"

"Dead." Why was I telling him all this?

"Ah. Who?"

Enough. He was still nearly a total stranger. "I really don't want to talk about this."

"Then what would you like to talk about?"

"How about you?"

"Me. Well." He shifted in his seat. "You already know I'm an investment banker."

"And I'm having dinner with you anyway. I don't want to hear about that. What do you do for fun?"

"Nothing."

"You enjoy driving your motorcycle too fast and scaring the girl sitting behind you."

"You weren't scared."

"How could you tell?"

"I could tell."

That sounded like he had plenty of basis for comparison. "Given lots of girls rides, have you?" Yes, the double entendre was intentional.

"Not like you."

About here, Eddie ordered another bottle of the wine. He was quite right. It kept opening up, changing minute by minute. Kind of like him.

"Are you dating anyone?" It seemed like a fair question.

"Let's see." He looked at his watch. I couldn't tell the brand, but it was plainly expensive. "At this precise moment, I believe I'm dating . . . you."

"I mean, are you dating anyone regularly?"

"What are you doing tomorrow night?"

"What should I be doing?"

His answer to that question was crucial. If his response made any suggestion involving sex, we were done. Don't get me wrong. I've had second-date sex plenty of times. First-date sex, too, for that matter— and I certainly wasn't ruling anything out. On the contrary. But even in spite of his white shirts and business suits, Eddie seemed to have potential that went way beyond a quick bang. If his answer was about sex, then he was just chasing the quick bang after all, and my estimation of him was wrong.

"Anything. Dinner. Movie. Motocross race. Or nothing. Sit in the park, listen to the grass grow. Just as long as you're doing it with me."

Good answer.

essert was as divine as the rest of the meal. Eddie had a soft-centered chocolate cake, I had a lavender-scented crème brulee, and we both shared. Then Brigitte brought us two small glasses of limoncello, as if we needed more alcohol. Finally Fabrice himself delivered two chocolate truffles, which he had just made specifically for us. He wore a black chef's tunic with his name embroidered in red on the breast, and he was intensely interested in whether we had enjoyed our meal. When we made it clear to him how happy we were, he radiated joy.

As we savored the limoncello and the chocolates, my attention was captured by the view of the bridge. At the end of the span nearest to us, a tall pillar rose up, and it was crowned by the stylized sculpture of a woman.

"Who is she?" I asked Eddie.

"Saint Genevieve. She's the patron saint of Paris."

"What did she do?" I'm not a religious person, but to be the patron saint of a place as fabulous as Paris, I assume you have to do something pretty terrific.

"In the fifth century, she saved the city from Attila the Hun."

"Wow. Strong woman."

"I like strong women."

I looked him in the eyes again. "Good thing."

He got the check, and paid quickly. In cash. I couldn't help but notice that his wallet was filled with big bills, 100s and 200s.

Outside, we both looked at Eddie's motorcycle. I handle my liquor pretty well, but we'd just put down two champagnes, two bottles of wine and two limoncellos. In any event, I wasn't sure where we would go, and what I was prepared for us to do when we got there. "Let's take a walk," I suggested.

Eddie took my hand in his and we ran across the street. Soon we found a stone stairway that descended to a broad cobblestone walkway. Just a few feet below us, the river flowed quiet and dark.

We walked. The air hung in a perfect balance between cool and warm, so that the touch of our hands and the glow of heat from our bodies surrounded us in comfort. The sky wasn't quite black, more like navy blue just a shade darker than Eddie's suit.

"Don't you ever take your suits off?"

"I don't sleep in them, if that's what you mean."

I almost asked what, if anything, he did sleep in. *Not so fast, girl, not so fast.* "I just mean, don't you ever unbutton your collar?"

"Just before I take my shirt off."

"In public."

"No."

"Never?"

"No."

No? That was weird. Who never unbuttons his collar in public, ever? "Why not?"

"Because."

Eddie was a very smart, highly educated man. *Because* is the sort of answer that is usually given by, or to, small children. For whatever unfathomable reason, he didn't want to answer the question. I left it alone.

We kept walking. Soon, we were directly across the river from the cathedral of Notre Dame. It's a complicated, confused, contradictory structure: beautiful and ugly, square and round, earthbound and soaring. I guess I was paying too much attention to the cathedral and not enough to where I was walking, because I tripped on the cobblestones.

I started to fall, but somehow Eddie caught me as I was just inches above the ground. He held me like that for a few seconds. He was very strong. Then he pulled me up, and turned me around so I was facing him. He drew me close to him. Closer.

An old sightseeing boat puttered by. From the sounds of it, the entire load of passengers consisted of German men. They were singing a song in unison, badly. They sounded very drunk, and I have no doubt that if I understood German, I would have been offended by the lyrics. In other words, it wasn't the most romantic moment in the history of Paris.

None of that mattered.

Eddie kissed me.

Everything else went away. The crass party boaters. The cathedral. The river. The stones beneath our feet, the velvet sky above. All were suddenly and completely gone.

What was left was the point of intense contact between us. Mouths. Tongues.

From that center of the universe, a wave of energy flowed outward. Now I could feel our hands wrapped around one another, our bodies pressed together.

I don't know how long the kiss lasted. A minute. An hour. Whichever it was, when we finally separated, it was only to realize that we wanted, needed to kiss again. The second kiss went on even longer than the first.

When I finally released him, it was only so I could look around to see if there was somewhere nearby, anywhere, that I could tear his clothes off and release us both.

Cobblestones. Everywhere.

"Let's go someplace," I said.

Those are the precise words I said. What I actually meant was, *Let's go someplace where we can have wild hot monkey sex, right now.* The expression on Eddie's face made it quite clear that he understood my meaning completely.

So I was taken entirely by surprise when he said, "Not yet."

"Not yet?"

"No." He paused, and a mischievous light seemed to sparkle behind his dark eyes. "First . . . let's play."

lay?

I didn't have a chance to ask Eddie what that meant. He grabbed my hand and pulled me toward a flight of stairs. We raced up, and in seconds were back at street level.

Even though I didn't know where we were going, I wondered how we would get there. I thought about how wild our first motorcycle ride had been, back before all the drinking. "I don't think you should drive yet."

"I don't intend to."

He tugged me along, never letting go of my hand. We were almost running.

"What's the hurry?" I asked.

"I want to get there before it closes."

I was aching to know what *it* was, but I didn't ask. Eddie was being fun and mysterious, neither of which I would have expected from an investment banker who never unbuttons his shirt in public. The mystery, and his giddy mood, were as intoxicating as any drink. He was taking me to play, and that was good enough for me—so we cantered down the broad sidewalk that overlooked the Seine without another word, just the occasional giggle.

We practically skipped across a wood-planked footbridge that spanned the river, then raced over the large cobblestones that led into the courtyard of the Louvre. In seconds we were surrounded by ancient palatial walls, and it was as if we had been transported back in time. The setting was beautiful . . . but not playful.

"Where are we going?" I finally asked.

Eddie stopped for just a second and looked into my eyes. "Trust me." He smiled again.

Something in those eyes spoke even more convincingly than his words. I *did* trust him.

We hurried through an arched passageway. Ahead of us opened a broad plaza. In its center was a glowing glass pyramid, and it was flanked by the enormous wings of the museum. The scene was breathtaking and romantic.

Play?

Eddie hurried us past the pyramid. A warm breeze blew across our faces, and as if from nowhere, I thought I detected a whisper of music carried on the wind. Beyond the plaza was a park with immaculate hedges and neat white footpaths. As we passed the tall façade of the Louvre, suddenly a wave of sounds swept over us: music, and bells, and laughter. I looked to my right to find the source of the sounds, and what I saw made me catch my breath.

Lights: spinning, dipping, whirling. Some of the lights spun slowly, bobbing up and down as they went. Others rose and fell rapidly. Most glorious of all were the rainbow lights that rose up in a giant wheel outlined against the backdrop of Paris at night.

It was a carnival.

As we approached, the details came into focus. The slowly turning, bobbing lights belonged to a merry-go-round that must've been a hundred years old; the carousel was covered with gorgeous Art Nouveau murals, and the carved wood horses and elephants and zebras looked ancient and timeless. The lights that climbed and dropped in an instant were attached to a tall crane that hoisted brave souls skyward and then let them fall in a shrieking rush. And the enormous circle of rainbow lights was a huge Ferris wheel.

Eddie bought a long string of paper tickets. "Let's play," he reiterated.

We played. We climbed a tower of stairs and then spun like lunatics down a tall corkscrew slide. We careened around a huge bouncer like four-year-olds hopped up on ice cream and Coke. On a ride comprised of scores of flimsy chairs that hung down from chains, we took adjacent seats; as the whole thing spun faster and faster and centrifugal force lifted us higher and higher, I held Eddie's hand the whole time and laughed until there were tears in my eyes. At the carousel, I sat on an adorably aged carved wooden pig, but Eddie couldn't decide which animal he wanted to ride, so he climbed from one to the next to the next until a sweet-faced little boy atop a rabbit cast Eddie a withering glance and said, "*Petit con.*"

Which is French for *asshole.*

We skipped the flume ride because I was pretty sure my outfit wouldn't forgive me if I got it totally soaked. Eddie dropped a pile of euros trying to shoot a crossbow bolt through the center of a tiny star on a little target. He never got close, but finally the barker felt sorry for him and handed me the yellow stuffed animal Eddie had been trying to win for me. I've never been one for plush, and the thing was ugly to boot, so when I spotted the profane little kid from the merry-go-round, I handed it to him and we were all happy.

I have no idea how long we were there. It must've been hours, but it felt like seconds. I've never had so much fun—I mean just plain laugh-out-loud, giddy-headed, I'm-a-little-girl-again *fun*—on a date.

Finally, Eddie looked at his watch. "Closing time," he said. I looked around, and sure enough, the crowds had thinned almost to nothing. "One more."

We ran for the Ferris wheel and caught the last ride of the night. Although the wheel looked sturdy enough from the ground, our gondola was open to the air, with just a short railing holding us in. Plus, the thing creaked something fierce.

Eddie looked at me. I had one hand on the steel rod from which we were suspended, and my other hand clenched the railing. "Scared?"

"Nah."

He put his arm around me and hugged me close, which made me feel a lot safer. Then the big wheel lurched into motion, and Eddie's free hand made a desperate grab for the steel rod. He smiled. "Yeah. Me neither."

As we ascended, though, any acrophobia yielded to awe at the views. To the north, a stunning white structure that bore a resemblance to the Taj Mahal rose up on a high hilltop; Eddie told me that was the church of Sacré-Coeur. To the west, auto lights painted a glowing red and white path down the Champs-Élysées to the Arc de Triomphe. Southward, the Seine wove its dark glittering path, illuminated by the lights of bridges and sightseeing barges. And east, closest to us was the Louvre with its glowing pyramid; beyond, when the Ferris wheel reached its apex, we could just make out the towers of Notre Dame. It was the most beautiful collection of vistas imaginable.

Then Eddie kissed me again, and Paris went away for a while.

In fact, having missed so much of the sightseeing while we were kissing, and despite my discomfort with the heights, when the wheel stopped, I said, "Let's ride it again." But the carnival was closing for the night, so we had to dismount.

Once our feet were on the ground, I asked Eddie, "Now what?"

"That's up to you." His eyes sparkled again. "We can head back. Or . . . we can keep playing."

Part of me wanted to rush back to Eddie's place and tear his clothes off. Okay, a big part. But let's be blunt: I've had sex before. Lots of sex. Even, on occasion, truly great, re-enact-the-creation-of-the-universe-Big-Bang sex. However, I had literally never had as much fun as I was having in the middle of the night in Paris with this handsome overdressed deliciously perplexing man. And I just wasn't ready for that to end.

"So?" He looked at me expectantly. I wondered if this was a test, and if so, what the correct answer was. "What do you say?"

"Let's play."

48

*O*nce again, Eddie led the way. We strolled through the Tuileries Gardens. At the far side, we descended a stairway that led down to the bank of the Seine, and, conveniently, to a walk bridge that spanned the river without the distraction of cars. Eddie pointed out an elegant, enormous structure across the way. "That's the Musée d'Orsay," he said. "It used to be a train station." As I've already observed, the French clearly care more about their train stations than Bostonians do. The structure was crowned by two huge illuminated clocks, whose roman numerals and giant hands informed me it was almost one thirty in the morning. "Now it's an art museum. Let's go there."

"Now?" I wasn't sure how one would play in an art museum in the middle of the night, but so far, Eddie had proved pretty resourceful.

He gave me a puzzled look. "No, not now."

"I thought you wanted to go play."

"I do. But that's an art museum."

"I'm confused."

"So am I."

"Where are we going?"

"To play."

Who's on first? I don't know. Third base. I gave up. "Never mind," I said. "I'll just trust you." And to seal the deal, I kissed him.

Briefly, I considered just standing there all night, kissing him. It was that good. But I was pretty curious about how we were going to continue our fun and games in the middle of the night. So at some point I said, "Come on," and we kept walking.

On the other side of the river, we wended our way down tiny little streets that ran at odd angles. I held tight to Eddie's hand. I liked the feel of my hand in his; it felt like it belonged there.

Finally, we reached a large park surrounded by a tall black iron fence. We checked an entryway, only to find it sealed by a locked gate. We headed around the corner to another entrance, which was padlocked as well.

I was crestfallen. Playtime was over. And, even though this was hardly fair of me, I felt as if Eddie had let me down. Why hadn't he known the park would be closed?

I turned to him, expecting him to apologize. But he didn't look apologetic at all, or even discouraged. On the contrary, he was smiling, even more mischievously than before.

"What are you smiling about?"

He didn't even answer. Instead, with one hand and one foot on the bars of the fence, and the other hand and foot on a large tree, he started to climb. He looked like something out of Cirque du Soleil, only in a three thousand dollar suit. When he was about six feet above the pavement, he looked down at me. "What are you waiting for?"

What, indeed? I climbed.

After several breathless minutes, I dropped down inside the park. Eddie was already there, waiting for me. Remarkably, neither we nor our clothes were the worse for wear.

He was grinning hugely. "I can't believe you did that."

"Why not?"

"I never dated anybody who would break and enter the Luxembourg Gardens."

Hmm. I wondered it this was some kind of weird litmus test. "How many girls have you invited to break and enter the Luxembourg Gardens?"

"Counting tonight?"

"Counting tonight."

"One."

Oooh. I was his first.

Wait a second. "If you never asked anybody else to do this, how can you say you never dated somebody who would do it?"

"I never bothered asking because I knew they wouldn't."

"And you thought I would do it."

"Maybe. Yeah."

I kissed him: a quickie, but intense. "Yeah. Well, you were right."

Eddie gave me a tour. It's a big park, with lots of discrete areas: the botanical garden, with roses of all kinds, and lemon and pear trees, and honeybees buzzing in their combs; the sports park, with rows and rows of tennis courts; the pond, where Eddie said kids float toy sailboats during the day, but where now only a few sleeping ducks bobbed aimlessly; and the children's playground, surrounded by a three-foot chain-link fence.

"Come on," I said, hopping the fence.

"Where are we going?"

I smiled in the darkness. "You said you wanted to play."

I guess this was my test for Eddie. But investment banker or not, custom suit or not, he was game. Once we had mutually agreed to skip the sandbox, all bets were off. We climbed the vertical rope spider webs, slid down the slides, shimmied up and down the fire poles, bounced on the seesaw, rocked on the spring-mounted scooters, and spun in the whirlers until we were dizzy. Then I spied it.

"Last one to the top is an investment banker!"

49

*M*y destination was the most elaborate climbing structure I'd ever seen, not to mention the most Parisian. It was a squat version of the Eiffel Tower, made entirely of thick ropes. The ropes formed a complicated network of triangles and rectangles to provide plenty of hand- and footholds, and the whole thing rose to the peak of a steel column at least thirty feet high.

I sprinted, and even though my head was spinning, I got there first. I had a pretty good head start, but once Eddie got moving, business suit or not, he climbed like a chimp.

We both reached the top at exactly the same moment, and crowned our achievement with a kiss. Then we sat as comfortably as we could on ropes, holding on to the column and each other, and surveyed the empty park, lovely in the darkness.

Eddie looked straight down. I followed his gaze. Not such a good idea: it was a long way down.

He turned to me. "They let *kids* climb this thing?"

I shrugged. "They let *investment bankers* climb it, so I guess they're not very discriminating."

"They let beautiful women climb it, too."

I swear, it took me at least ten seconds to realize he was talking about me. Giancarlo at the Crazy Horse was the first man who ever told me I was beautiful, so Eddie was only the second. Coming from Eddie, though, it meant so much more. It meant . . . everything.

I kissed him again, softly this time. The ropes swayed gently under us. The warm breeze caressed our skin.

Then the flashlights flared in our eyes.

When we decided to break and enter, Eddie had neglected to tell me that the big building bordering the north side of the Luxembourg Gardens is the French Senate. Consequently, I guess they take security somewhat seriously.

I daresay we set a record for descending the rope Eiffel Tower.

We didn't get arrested, but only because we didn't get caught. The gendarmes on night duty were quite a bit older then Eddie and I, and they had clearly spent those years indulging themselves with French pastry. Also, after apparently spotting us from outside the park and unlocking the gate so they could come in and chase us, they were kind enough to leave the gate open and provide us with an exit that did not involve tree climbing.

And yes, they really do wear those funny hats.

In retrospect, it sounds pretty comical. At the time, though, I was scared. I think Eddie was, too. We ran like hell. In fact, we didn't stop running until we had reached the Seine, not far from where he'd kissed me the first time.

I took a long look at Eddie. He was a little winded, and a sheen of perspiration moistened his upper lip. He was grinning like a kid, and the expression suited him.

I still couldn't begin to fathom how the disparate pieces of this man fit together. But I wanted to find out. No man had ever treated me the way Eddie did. And strange as it seems, since he and I practically just met, no man had ever made me feel the way I was starting to feel about Eddie. Despite the fact that, in many ways, he was still a total stranger, he and I had just spent the most romantic, exuberant, ridiculous, *perfect* night together—and we hadn't even had sex.

Yet.

Eddie and I were both still breathing hard. Maybe it was from running, or from the adrenaline, the fear, the exhilaration that was still coursing through us. Or maybe it was just our personal chemistry, stirred into the magical elixir of Paris at four a.m. Whatever it was, it pulled us together, and once again, with Notre Dame as our backdrop, he kissed me.

Oh my.

This time, I couldn't wait any longer. If we couldn't find our way to a bed, and soon, I really was going to rip his clothes off and ravish him on the spot, cobblestones or no.

"Let's go," I said, and dragged him toward the broad street that bordered the Seine. Fortuitously, a taxi appeared, and Eddie flagged it down. We rushed into the back seat. The driver started the meter.

"Where are we going?" asked Eddie.

"I don't know. Where do you live?"

"We're not going to my place," he said.

"Why not?"

"We're just not."

"That's not a reason."

"I don't care."

Okay, childish fun is great, but childish *childish* is intolerable, particularly when life-altering sex is in the offing. "Would you please just tell the driver where you live?"

"No." The word hung in the air of the cab like smoke. Eddie waved his hand in front of his face, as if trying to waft it away. "It's not a big deal. Let's just go to your place. Where are you staying?"

"It's none of your business."

"You won't tell me where you're staying?"

"No."

"We just had the most amazing night, we barely eluded the French police, you're ready to have sex with me, but you won't tell me where you're staying."

"Apparently. Why can't we just go to your place?"

"Because."

"That's not a reason. Is it too far?"

"No. We could walk there."

"So why are we taking a cab?"

"Because we're not going to my place."

"Why not?"

"Because."

"That's *still* not a reason." A chill ran through me. "There's some-body there."

"What?"

"There's somebody else there. Another woman. Or another man, for all I know. But there's somebody there, so you can't bring me home."

"There's nobody there."

"I don't believe you."

"You have to believe me."

"Why?"

"Because it's true."

"How do I know that?"

"It just is."

"Then why can't you take me home?"

"I can't tell you."

"What kind of a secret are you hiding from me?"

"What kind of a secret are *you* hiding from *me*?"

Neither one of us spoke. There was still enormous electricity be-tween us, only the connection had short-circuited. The air in the cab crackled with our silence.

I had the sudden overwhelming sense that I'd made a terrible mistake, and had completely misjudged Eddie. At that instant, a question popped into my head. "Where did you go to business school?"

It took him by surprise. "What?"

"You're an investment banker. You have an M.B.A. Where did you go to school?"

"Harvard," he said.

I *knew* it.

No matter how attractive and charming and fun Eddie might be, deep down, he was just another snooty big-money pseudo-intellectual brat. He was the enemy. No matter how comfortable I felt in Paris, deep down, I was still a Somerville girl. And I don't date Harvard guys. Ever.

"I think you'd better go," I said, as coldly as I could.

He recoiled as if I'd slapped him. Seconds passed; maybe he was waiting to see if I would change my mind. I didn't. Finally Eddie opened his door. "Fine," he said, and got out. He handed the driver forty euros. "Take her wherever she wants. But you'll have to ask her where she's going. Because she won't tell me."

He slammed the door and stormed away.

50

The cab driver was wise enough not to ask any questions. He pulled the car into traffic. Only after we had ridden a safe distance did I tell him where we were headed. And even then, to be safe, I had him drop me at Jeff Hotel Jeff. I didn't put it past Harvard brat investment banker Eddie to call taxi companies and flash money around until he got what he wanted. This way, the driver literally couldn't tell Eddie where I was staying.

When we arrived, the fare was barely over twenty euros. I gave the driver all forty. I didn't want to keep Eddie's money.

Only when the cab drove out of sight did I walk down the street and go home.

Although hours earlier I had fretted about whether I could bring myself to sleep in my mother's bed, by the time I reached the top floor landing, the issue was resolved. I was beyond tired. Drained. I entered the apartment, locked the door, took off my clothes and hung them in the dressing alcove, then slipped myself naked between the sheets. I could feel that they were the finest linens my skin had ever touched. Under different circumstances, the sensual brush against my flesh might have gotten me started thinking about sex.

Instead, I fell asleep immediately.

I was awakened by a gentle knock on my apartment door. Instantly, I knew it wasn't Eddie; he would have pounded.

"Good morning," Madame Renard said from the landing. "I have your breakfast. Do I have your permission to enter?"

"Of course." I looked at a clock: it was past eleven.

She opened the door with her own key, and carried in one of those breakfast-in-bed trays that you see only in movies or in Macy's for Mother's Day sales. She plumped pillows behind me so I could sit up in bed, then set the tray down in front of me.

"I really don't need to eat this in bed, thanks."

"It is no trouble."

I looked at the tray. "I mean, I'm not really *comfortable* eating like this."

"This is how your mother had her breakfast."

I thought about that. Tradition was a very powerful force here. Still, I really wanted to sit on a chair to eat. "I'm my mother's daughter, but I'm not my mother. *Please* put it on a table?"

She did, and excused herself. The breakfast was totally French, and couldn't have been more different from my usual *Americain* fare at Montana. There were amazing fresh croissants and miniature baguettes, with the most delicious strawberry preserves I've ever tasted. There were three different kinds of cheese, soft, medium and hard, with three incredibly different flavors. The ham was sliced so thin it was translucent, and the egg was perfectly poached. Finally, the coffee was hot and brutally strong; in other words, perfect.

I was famished. The last thing I'd eaten had been the dessert at dinner last night with Eddie. Eddie, who'd duped me, who'd used a perfect night and a playful exterior to conceal who he really was.

I wasn't going to think about him. I wasn't. I'd distract myself. I'd think about other things. Like, for example . . . the weather.

I looked out the window. The sky was gray, and judging from the outerwear on the pedestrians below, the temperature had cooled. Except for dressy things, my wardrobe for such weather consisted of my old jeans and sweatshirt. Oddly, I didn't relish wearing those. They were so . . . unfashionable.

Clothes. Perfect. Another distraction to keep me from thinking about . . . him.

Although I was still reluctant to investigate the high fashions in the closets, I decided to check my mother's dressers to see what I might find. I skipped the top drawer, which I assumed to be filled with lingerie; too private. The second drawer contained blouses, and the third sweaters. I found just what I was looking for: a close-fitting thin black pullover with a crew neck. Emboldened, I opened the closets. I still avoided the bagged gowns, and searched for pants. Sure enough, there was a matching pair of black capris. The sweater and the pants both felt more like cashmere than wool. I looked at the tags. There was no fabric content. In fact, there was only a single word: Givenchy.

I donned the clothes and looked in the mirror. To my surprise, the woman I saw looked less like my mother than like Audrey Hepburn. Not that I claim any resemblance to Audrey Hepburn, who was the most beautiful creature ever to grace a movie screen. But in attire and build, I looked very much straight out of *Sabrina*. All I needed to complete the ensemble was a pair of black slipper flats. I checked the closet, and sure enough, there they were. With earrings and a different haircut, I would've been perfectly poised to convince stuffy businessman Humphrey Bogart to forget his obsession with the bottom line, succumb to the Parisian mindset, and fall hopelessly in love.

My mission for the day was to search out the vintage clothing shop that Marie at the Moulin Rouge recommended. My attention had been distracted by Eddie Atkinson. Now, though, I knew that Eddie was not just a buttoned-down stuck-up snooty Harvard investment banker, but also an idiot who would let some dumb secret about where he lived get in the way of sex that would've registered on the Richter scale. I was shoving him out of my mind, out of my life, and the distractions were gone. I was back on track to trace every part of my mother's history, including her fabulous, decadent costume that had set me on this journey in the first place. And the vintage shop was my only lead.

I was ready to leave, and actually had my hand on the doorknob, when there was another knock on the door. I opened it. There, again, was Madame Renard.

"There is a gentleman downstairs to see you," she said.

Eddie. How did he find me?

"I don't want to see him."

"Oh, but I think you do."

"No, I really don't."

"How do you know?"

"Because he and I had a fight last night, and I'm done with him."

The old lady looked confused. "You saw him last night?"

"If you must know, yes."

"But that is quite impossible."

"I should know. I was there."

She shook her head slowly. "I simply do not understand."

"Which part of this is confusing you?"

"I only told him this morning."

"Told him what?"

"That you were here."

"You did what? I thought you were the soul of discretion."

She looked stricken. "But I am."

"Then why did you tell Eddie where I was?"

"Who is Eddie?"

"The man I was with last night. The man who is apparently waiting for me downstairs, thanks to you."

"There is no Eddie downstairs."

"Great. What now, is he making up phony names?"

"He has many names, but they are all real."

"What are you talking about?"

"The man downstairs."

Now I was the one who was confused. "Okay—you tell me. Who is the man downstairs?"

"He is"—she leaned close and whispered—"one of your mother's lovers."

Wait just a second. Eddie was, I don't know, thirty years old. Thirty-two at the most. Meaning he was born, at the earliest, in 1975. Maggie arrived in Somerville, Massachusetts in 1979. He couldn't have been her lover. It was mathematically impossible.

"This man. The one you told I was here. What's his name?"

"His full name?"

"Sure. His full name."

Madame Renard stood up straighter. "Don Marcos Miguel Alonso Felipe de Bourbon."

I thought she was done. I was about to ask her what I should call this multi-named fellow, but she cut me off with a raised palm.

"Prince of Spain," she added.

51

I sat down, hard, on the divan.

"Prince?"

"Of Spain," Madame Renard confirmed.

"A real prince?"

"He is King Juan Carlos's second cousin."

"And he was my mother's . . ."

"Lover. Yes. One of them."

"*One* of them."

"There were many."

I almost asked *How many*—then decided I didn't want to know.

"But only one at a time."

Well, that was something. If my mother had to have *many lovers*, I guess I preferred that she was a serial monogamist than a nympho- maniac slut.

Madame Renard cleared her throat, the way people do when they're waiting for something.

"Yes?"

"The Prince," she reminded me. "He is downstairs."

"Oh. Right." I tried to think what was the appropriate thing to do in such a situation. I had no idea. Back in Somerville, several of my friends had slutty moms, but to the best of my knowledge, none of those moms ever had a Spanish prince for a lover. "Well . . . send him up."

"Thank you." She looked relieved as she left the apartment.

I waited. For the Prince. Of Spain.

Several minutes passed. Then I heard footsteps coming slowly up the stairs. Step. Step. Step.

Finally, a tap at the door. Tap. Tap tap. Tap tap tap.

I hadn't bothered to lock it. "Come in," I called.

The door opened, and in stepped the most elegant man I've ever seen. He was perhaps seventy years old. He had a full head of beautiful silver hair, twinkling black eyes, and an Errol Flynn moustache that would have appeared silly on a younger man but looked quite dashing on him. His back was as straight as a ramrod, and he was just as slender. He wore a pearl gray suit with silk accents and touches of brocade that hinted at his royalty without flaunting it. And he carried a gold-handled walking stick, although he moved without the slightest hint of impairment.

He strode up to me and bowed deeply. Then he put one knee down on the floor, took my right hand in both of his, and kissed it. He released my hand, but didn't stand.

Seconds passed. He didn't move.

"Please," I finally said. "You can get up."

He stood instantly and bowed again, a little less deeply this time.

"I am His Royal Highness Don Marcos Miguel Alonso Felipe de Bourbon," he said in a voice that sounded uncannily like Mandy Patinkin's character, Inigo Montoya, in *The Princess Bride*. So much so, I half expected his next words to be *You killed my father. Prepare to die.*

I had to remind myself that this wasn't a movie. It was real.

"Prince of Spain," I added.

"Your humble servant."

I didn't have a clue how to entertain royalty. Or anyone else, for that matter. "Please." I looked around. "Sit down."

He sat in the leather club chair. He looked so much at home sitting there, I guessed it was his usual seat in the old days. I chose the divan, and he smiled. "That was where your mother sat, when we talked."

"You talked?" What a relief. I thought he was going to regale me with tales of their lovemaking.

"Of course," he said. "Almost as much as we made love."

Oy.

I'm happy to say that the prince clearly had no designs on me, despite observing my remarkable resemblance to my mother. I'm less happy to report that he had come to reminisce, and a good part of what he wanted to reminisce about included sex. He told me that *La Gazelle* liked to do it standing up, that she also liked to be on top, and that she had a fondness for a position he called the Seventh Posture, which I'd never heard of and didn't ask him to describe.

Fortunately, they had done much more together than screw. She adored the opera, he told me, and *La Bohème* was her favorite. She very much enjoyed horseback riding. She shared his passion for pheasant hunting, and was an excellent shot.

He went on and on, describing idle pastimes of the rich and royal. I could tell he found them fascinating, and so, too, did my mother. At least, that's what he said. Truth be told, though, almost everything he talked about sounded dry as dust.

After four hours, he was still talking. I had difficulty picturing my mother blasting little birds with a shotgun, but of one thing I was sure: she must've been a hell of a listener.

Finally, His Royal Dullness said something that caught my attention. "I would have married her, you know."

I sat up straight. "You would?"

"Of course. I adored her. I proposed to her. Several times. It was quite a scandal." He smiled, and I gathered that he had enjoyed being the subject of such notoriety. "The newspapers might just as well have minded their own business. Because she turned me down. Every time. Eventually, I stopped asking."

Wow. If she'd said yes, I could've been Princess Linda. Instead of cutting class, I could've played polo.

Then again, I'd have been stuck with Prince Blowhard as my father.

He was still talking. "Your father. To have won the heart of *La Gazelle* . . . when I, and so many others, failed. He must be a very special man."

I pictured Jack, sitting at the kitchen table in his boxers and ratty bathrobe, reading the *Boston Globe*, farting a cloud that sent the dog running for air.

"He is . . . unique."

"Perhaps someday I will have the honor."

"Perhaps." Oh God, I hope not. For both their sakes.

Don Marcos drew an antique watch from his pocket. "Gracious," he said, "look at the time. I fear I have talked your entire day away."

Yes, you have, you windbag. That's what I thought. "Don't be silly," I said. I guess I was learning tact.

"Forgive an old man remembering the love of his life. Seeing you has given me the opportunity to relive my most joyful days."

Well, that was sweet, anyway. "I'm glad," I said, and meant it.

He stood. "It has been my great privilege." He strode to the apartment door, opened it, turned toward me, bowed again, and departed.

I listened to his footsteps fade down the stairwell. When I couldn't hear them anymore, I walked to the window and looked down. Eventually, I spotted his silver hair and gray suit. A long expensive car was waiting. After a moment more, the car pulled away.

Elvis has left the building.

was still gazing out the window when there was a knock on the door. It was Madame Renard; by now, I recognized the sound of her tapping.

"Come in."

She entered and regarded me with an expression of extreme sympathy. "You are tired."

"Yes. How did you know?"

"Your mother was always exhausted after the Prince left."

I tried hard to keep pictures from forming in my head. "From the—"

"From the *conversation*. Simply because he is royalty, the man believes it is his God-given right to talk until everyone around him has died of old age."

In fact, Don Marcos had yakked his way straight through lunchtime and past high tea. I realized I was quite hungry. I decided to opt for an early dinner and skip the vintage shop, which, for all I knew, might already be closed. Once Madame Renard headed off to her kitchen, I carefully removed the Audrey Hepburn outfit and slipped on my mother's black silk robe. The fabric whispered against my skin, and I shivered. It was a good shiver. I wondered if the touch of the robe had made Maggie shiver.

The apartment had a TV and a stereo, but I was in the mood for neither. Instead, I perused the living room's small bookshelf. There weren't many volumes, but they were choice. *Madame Bovary. Anna Karenina. Wuthering Heights.*

Jesus, I thought. *Could she have picked any more books with dying heroines?*

At least *Love Story* wasn't on the shelf.

I wondered at my mother's taste in men. The prince didn't seem to have an ounce of fun in his entire regal body. Unlike Eddie.

About whom I refused to think.

Madame Renard brought me a tray with the most delicious roasted chicken I had ever eaten, coupled with creamy mashed potatoes and haricots verts, delectable little green beans. Also a lovely half-bottle of Meursault.

With service like this, it was no wonder my mother had stayed in Paris for nineteen years. The mystery was why she'd ever left.

The next day, Saturday, I rose earlier. Somehow Madame Renard intuited the moment I was out of bed, because she appeared almost instantly with a breakfast tray. I ate, showered, and dressed, this time choosing an outfit that was more reminiscent of Jean Seberg in *Breathless.* I was ready to head out the door by ten a.m.

Before I could open the door to leave, though, Madame Renard knocked. I opened it.

"There is a man here to see you."

"My mother's or mine?"

It just slipped out. Madame Renard glanced at me. I hadn't told her about Eddie. "Your mother's. It is Monsieur Garrond."

"Garrond. Like the car." Not surprisingly, the streets of Paris are filled with French cars. Renaults seem to be most common. Then there are Peugeots and Citroëns. Coming in a close fourth are Garronds.

"Exactly like the car. Monsieur Garrond is *the* Monsieur Garrond. He is a great industrialist. A renowned philanthropist. And—"

"My mother's lover."

"Yes."

"He knows I'm here because you told him."

"Yes."

We were definitely going to have to review the rules on the whole discretion thing. "And he'd like to see me."

"Yes."

"Does he talk as much as the Prince?"

"No."

I looked at my watch. If I could hold the industrialist down to two hours, I'd have the entire afternoon. "Send him up."

She didn't budge.

"Is something wrong?"

Gradually, Madame Renard's gaze shifted downward until she was looking at my feet. I was wearing the same slipper flats I'd chosen the day before. "A word of advice."

"Yes?"

"Keep your shoes on."

Before I could ask what that was supposed to mean, she was gone.

A few moments later, I heard a new sound: the squeak and groan of stairs complaining under a great weight. I wondered if Monsieur Garrond was enormous. I had trouble picturing my beautiful tall slender gazelle of a mother with a hippo.

I heard steps on the landing. Even before the knock, I said, "Come in."

Slowly, the door swung open, revealing . . . no one.

No one that I could see, anyway. The person in the doorway was almost entirely concealed behind the huge steamer trunk he was carrying.

Slowly, the trunk edged into the apartment. When it cleared the door frame, I saw that it was borne by a large sweating bald man in shirtsleeves. Not exactly my mental image of a captain of industry.

"Set it down over there, Jacques," instructed a commanding voice.

I turned back to the door. The figure I saw there was perhaps seventy-five years old, well fed but not fat, clothed in a double-breasted suit that made Eddie's clothes look off-the-rack. His fingernails and his shoes were buffed to perfection. This man was undoubtedly Monsieur Garrond.

Jacques put the trunk down and left the apartment without a word, closing the door behind him.

The trunk was enormous, probably four feet high, and three feet wide and deep. It was a gorgeous old piece; its surface was covered entirely with the classic Louis Vuitton pattern that even I, the fashion neophyte, recognized. Considering the price of a Vuitton wallet, you could probably buy a whole house in Somerville for what such a trunk must cost. Still, my primary interest wasn't the outside of the trunk. It was the inside.

My pulse quickened. Had my mother's former lover brought me the object of my quest, my mother's showgirl costume from the photograph?

Monsieur Garrond obviously was not interested in playing second fiddle to a piece of luggage. He stepped between me and the trunk. Then he approached me slowly, moving first to my left, next to my right, all the while never taking his eyes off me. His gaze swept up to the top of my head, then down to my feet, where it seemed to linger . . . then back up. He studied my face. Finally he broke into a huge smile. His formal demeanor cracked and fell away, leaving genuine exuberance. He hugged me and kissed both my cheeks. Then he stepped back. "It is like a miracle," he said. "As if she had returned."

His genuine affection for my mother was obvious. It made me like him instantly, even to the point where I was willing to take my mind off the mystery of the trunk, at least for a little while, and listen to Monsieur Garrond reminisce.

He described how he had been my mother's sole consort not once but twice—first, shortly after she was proclaimed *La Gazelle* and took Paris by storm, and then again years later, near the end of her career.

Why had they parted the first time, I asked.

"My wife did not approve," he said.

Oh.

And the second time? Again, his wife?

"No. By that time, the old bag didn't care." He sighed. "My *mistress* did not approve."

Oh.

Still, after all these years, my mother held a place in his heart that no other woman had ever possessed. "She was an extraordinary creature. Did you know, she was endlessly fascinated with business?"

"Business?"

"Industry. High finance. The stock market."

I wondered how that fit together with the woman the prince had described only yesterday. "What about horses?" I asked.

"What about them?"

"Did she ever take you riding?"

"I should say not. She was afraid of the ponies at the *Jardin du Luxembourg*." Monsieur Garrond snorted at the absurdity of the notion.

"What about pheasant hunting?"

He stared at me. "You mean with guns?"

I nodded.

"Your mother?"

I nodded again.

The old man started to chuckle. Then he chortled. Finally he outright laughed. "Absurd," he finally said, wiping his eyes. "She abhorred loud noises. Once, a car backfired, and she leaped six feet up the nearest lamp pole. I almost had to call the fire department to get her down. Honestly, child, I can't imagine where you get your ideas."

I didn't mention yesterday's visitor. I was too busy puzzling through the incongruent fragments that had somehow fit together to comprise my mother.

"So," Monsieur Garrond said, "I have talked for a long time. Now tell me: do you have any questions?"

I sure did.

"What's in the trunk?"

53

"*A*h," said Monsieur Garrond. His face lit up as if illuminated from within. "When your mother announced that she was leaving France, she bestowed upon me a very great gift. For many years, I have been the guardian of her legacy. But now, her daughter has come to Paris. You. And it is only fitting that I give to you the heritage that is rightfully yours."

That was a lovely little speech, and I could tell it was entirely heartfelt. It struck me as only a little odd that, as he concluded, the great industrialist was looking down at the floor. At my feet, if I'm not mistaken.

He looked up and smiled. "Would you like to open it?"

I nodded, yes. He handed me a small brass key. I turned the lock and swung the trunk open.

For an instant, I felt a flash of disappointment. There was no glittering, scandalous dress.

But my disenchantment lasted only an instant. Because the trunk held other treasures.

Shoes.

I had already seen many of my mother's shoes, and was even wearing a pair. All of the footwear in her closet was beautiful, but considering who my mother had been and what she had done for a living, those shoes had seemed just a little . . . conventional. Safe.

The shoes in the trunk were dangerous.

All the heels I could see were stilettos. The shortest were three inches, the tallest at least four-and-a-half. If my mother and I were the same height, as I suspected, she would've towered a full six foot five in her highest shoes.

Many of the shoes were strappy things, narrow slashes of black leather with a touch of bondage, or gold or bronze, which looked as if they might have graced the feet of Helen of Troy, assuming she knew how to wear high heels.

And the glitter! Several pairs were encrusted with fine crystals that caught the light and sparkled like diamonds. The stones on one pair were such brilliant white and blue that I wondered if they might actually be diamonds and sapphires.

There was even a pair made of glass. I picked up one of the shoes and studied it, trying to discern whether these were just a curiosity, or if she had actually worn them.

"They're quite real," said Monsieur Garrond. "And surprisingly strong. She wore those for me on several occasions." He seemed to flush slightly. "She wore all of these for me."

Then I saw them. Down in the row of compartments at the very bottom of the trunk. I reached down and carefully lifted them out: two delicate, beautiful, glittering high-heeled sandals.

I recognized them instantly and certainly. They were my mother's shoes from the snapshot. Her showgirl costume shoes from 1960. They looked brand new, perfect.

They also appeared to be my size.

"Would you like to . . . try them on?" asked Monsieur Garrond.

Of course I'd like to try them on.

I was sure they would fit. Once I put them on—literally stepped into her shoes—I somehow knew that I would feel some of what she had felt, understand viscerally how the disparate pieces of her life fit together.

I also knew they would make me—*me*—feel elegant. Glamorous. Beautiful.

I bent down to remove my flats.

Keep your shoes on.

I stopped. That was what Madame Renard had said.

I looked over at Monsieur Garrond. He was staring intently at me. More precisely, at my feet.

His face was flushed, and his breathing uneven.

I sat up straight. Both shoes were still on.

"Don't stop," he said.

I've heard about foot fetishists. I never really believed they existed, though. Much like leprechauns and Easter bunnies, I assumed they were fictional—probably because I'd never met one.

Until now.

I pointed at the trunk. "My mother wore these for you?"

"Oh, yes." His voice was a little hoarse.

"And you . . . enjoyed it."

"Oh, yes."

"Did she . . ."

"She enjoyed that I enjoyed it."

"What about . . . I mean, besides the foot thing—did you also . . ."

"Of course!" He seemed in somewhat better control of himself now. "All the time. But the shoes . . . the shoes were special."

"Standing up?"

"I beg your pardon?"

"Did she like to do it standing up?"

He seemed offended. "That's a rather personal question."

"No more personal than you and her shoes."

I guess he couldn't argue with that. "All right, then. In any event, the answer is no. She was actually quite . . . conventional. Spirited, to be sure, but conventional all the same. Standing up? I should say not."

Doctor Freud and I had no further questions on this particular subject.

"Aren't you going to try those on?" Monsieur Garrond asked, referring to the showgirl sandals I was holding.

"I might," I said.

His eyes started to glitter.

"But not while you're here."

The smile dropped off his face.

"I'm not my mother."

He looked tragically sad.

Maybe he was a weird foot freak, but Monsieur Garrond really did appear to have loved my mother. If I could do something for him that didn't make me a podiatric whore, I wanted to. I got an idea.

"May I keep these?" I asked, indicating the glittering sandals.

"Of course. You may keep all of them."

"No," I said. "You're very sweet. But she wanted you to have the shoes in that trunk. Obviously, they're very special to you."

"That's true," he admitted.

"In that case, I want you to have them, too. I just want this one pair."

"You are very kind." He said it with such relief, I couldn't fathom how hard it must have been for him to offer the contents of the trunk to me in the first place. Twisted fetishist or not, he had obviously really adored my mother—and not just her feet, either. All of her.

Within seconds, Monsieur Garrond had fully collected himself. He opened my door and bellowed into the stairwell: "Jacques!"

Almost instantly, the bald man was back. I closed the trunk, locked it, and handed the key to my mother's former lover. Jacques hefted the trunk and hauled it out of my apartment.

"Thank you for the shoes," I said.

"And thank *you* for the shoes," Monsieur Garrond replied. He gave me a perfectly proper hug, kissed both my cheeks again, and took his exit. Leaving me alone.

In my mother's apartment. With her monumental, flamboyant headdress and her daring, glittering sandals.

To complete my quest, all I needed now was her beautiful, shocking, sexual dream of a dress.

And I knew exactly where to look.

54

The business card for the vintage shop on Rue de l'Échaudé pulsed in my pocket like a living thing.

Maybe I was kidding myself. After all, old Marie at the *Moulin Rouge* hadn't promised my mother's showgirl dress was at this shop; on the contrary, she'd only told me that the person whose name appeared on the business card might know.

I tried to give myself a reality check. Maggie had worn that dress in 1960. What were the chances of finding it forty-seven years later?

Then again, what were the chances of finding her headdress, and her shoes? Yet now, almost magically, I had them both.

I had already tried on the headdress. I hadn't yet stepped into her shoes.

The vintage shop could wait a few minutes more. I slipped off the black flats, picked up one of the sparkling sandals, and examined it. The heel was not quite three inches high. Out of all the shoes in the trunk, these probably had the shortest spikes—but to me, they might as well have been the Hancock Tower. I've never worn high heels. Ever.

Still sitting down, I slipped the sandal onto my right foot and adjusted the ankle strap. It fit perfectly—as if it had been made for me. I extended my leg, pointed my toes, raised my foot until it was pointing up at the ceiling. The light from the small crystal chandelier caught the rhinestoned straps. The shoe was dazzling.

I lowered my leg, put my right foot down on the floor, and donned the left sandal as well—another perfect fit. If only I could walk in them.

Slowly, carefully, I stood up.

For a second, a wave of vertigo washed over me, and the room spun. Then, just as fast, it stopped. I was standing. On high heels.

I took a step. Another. I didn't teeter. I didn't trip. I walked. Somehow, despite the fact that my feet were now tilted at an angle they'd never experienced, I felt fine. Natural, even. As if I'd been waiting to put on those shoes my entire life.

My comfort in my mother's shoes further convinced me that I would, in fact, find her dress. Once I had stowed the glittering sandals safely in the closet, I put the black flats back on—and how very flat they suddenly seemed. Then I locked the apartment, ran downstairs and got directions from Madame Renard. The vintage shop was almost a straight shot south, about two miles. When I told her I was walking, the old woman tried to encourage me to take a more scenic route. I thanked her but explained that I was more interested in speed than sightseeing just now.

As I hurried through the narrow streets, I understood why Madame Renard had tried to direct me to a different route. I walked several blocks that were not just unattractive, but which bore neon signs, currently unlit, advertising XXX peep shows and DVDs. I appreciated her protectiveness, but compared to the sexual smorgasbord that surrounded the *Moulin Rouge,* this was downright tame. In any event, after a few minutes I had emerged into a lovely green park. I passed the Metro station for Les Halles and kept walking.

A short ways beyond the park, I reached the Seine. A bridge of beautiful white stone arched gracefully over the river; from its span, an endless array of grotesque carved faces frowned and glowered and scowled. A plaque identified the bridge as the Pont Neuf. I crossed its first span, which bisected the western tip of the Île de la Cité, an island that lay in the middle of the river like a huge ship run aground. I continued across the second span of the Pont Neuf, and in minutes I was on La Rive Gauche, the Left Bank. Every store window I passed was either a restaurant, gallery, bookstore or upscale clothing boutique. I saw no vintage shops.

Here, the streets ran at crazy angles. I adhered to Madame Renard's detailed instructions: a right turn onto a street that then curved left; followed by another right, then a hard left turn. This should be it.

I wondered if I was in the correct place. The narrow passageway in which I stood was barely more than an alley. Then I looked up and saw a blue street sign mounted on the wall of the nearest building: RUE DE L'ÉCHAUDÉ. I took the business card out of my pocket. The name of the street matched.

Despite having hurried to get here, now my pace slowed almost to a crawl. I passed a gallery. A tiny shop selling delicate antique knickknacks and jewelry. And then, there it was.

The exterior consisted almost entirely of a large glass window set into a flat white façade. An enormous, ancient wooden beam capped the window like a hat. On display were garments the likes of which I had never seen: a sleeveless gown seemingly woven entirely of gold; a silver mesh tunic, almost transparent, over which was layered an even more revealing silver mist that was nearly invisible, but for the detailing of edges and buttons. The clothes hovered in front of an ethereal background of blue and gold silk.

For a moment, all I could do was look and wonder: *What exquisite female creatures must have worn such remarkable dresses?* No wonder Marie had sent me here.

On the glass door, small gold lettering identified the establishment: JAZZ. And below the store name: FRANÇOISE MALRAUX, EXPERT. This was it. I took a deep breath and opened the door.

Inside, the place was tiny, and it felt even smaller, crammed as it was with racks and racks of antique garments. Silks and beads and furs were everywhere. Directly in front of me was a huge ornate old cash register with a crank handle. Beyond the cash register, a spiral staircase rose straight up into the ceiling, and even more fine garments hung from the staircase railing. To my left was a small old wooden desk, its surface cluttered with bolts of fabric, pincushions, a large square glass ashtray, and a small television set flickering soundlessly. Behind the desk, watching the TV, sat a woman. She was younger than Madame Renard, older than my mother would be now if she were still alive. She was dressed simply but elegantly, and even just sitting there she conveyed an air of authority.

She looked up at me, her expression bemused. I got the impression that she had been expecting me. After a moment, she stood. She was far shorter than I, and wider. I looked down at her. Her eyes twinkled with the light of secrets soon to be discovered.

"Welcome," she said in a throaty alto. "I am named Françoise."

55

*S*he held out her hand and we shook hands, very formally.

She looked up at me. Her eyes met mine and held them. "You have need help?" She asked it like a question, but I could tell that she already knew the answer.

"Yes," I said. "Please." I offered her the old snapshot of my mother and Dixie. "Do you have this dress?"

She glanced at the picture for only a few seconds, then passed it back to me. "It is very pretty."

"I know."

"This dress is very special."

"Yes."

"Full of glamour. Decadence. Magic."

"Yes."

"From *Les Folies*."

Hope sparked within me. "So you have it?"

"No."

Hope crashed.

Then again, maybe she wasn't sure. I handed the photo back toward Françoise. "Do you want to take another look?"

She sniffed at me and turned away. "I do not need another look. When I tell you I do not have this dress, it is because I do not have this dress."

Not only did I want to cry, but I felt guilty, having apparently hurt her feelings. "I'm sorry. I believe you. It's just . . . the dress is very important to me. And you were my only hope of finding it."

The old woman turned back to me. From the warmth on her face, I could tell that I had been instantly forgiven. "You are a sweet girl."

"Thank you."

"You have great respect for your mother."

I hadn't said anything about the girl in the photo being my mother, so her comment took me aback. Then again, I guess the resemblance was pretty strong. "Yes." It was only a single word, but it reverberated through my body and my brain. *I had great respect for my mother*—the woman I had never known, whom I had grown up hating.

"It is good for a daughter to respect her mother. She would be proud of you."

I couldn't tell if she was speaking hypothetically, or if she had actually known Maggie.

Françoise was still talking. "Maybe I have something else you would like."

"That's all right. I'm really only looking for this dress."

"Maybe I will look anyway."

"You really don't have to."

Her old eyes twinkled. "Maybe you will humor me."

With that, she brushed past me and tromped up the iron spiral staircase. It hadn't occurred to me that the stairs actually went anywhere. At the top, Françoise stopped and looked down at me. "You are coming?"

"Coming where?"

"To see the nice things."

I looked around the crowded shop. The racks were overflowing with nice things. I wondered what she meant. Still, I didn't move.

She shrugged. "Very well. I will simply pick something out for you."

With a shove of her shoulder, she opened a door above her and disappeared into the ceiling. Through the little door, a light clicked on. Craning my neck, I could see that there was a tiny space above the store. It appeared to be literally filled with clothing.

For several minutes, Françoise remained out of sight. From the ceiling, I heard the rustle of fabrics: taffetas and crinolines being pushed out of the way. Then, a single word: "Ah."

Another full minute passed. Finally, the light in the tiny room clicked off, and the old woman descended. Something was in her hands. Whatever it was, it appeared to be as insubstantial as a spider web. She carried it so carefully and walked down the stairs so slowly, you'd have thought she was holding the Holy Grail.

Finally she stood before me. "This is very special," she announced. "This is . . . four hundred euro."

"I'm really not shopping for anything."

She thought for a bit. "I will give to you for . . . three hundred euro."

Her persistence was mystifying. I still couldn't tell what she had in her hands, but whatever it was, why would I care, much less spend hundreds of dollars for it?

"She wanted you to have it," said Françoise.

Her words froze me. "She?"

"Your mother. I am sure."

"My mother?"

"You would like to see it?"

I couldn't speak. I nodded my head: *Yes.*

The old woman unfurled the thing in her hands, holding it by the shoulders and letting it hang down its full length. It was a bodysuit made of the finest silk mesh I had ever seen, like antique stockings, only much more sheer. The mesh was virtually transparent but had a slight fleshtone hue. Patterned throughout the almost invisible garment were graceful veins in a darker shade. One of the veins climbed seductively up the left thigh of the bodysuit. Another coiled intimately around the right breast.

"You know what this is?" she asked.

I shook my head, *No*, even though I was pretty sure I did know.

"This," Françoise proclaimed reverently, "is the costume of *La Gazelle.*"

started to shiver, and even though it was perfectly warm in the shop, I couldn't stop. My arms were covered with goose bumps. The hairs on my neck stood up as if someone had just plugged me into a socket.

Françoise had a three-panel folding mirror on the far end of the shop. "Come," she said. "Come see."

I crossed the room. I felt like I was floating. If my feet moved, I wasn't aware of it.

I stood before the mirror. Every way I looked, there I was. Françoise held the ephemeral garment up in front of my body. It brushed lightly against me. Even though I was fully clothed, a charge like static electricity sizzled across my breasts, my belly, my thighs.

I looked in the mirror. There I saw my mother, wearing only this costume, if one could call it that. This whisper, this dream. She looked clothed, and yet more naked than if she were standing there in nothing but her skin.

I blinked. When I opened my eyes, my mother was gone—yet the image of the woman in the blatantly bare outfit remained. Now, though, that woman was . . . me.

"I'll take it," I said.

I paid Françoise, and as I signed the credit card receipt, I vowed this would be my last fashion purchase. The old woman took the remarkable garment and folded it very carefully, until it was no bigger than a paper napkin. She wrapped it first in white tissue, then surrounded that with sturdy brown paper. Finally she handed the small package to me.

Françoise got up on her tiptoes and kissed me on my cheeks, right and then left.

"Thank you," I said.

"Now go and make her proud."

I wasn't at all sure how to do that. That didn't change my answer, though.

"I will."

The package in my hands was almost weightless. Just thinking about it made my heart flutter. I wondered how long it would take me to get up the nerve to put it on. I wondered if I would ever have the nerve.

I retraced my steps to Rue Dauphine, the street that led back to the Pont Neuf. Two blocks before I reached the Seine, I glanced to my right down narrow Rue Christine. The street ran for only a single block, and midway down its length, a crowd had gathered. I wasn't in a rush to get anywhere, so I decided to see for myself what everyone found so interesting.

As I approached the assembled people, I saw that there was a small movie theater, dubbed *Action Christine,* tucked into the surrounding ancient façades. The people were waiting in two lines. From the orderly highbrow crowd and the modest frontage, it was clear to me that this was an art-house cinema. I felt a sudden pang of homesickness for my beloved Brattle Theatre in Harvard Square.

There was no marquee here; instead, there were two doors, each leading down a flight of steps to a separate theater, and above each door was a small board identifying the featured movie. Theater 1 was showing something called *Le Mepris.* There was a poster on display, which depicted Brigitte Bardot, her blonde hair tousled, her voluptuous breasts almost spilling out of a low-cut pink dress. She was the embodiment of desirable femininity. Seeing that poster reminded me just how much I didn't look like what men wanted— skinny me, with my dark hair and too-long legs and too-small breasts.

I looked at the sign over Theater 2, and I almost shouted with joy.

Sabrina was playing. The original, of course, with Audrey Hepburn, in glorious black and white.

Maybe a dark-haired skinny girl with long legs and small breasts had a chance after all.

The crowd had already started to filter in to Theater 2. I checked the showtimes posted at the box office window: the movie was due to start in two minutes. I simply couldn't resist the idea of seeing *Sabrina* in Paris. The fact that the little purple ticket cost me only three euros made it even more perfect.

Downstairs, the small screening room was already dark. I found an open seat in the last row just as the screen sparked to life. Blessedly, there were no Coke commercials and no Jerry Bruckheimer trailers; we went straight to the film.

When Sabrina, the lovely but sad chauffeur's daughter, sat in the tree, hopelessly adoring wealthy playboy David Larrabee from afar, I was the one sitting in that tree. When the tear rolled down her cheek, I was the one who dabbed my eyes with Kleenex. When motherless Sabrina was sent off to Paris to forget her crush on David and find herself, I went with her. When she returned, triumphantly glamorous in Givenchy, and pragmatic older brother businessman Linus Larrabee began to woo her in David's place, I was the one who sailed on Linus's boat and felt the wind and the spray on my face. And when Linus abandoned his obsession with business to join Sabrina on her return to Paris, the romantic triumph was mine.

Every time I've ever seen this movie, I've always been Sabrina. This time was different, though. This time, I actually was in Paris. I had met, and nearly fallen for, my own real-life business-obsessed Linus Larrabee—only mine was named Eddie Atkinson. And, with due respect to Humphrey Bogart, Eddie was much better looking.

No matter how much I associated with it, though, *Sabrina* was still just a movie, whereas my life was real. Humphrey Bogart might hitch a ride on a tugboat to catch up to the ocean liner sailing Sabrina to France, but no matter how much chemistry we might have or how much fun he could be, Eddie and I had no cruise in our future. That ship had already sailed.

When the movie ended and the lights came up, I made sure I had my precious package from the vintage shop, and headed for the stairway to the street. On Rue Christine, I stopped for a moment, blinking in the sunlight while I got my bearings.

"Hey!"

The word came from behind me, spoken by someone still on his way out of the theater. I ignored it. I wasn't with anyone, and, outside of my own small neighborhood near the *Folies Bergère*, I didn't know anyone in Paris. I started to walk back toward Rue Dauphine.

"Lindy!"

That stopped me cold. I had only ever used that name with two people. Dixie was back in Las Vegas. And Eddie was—

right here, grabbing my hand and refusing to let go.

"Eddie!" I was shocked to see him.

But, inexplicably, I was happy, too. He was as handsome as ever— maybe even more so. He was still buttoned up, of course; although it was Saturday, he wore a navy blazer, gray slacks, a perfect white shirt—what else—and a classic striped tie.

"What are you doing here?" I asked.

"Same thing as you. I just saw the movie."

"You did not."

"Of course I did. *Sabrina* is my second-favorite movie."

I looked around to see who might be with him. He appeared to be alone. "Where's your date?" I asked.

He looked puzzled. "I don't have a date."

"Nobody goes to the movies alone."

"You just did."

"That's different," I said, although I couldn't think of how it was different, or why.

"Never mind about that. Where have you been?" he asked. "Nobody at your hotel named Jeff knows where you are."

"I haven't told them."

"I've been looking for you."

"That's why I haven't told them."

"Please," he said. "I need to see you again."

"You're seeing me right now."

"I mean it. I'm sorry. I was an idiot. Please: have dinner with me. Tonight."

"I'm busy." *I don't know why I didn't just say* no.

"Tomorrow night, then."

"All right." *Wait a second. Who said that? What about how obnoxious he'd been in the cab? What about my rule against dating Harvards? What was I doing?*

"I'll pick you up."

Did he really think I would fall for that? "I'm still not telling you where I'm staying."

"I'm not asking. Just be in front of the Jeff. Nine o'clock tomorrow. I'll come get you."

"On that motorcycle of yours? I think I'd rather walk."

"No motorcycle. Okay?"

In spite of myself, I smiled. "Okay."

He glanced at his expensive watch. "Oops. Gotta run. Conference call in ten minutes."

He started to hurry away.

"Eddie!"

He stopped and turned back to face me.

"What should I wear?"

Eddie smiled hugely.

"Something fabulous," he said, and then he was gone.

walked all the way back to my mother's apartment. My apartment. Although *walked* doesn't describe it. More like *floated*.

My mind swirled with questions:

Eddie was a buttoned-down, stuck-up, Harvard-educated investment banker—so why did he have this effect on me?

If *Sabrina* was his second-favorite movie, what was first?

Where would he take me for dinner?

And what would I wear?

I didn't have the answers to any of these questions, but for the last one, at least I knew where I would look: in my mother's closets.

Madame Renard had dinner waiting for me, a delectable duck accompanied by a half-bottle of a divine red Bordeaux. It was no wonder my mother had stayed in Paris for so many years; in just two days, I had already become addicted to having someone provide me with free rent, fabulous meals and immaculate laundry service. Under such circumstances, it was hard for me to imagine why she ever left.

I thought about beginning my search of her closets, but the idea of delving into the mysteries hidden in all those garment bags was still daunting. I convinced myself that I would be braver in daylight, and went to bed.

The next morning, I was rewarded with the most glorious day since my arrival in Paris. I drew back the curtains on every window, and the apartment was flooded with a rich light that blessed everything it touched. I opened the French doors to the air outside, and, even though it was still only May, I was embraced by a gentle summerlike warmth. The sky was perfectly blue, with not a hint of cloud or haze. *On a day this beautiful*, I thought, *anything is possible.*

I approached the closets. Now they were intriguing, beckoning— not frightening at all.

I zipped open the first garment bag, revealing a glittering dress fashioned entirely of silver tube beads. It was lovely, but very formal, and very heavy, neither of which seemed the right choice for this evening. The next bag contained a black silk ensemble trimmed in a fur I guessed was chinchilla. Surmising that I had inadvertently begun my search in the winter closet, I closed that door and opened the next one.

When I unzipped the first bag, I gasped. Literally.

The gown was floor-length. It was fashioned from a silk jacquard, with a pattern of impressionistic roses giving the fabric a texture that begged to be touched. In the front, the neckline was high and modest, but in the back, the slender shoulder straps dropped down in a cowl that scooped daringly low. The gown was fitted at the waist and hips, but flared out at the knee like a mermaid's tail. The whole thing was a vibrant crimson: not the tired maroon that every piece of Harvard logo wear inexplicably calls *crimson*, but a radiant shade somewhere between scarlet and rose. In a word, it was fabulous.

Instantly, I knew two things. It would fit me as if it had been custom-made. And this was what I would wear for my evening with Eddie.

I removed the gown from its padded hanger and held it up in front of me. At that moment, I heard Madame Renard's gentle knock on the door. "Come in."

She entered. When she saw the stunning dress, she did a double take, and I knew that for just an instant, she'd thought I was my mother. Then she broke into a huge smile. It was an expression I'd never seen on her face before.

"This was one of your mother's favorites," she beamed.

For reasons I can't explain, that made me happy.

"She particularly loved the Sabrina neckline," Madame Renard continued.

This time I was the one who did the double take. "The what?"

"The neckline. Monsieur Givenchy designed it for Miss Hepburn. She wore it in the movie *Sabrina* and made it famous. The American costume designer won an Oscar for Monsieur Givenchy's gowns. In France it was a great scandal. Anyway, although your mother was taller than Miss Hepburn, their physiques were quite similar. The Sabrina neckline was very flattering on her." If it was possible, she smiled even wider. "And it will be very flattering on you, too."

I blushed.

Madame Renard made a visible effort to restore her usual stern demeanor. "Mademoiselle has a visitor," she said.

"You're kidding."

Of course, she wasn't.

"A man?"

"Naturally."

"Another one of my mother's . . . friends?"

"This man was much more than a friend."

How many of Maggie's *more than a friend* men would I have to endure? "Okay," I said. "But first, do me two favors."

"Of course."

"Let me put some clothes on. And"—I looked at the gown—"pick me out some shoes that go with this?"

It occurred to me that there was something slightly weird about my mother's former suitors seeing me—by all accounts, her look-alike—wearing her outfits. Instead of her clothes, I slipped on my IKKS parachute pants and funky T-shirt.

Madame Renard approached the dressing area with a pair of shoes in her hand. They were delicate jeweled wonders: pale rose in hue, with tiny pearls and crystals that made them sparkle and dance in the daylight that filled the apartment. They were so perfect for the dress, I didn't hesitate even when I saw the two-and-a-half inch spike heels.

The old woman looked at me expectantly. Now that I was dressed and had chosen my outfit for the evening, I was out of excuses. "All right," I said. "Send him up."

She vanished out the door. Barely a minute later, she was back.

"Allow me to introduce . . . Monsieur Michel Petit."

In strode a man of about sixty. Despite the warm weather, he was dressed in a black turtleneck, black slacks, and a white double-breasted jacket.

I didn't laugh, but it wasn't easy.

Petit is the French word for small. Monsieur Petit was, by my best estimate, five foot two.

And he was wearing lifts.

"My darling girl," he exclaimed, and kissed my cheeks, not twice but four times. I had to bend down quite a ways to let him do it. Then he stepped back and looked at me appraisingly. "You don't know who I am, do you?"

I had a scary Luke Skywalker flash and feared for a moment that he was about to proclaim himself my father. "No," I said. "But can we get one thing out of the way first? What sexual positions did you and my mother prefer?" Forgive my bluntness, but let's cut to the chase.

The question seemed to take him aback. "She and I did not have sex."

"Don't tell me—you just liked to watch."

He shook his head vigorously. "Your mother was . . . not my type."

Oddly enough, instead of feeling relieved, I took that as an insult. "How could she not have been your type?"

"She was not a man."

Oh. Well, let's look at the bright side: at least I wouldn't have to buy him a Father's Day card. I steered him back to where I had interrupted. "You were about to tell me who you are."

"Ah. Yes." He straightened up to his full height, such as it was. "I am the most important man in your life."

Huh? "You mean, you were the most important man in my mother's life."

"No. Silly child. Monsieur Gyarmathy was the most important man in your mother's life. Or perhaps Monsieur Petsch. Not I," he said, in an imitation of humility. "But I *am* the most important man in *your* life."

Notwithstanding that we'd just met. "And why is that?"

"Because I am the man who is about to make you the star of the *Folies Bergère.*"

$\mathcal{I}$ sat down. Hard.

Reality check. "The *Folies Bergère* is closed."

"Temporarily," he admitted.

"Since nineteen ninety-three."

"Awaiting only a star whose brilliance can propel the *Folies* into a triumphant new era."

"So where exactly do I fit in?"

"You are the daughter of *La Gazelle*."

"And?"

"You look like her."

"And?"

"You move like her."

No one else had told me that before. Even coming from this strange little man, I enjoyed hearing it. Still, I didn't see where he was going with all this. "So?"

"So. For years, I have labored to restore the *Folies* to its place in history. I have raised millions of euros. I have conceived a spectacular new revue. I have assembled the dancers. The nudes. The comedians. The musicians. The costumers. Everyone and everything now awaits only one person. The headliner." He paused dramatically. I held my breath. "You," he finally proclaimed.

"Me?"

"The daughter of *La Gazelle*."

"Why would anybody come see me in a show?"

"Because only you can recreate your mother's immortal act."

He kept talking. At least, his lips kept moving. But I stopped hearing him, or anything else, for a while. The enormity of what he'd just said had rolled over me like a tidal wave, and I could feel it carrying me out to sea. The ocean roared in my ears—or was that my own blood coursing?

Gradually, my hearing returned. Monsieur Petit was still speaking. "With your participation, I could stage the entire show in a month."

Having witnessed the backstage mayhem at the *Folies* show in Las Vegas, some part of my brain was astonished that someone could assemble such a complicated extravaganza in only four weeks. Most of my gray matter, though, was consumed with a very different thought.

"You want me to have an orgasm on stage?"

He smiled the most cryptic smile I've ever seen. "Perhaps."

Michel Petit proceeded to explain his dream. It was no wonder he'd been able to raise a fortune and muster a creative army. He was captivating.

He had served as the assistant to Monsieur Gyarmathy, the creative genius who had conceived and staged the *Folies* revues for half a century. Ever since the theater closed for financial reasons, Monsieur Petit had dreamed of becoming the impresario who could return it to its former glory. Over the past fourteen years, he had planned and sketched, choreographed and orchestrated, ever refining his creative vision. He had also enlisted a cadre of investors including a Russian oil baron, two Silicon Valley dot-commers and the drag-queen brother of China's forty-first wealthiest man. They were a ragtag bunch with only three things in common: they had money they could lose without flinching, they were in no rush, and they were all intrigued by the prospect of restoring Paris's decadent goddess.

Six months ago, Petit had been on the verge of launching his revival. For his star, he had enlisted a Polynesian chanteuse who claimed to be descended, illegitimately of course, from the brilliant and legendarily amoral artist Paul Gauguin. The young woman, who billed herself as *Lily G,* wasn't much of a singer, but Petit was gambling on her exotic beauty and decadent French pedigree to draw the crowds. He stuck with Lily even after it was revealed that her most recent gig had been as a high-priced Thai hooker. But when several of the famed painter's *legitimate* illegitimate heirs challenged her claimed patrilineage, DNA tests were in order, and it was revealed that she was even less a Gauguin than a songstress. Looks alone would not translate to box office. Petit was left without a star, and the new revue was put on indefinite hold.

"Until now," he declared fervently. "Now, destiny has brought you to Paris. To me. To *Les Folies Bergère.*"

Strangely, I didn't immediately say no. "What makes you think I can do my mother's old routine?"

"I told you, you look like her, and you move like her."

"Maybe I don't move *exactly* like her." Given the nature of my mother's act, it occurred to me that even little differences could be critical.

He clapped his hands together. "Well, then, let us see." He gestured at the floor. "Will you walk for me?"

"Just walk?"

"Just walk."

I stood up, and walked. Just walked.

"Spectacular," he said.

"All I did was walk."

"No. You walked . . . *exactly* like her."

"Really?" Maybe it was a sales pitch. I didn't care. I was buying.

"Really."

"Her routine was more than walking."

"You can do it."

Wait a second. "But . . . what if I can't . . ."

"Yes?"

"You know." He stared at me blankly. Jesus, he was really going to make me say this. "What if I can't . . . *come* like her?"

The little man's eyes twinkled. "History has only a few great mysteries," he said, his voice low. "Why was the Mona Lisa smiling? What was the secret of the sphinx? And . . . was the grand release of *La Gazelle* genuine? For years, all of Paris debated this question. Your mother never told anyone. Not Gyarmathy, and not me." He shrugged. "So. Perhaps it was all stagecraft of the highest order. Or perhaps it was entirely real. Only one person ever knew. Now, a second person can learn the secret."

"Me?"

"You. I can teach you the steps, the gestures, the timing. But the magic, the fire, the explosion . . . those are within you."

Incredibly, he believed I could do it.

Even more incredibly, so did I.

My whole body tingled. Maybe that was a good sign.

"Okay."

59

*M*onsieur Petit broke into an extravagant dance, right there in the middle of the living room. He was an excellent dancer.

While he was spinning, I looked at my watch. He had talked for hours. It was the middle of the afternoon. I had plans for what might prove to be an extraordinary evening, and I wanted ample time to get ready. When Petit paused, I grabbed his elbow and told him we'd have to continue our discussion at another time. We agreed that he would return the next afternoon. I escorted him to the door, and he jigged down the stairs.

Bless her, before my visitor had even reached the ground floor, Madame Renard appeared in my doorway. "You must prepare," she proclaimed.

First, she fed me a light lunch of fresh-baked bread and a thick soup. Then, while I showered and shaved, she rounded up a roster of personal care professionals: one woman for my manicure, a second for my pedicure, a waxer, a hair stylist, a makeup artist, and a fragrance consultant.

Up until this day, I had never had a manicure or a pedicure. My only prior experience with a wax left me blotched and half-finished. I hadn't worn makeup since I was fifteen, unless you count that black stuff during my brief Goth phase, and the only perfume I'd ever tried would've smelled right at home on Lily G, the Thai hooker. The treatment I was receiving now, however, I could get used to.

"Who's going to pay all these people?" I whispered to the old lady between hair and makeup.

"No one," she said. "They do it for the glory."

Finally I was ready to dress. There was no issue of a bra, because neither the gown nor my body called for one. Too late, however, it occurred to me that my own panties weren't nearly fit for the outfit I was about to don. My only option would lie in my mother's lingerie drawer.

Madame Renard rescued me from years of psychoanalysis. "Here," she said, handing me a small package. "They are your mother's favorite brand. But brand new, of course. Every woman should have her own."

Inside was the most beautiful, delicate, sensual black lace thong I had ever seen. Just putting them on sent waves of heat radiating out from my pelvis.

Maybe I really could do my mother's act.

Madame Renard helped me into the exquisite crimson gown and the jeweled shoes. "Walk," she instructed.

I walked. Effortlessly. When I reached the end of the room, I spun gracefully and waltzed back. Halfway, I caught my reflection in the large mirror that hung over the mantle. I froze.

The woman in the mirror was beautiful.

Madame Renard had tears in her eyes. "You are extraordinary," she said. "Your mother would be so proud."

My own eyes started to well. I willed them to stop. The makeup artist had already gone. Besides, time was short: it was past eight forty.

Madame Renard lifted my long sweeping skirt and assisted me as I walked downstairs. When we reached the bottom, before I stepped out into the courtyard, I took both of her hands in mine. "Thank you," I said.

For being my mother's guardian, the keeper of her flame. And for helping me discover . . . me.

I didn't say all those words, but I think she heard them.

As I walked down the street, I realized that I couldn't wait to see Eddie. My body literally tingled with anticipation.

At eight fifty-eight, I reached Jeff Hotel Jeff. Three orange traffic cones occupied the street directly in front of the hotel.

At eight fifty-nine, the desk clerk, Claude, emerged and removed the traffic cones.

At nine o'clock sharp, a black limousine pulled into the newly created space.

From inside the limo, the rear door opened. Eddie Atkinson stepped out.

He was transformed. Notwithstanding that I'd always seen him in perfect suits, shirts and ties, he'd always looked like, well, an investment banker, and a Harvard-educated one at that. Buttoned-down, stiff, formal, in spite of his good looks. Now, though, Eddie was wearing a *tuxedo*. He looked simultaneously flawless and reckless, elegant and dangerous. Move over, Cary Grant, Humphrey Bogart and Sean Connery—there's a new leading man in town. With a change in wardrobe, he'd gone from Steady Eddie to Fast Eddie. I liked it. I more than liked it.

Eddie looked at me. Stared. "Wow," he finally said.

In the movies, suave leading men don't stare, and don't say *Wow*. Who cares? Eddie was real.

And in that instant, I knew that if I wanted him, he was mine.

I was pretty sure I wanted him.

The limo wound through the narrow streets toward the Seine, near where we'd gone to dinner the other night. Instead of crossing the river, though, the long car turned down a sloping drive and pulled to a stop next to an elegant dock. Tied up at the dock was a stunning, timeless white vessel. On its side was emblazoned YACHTS DE PARIS, and across its stern, below the tricolor French flag, was the name ACTE III. We stepped across a gangplank and onto the rich teak stern deck.

Eddie escorted me into a long cabin of gleaming pale wood. Polished dark wooden beams crossed the arched ceiling. He led me up three stairs to a forward cabin that looked like the bar of a wealthy men's club, then beyond, to the teak foredeck. I touched my hand to the gleaming brass railing. I half expected it to melt, the way dreams melt and vanish. The railing was smooth and cold. It didn't melt. It was real. All of it.

The yacht was perhaps a hundred feet in length. I'd seen any number of sightseeing boats plowing the Seine, ranging from rotting scows to elaborate platforms for dinner and dancing. This was clearly the finest of them all. From the size, I guessed it would accommodate twenty or thirty passengers. Yet, I hadn't seen anyone.

"Where is everyone?" I asked Eddie.

"The captain is at the wheel. The seaman is casting us off. The purser is fixing drinks, the chef is cooking, and the violinist is . . . I don't know. Around."

"I mean, where is everyone *else*?"

"There isn't anyone else."

"We don't have the whole thing to ourselves."

"We do."

With that, the engine roared to life, and we sailed off into the Parisian night.

60

I wish I could recall every single detail of that cruise, but I can't. My brain was just too overloaded with overwhelming sensations and perfect images. If I'm lucky, for the rest of my life, I'll have flashbacks from this evening.

Here are a few of the things I do remember:

We drank champagne, and four different wines, each of them exquisitely paired with whatever we were eating.

We ate lobster and foie gras and veal and cheese and chocolate, although not necessarily in that order. The lobster made me moan. So did the veal.

We sailed under thirty-six bridges, each of them different, each of them perfect. Eddie kissed me under at least seven of the bridges: one of them because it's a special bridge and good luck, and the rest, just because.

The Seine has its very own Statue of Liberty, albeit a little one. I waved to her. I swear she waved back.

The Eiffel Tower is a huge cliché. It is also, when it looms over your heads and explodes into dazzling sparkling light, the most romantic sight I've ever seen.

Eddie's favorite movie, ahead of *Sabrina*, is *An American in Paris*.

I asked the violinist if she could play the song from *Sabrina*, the one that Audrey Hepburn sings to Humphrey Bogart. *La Vie en Rose*. She could. She did. And, there on the foredeck of our own private yacht, Eddie and I danced.

He danced wonderfully. He held me close. Firmly, but gently. Together, we moved effortlessly. The boat swayed with the current. Our bodies twirled slowly. My head spun: from the champagne, the wine, the song, the dance, the romantic perfection of the moment.

I wondered what making love to him would be like. I hoped— intended—to find out. Soon. Tonight.

"We'll be docking soon," Eddie whispered in my ear.

According to the big clocks on the Musée d'Orsay, it was almost two in the morning.

I didn't want to leave him. Not yet—and maybe not ever. That made it even more crucial for me to keep my secrets from him.

This cruise must have cost him an absolute fortune: the type of money buttoned-down Harvard-man investment bankers make. I could only guess how badly he would react if he learned that I was the daughter of the notorious *La Gazelle*—and, even worse, that I was now planning to re-create her famous, infamous, shocking act of the ultimate public intimacy. If I wanted to keep Eddie, somehow, I'd have to keep those things from him.

He had his own secrets, too. I remembered how and why we had quarreled the other night. I wondered what he was hiding. He had erected barriers; I wondered if he would let me inside.

The seaman leaped onto the dock and tied the yacht fast.

Harvard or not, I didn't care. "Take me home," I said, looking down into Eddie's eyes.

"All right."

"*Your* home."

"All right."

Although the limousine was waiting, we didn't get in the car. Instead, we walked a little ways and crossed a short bridge. As we reached the far side, Eddie said, "This is the Île Saint-Louis." We continued a block more, and finally stopped in front of the massive wooden doorway of a stone building that looked like it must have been four hundred years old. Incongruously, there was a small key-pad mounted on the old stone wall; Eddie typed a combination of numbers on the pad and the huge door swung inward. We walked through a courtyard, past a garden. In the darkness, I could smell roses. Across the courtyard was another door. Through that one was an elevator. We stepped inside. Eddie took a key out of his pocket, inserted it in a keyhole at the top of the control panel, and turned the key. Slowly and silently, the lift rose.

At the top floor, the sixth, we stopped. The door slid open, and we stepped directly into an enormous loft. An entire wall of the space was made of glass, and the view was literally breathtaking. There below us was the Seine, glistening black in the night. Beyond were bridges, and then Notre Dame. The elevator door closed quietly behind us.

"This is where you live?"

In response, he kissed me. And kissed me and kissed me.

Finally, he stepped back. "This is where I live."

"Why is it a secret?"

"I've never brought a woman here before."

"Why?"

He said nothing, only turned slightly and looked at the stone walls behind us.

My eyes adjusted. Even in the darkness, with only the light filtering up from the street and the river, I could see that the walls were covered with huge canvases on which flowed lush curves. The paintings were captivating; I couldn't turn away from them. Eddie turned on a small lamp, and now I could see that they were gorgeous landscapes unlike any I had ever seen: sensuous rolling hills, valleys that descended into almost erotic mystery.

"Who painted these?" As I asked the question, I finally tore my gaze away from the art. I looked searchingly at Eddie.

"I did."

He did.

In that instant, everything changed. By day, Eddie was a custom-suited Harvard-educated all-business investment banker—but by night, he was a painter, an artist, enormously talented and overflowing with a creative force almost animal in its intensity. This new, hidden

Eddie, the one who had painted these nearly sexual landscapes—this Eddie might understand my mother's past, and even my own wild plans.

I looked into his dark eyes. They seemed to open up into bottomless wells. I felt myself falling in. I let myself fall.

I hooked my thumbs under the lapels of his tuxedo jacket and slipped it off him. Next, I tugged at his white bow tie. Naturally, he had tied it himself, and the bow untied easily. My fingertips touched his top collar button. I had never seen Eddie with his shirt unbuttoned. I waited for him to stop me. He didn't.

With just one hand, I undid the button.

As the collar spread open to reveal his neck, I caught a flash of vibrant red. I wondered what it was.

Eddie's tuxedo shirt was held closed by oval gold-and-onyx studs. I removed the first stud . . . then the next . . . and the next . . .

Eddie's chest was smooth and muscled. The flash of red I'd seen at his neck proved to be the barbed tip of the tail of a stylized dragon etched into his skin, simultaneously beautiful and fearsome. The tail coiled around the back of his neck. The dragon, its fangs bared and eyes flashing, was poised fiercely, standing guard directly over his heart.

I couldn't take my eyes off the tattoo. No wonder Eddie kept his collar buttoned. I wondered what his Harvard classmates and investment banking colleagues would think of *that*.

"I have one, too," I whispered. "Do you want to see it?"

He said nothing, just nodded.

Carefully, I slipped the gown off my left shoulder.

Eddie squinted. "Where is it?"

"Here." I pointed to a tiny red dot. "It was supposed to be a heart. A broken heart. But I had to stop." I blushed. "I have a very low threshold for pain."

"I like it the way it is," Eddie said, and kissed my shoulder lightly. I shivered.

"Wait," I said, and drew back a step.

Eddie had revealed his secrets to me. His intensely personal art, and the beast he kept hidden from the world. Now I could tell him my secrets as well. Before we went any further, I *had* to reveal everything to him. Then, there would be nothing to keep us apart.

"I have something to tell you," I said. I started to formulate the words in my head. But I never got to speak them.

Because at that moment, the elevator door opened.

$\mathscr{A}$ woman stepped out of the elevator and into the loft.

She was wearing a light coat, which hung almost to her knees. It seemed an odd choice of attire given how warm the night was.

She appeared completely at ease. She knew exactly where the switch was, flipping it on and filling the loft with light. As if she'd been there before.

She was everything I was not. She was a natural blonde, perhaps five foot five, and voluptuously curved—the embodiment of every cheerleader I ever envied and hated.

I know that she was voluptuously curved, and a natural blonde, because she removed her coat and tossed it over a chair. She was wearing nothing under the coat. She was entirely naked.

I looked at Eddie. He looked at the blonde woman, then at me. His mouth opened and closed, but nothing came out.

I've never brought a woman here before.

He had spoken those words only moments earlier. Obviously, he had lied. Not only had this woman been here before, she had her own key to the private elevator.

I realized she was looking at me. She took a step in my direction, then another. She scrutinized me from head to toe, with an expression I can only describe as . . . lustful. Apparently satisfied with what she saw, she reached up and stroked the line of my jaw with the long nail of her index finger. Then she turned to Eddie and cooed, "You are full of surprises." She licked her full lips. "Are you going to do just her? Or"—her voice was thick with sex—"both of us together?"

Before my eyes, Eddie shattered. Yes, he was devastatingly handsome, smart, amazingly talented, a big spender, a phenomenal kisser, unbelievably sexy, boyishly fun, and attracted to me. But none of that mattered. Because he was a liar: a filthy, horrible, despicable liar. He'd seduced me with yet another perfect evening, led me to believe I was special, convinced me that he cared about me—when in fact all he wanted was a tawdry threesome with his steady slut. He was like every other opportunistic Harvard snot who ever took advantage of a Somerville girl, only much, much worse. I'd convinced myself that he was different, but I'd been wrong. I could never believe anything he said, ever again. I would never trust him.

I looked at his face. He appeared unspeakably sad. So sad, I almost waited to hear what he might say, how he might explain away this carnal naked blonde woman with the key to his loft who had arrived unannounced at two thirty in the morning and hungrily suggested that Eddie *do* us both.

I turned my gaze from Eddie to the blonde. My eyes traced her curves. Then my focus shifted to the paintings behind her. There on the canvases were those same lush hills, those same sensual valleys. Suddenly the images transformed, and an awful realization struck me: Eddie had not painted landscapes at all, he had painted nudes. All of the paintings were of a woman. This woman. All of the sexual energies that radiated from Eddie's powerful brushstrokes had their source in her. I didn't need to hear any explanation from Eddie. I knew about artists and their models. She was his muse, and the intimate details of their relationship were displayed there on the walls.

I couldn't look at them any longer. Not at the paintings, not at the woman, and especially not at Eddie. I ran to the elevator, praying that the key was required only to enter but not to leave. My prayer was answered. I pushed the bottom button and the door slid closed. Just before it had shut completely, Eddie began to speak. Whatever he was saying, I didn't hear it.

The streets of Île Saint-Louis were empty. The night was silent, except for the echo of sobs. Someone was crying. Maybe it was me.

I couldn't possibly walk all the way back to my apartment in high heels. Given the hour, I figured my best chance of finding a taxi was to head toward Notre Dame. When I got there, the cathedral loomed overhead. I caught one of the gargoyles laughing at me. Ugly son of a bitch.

Finally a taxi turned the corner. I waved and got the driver's attention. Considering that I was wearing a stunning vintage crimson mermaid gown and that with the heels I was six-foot-three, I would've been hard to miss.

I caught a glimpse of myself in the rearview mirror. My tear-smeared makeup gave me the face of a raccoon. The cabbie drove his freakishly tall raccoon of a passenger home without a word.

The next day, I slept until almost one p.m. I showered away all vestiges of the previous night, and dressed in a pair of my old skinny boy jeans and my Aerosmith T-shirt. Glamour hadn't worked so well for me, so I was reverting to dour familiarity and comfort. Madame Renard frowned at my appearance, but made no criticism.

"A man may come looking for me," I told her.

"The man in the limousine."

"How did you know about the limousine?"

"I know everything that happens on Rue Richer."

"I don't want to see him."

"Very well."

"I don't want him to find me."

"He will not."

She said it with such certainty, I relaxed. She would take care of me.

At two thirty, Monsieur Petit arrived. He entered waving a contract, which he promised was extremely favorable.

Madame Renard snatched it out of his hand. "Mademoiselle's attorney will review this," she declared.

I didn't know I had an attorney. Neither did Petit. "And who is Mademoiselle's attorney?" he asked.

"The son of her mother's attorney."

The little man frowned, which led me to think that his proposed contract wasn't quite as favorable as he'd said. "Very well."

"I'd still like to start working," I interjected.

"You would?" He was pleasantly surprised.

"I want to."

If I'd been completely honest, I would've said *I need to*. I couldn't get Eddie out of my head. The swirl of our bodies as we danced on the yacht in the Paris night. The sensation of falling into his eyes. The ferocity of the dragon that guarded his heart. The tingle of his kiss on my shoulder. I desperately needed distraction: something, anything else to occupy my mind and body.

I accompanied Monsieur Petit downstairs. I was glad that he'd parked his car in the courtyard; I could avoid the street, and the risk of being spotted by Eddie, altogether. The car was the tiniest Mercedes I'd ever seen. Petit had the driver's seat adjusted all the way forward so he could reach the pedals. I slid the passenger seat all the way back to accommodate my legs. We made quite a pair.

He drove like a madman. Perhaps I shouldn't have told him there was someone looking for me and I didn't want to be found. Then again, maybe he was just a terrible driver. Finally, the car screamed to a stop in front of the ugliest building I had seen in Paris. There were chunks missing from its bare plaster façade, and what was there was covered in graffiti. I was having serious second thoughts as we ascended the steep narrow stairway.

The door at the top of the stairs opened into a huge complex of dance studios, and my doubts vanished. Entire rooms were filled to overflowing with elaborate costumes that were close cousins of those I'd seen at the *Folies Bergère* show in Las Vegas, barely ten days and a whole lifetime ago. Petit walked me from chamber to chamber, describing this tableau, that production number, all the while illustrating his talk by pointing to outfits that were as outrageous as they were glamorous: here, a set of full-length silver furs straight out of *Doctor Zhivago*; there, a rack of tiny jeweled G-strings paired with gold stiletto sandals, black top hats and enormous pink-and-white feathered bustles.

We reached the last studio. This one was completely empty.

"Here," said Monsieur Petit. "Tomorrow."

"Tomorrow what?"

"Tomorrow . . . you will begin to learn the dance of *La Gazelle*."

onsieur Petit phoned ahead to Madame Renard. By the time I returned home, there were several brand new leotards waiting in my apartment.

"Of course, you will wear the leotards only while you learn the dance," he explained. "The learning is slow. We do not want you to be cold. Or embarrassed."

"I wouldn't be embarrassed."

That's what I said. I wondered, though. I remembered the virtual transparency of my mother's historic costume. Would I actually have the nerve to step out in front of sixteen hundred people—or even one—so completely exposed? I told myself that I would . . . but in my heart, I was far from sure.

When Monsieur Petit pulled his little Mercedes into my courtyard, there was a tough-looking young man standing there. I'd never seen him before. He was doing nothing, just standing with his arms crossed and smoking a cigarette. His eyes were hidden behind dark sunglasses. Despite the fact that I had no idea who he was, he opened the car door for me, then held the stairwell entry door as well.

Later, I asked Madame Renard about the young man. "That is my grandson, Marcel," she explained.

She'd never mentioned having grandchildren. "What's he doing here?"

"He will see to it that you are not disturbed."

"He doesn't need to do that."

"He does what I ask him. My husband was a worthless bum. My sons never visit. But my grandsons are all good boys. They will take care of you."

Marcel looked pretty imposing to me. I didn't envy Eddie if somehow he found me and decided to make an unannounced visit. It would serve him right. The dirty stinking liar.

The next day I rose early, ate a big breakfast, donned a leotard and met Monsieur Petit downstairs at the appointed time. He drove us to the studios and, once inside, immediately began teaching me my mother's dance.

I had expected him to say something before we started. Something profound, or inspirational. After all, we were about to re-create history, weren't we? He didn't, though. He simply taught me the steps.

He described them first, one or two at a time, then demonstrated. Despite the fact that he continued to wear turtlenecks, blazers, slacks and dress shoes, he was surprisingly nimble and an excellent teacher. He seemed pleased with the rate at which I progressed.

"You are truly her daughter," he proclaimed at one point. Those words made me glow with pride.

The dance itself was not at all what I had expected. From Claudine's account of it, my mother's performance had sounded spontaneous, almost accidental, not to mention breathtakingly erotic. What Monsieur Petit was teaching me, though, was completely precise and calculated. *Here, you run across the stage at just such an angle, for eight steps—no, not seven, eight. There, you leap— from the left foot, onto the right. Hold the landing on the right foot for the count of three, then collapse suddenly—then just as suddenly, spring back up onto the balls of both feet. Arch the back—farther; no, farther. Stretch out the arms. Spread the fingers. Then throw the head back. Yes. Just so.*

Despite the fact that I hadn't taken a dance class since the seventh grade, the movements came wonderfully naturally to me. I recalled my ignominious dismissal from ballet class. *Linda has grown too tall.*

Kiss my ass, Miss Lynch. I am the daughter of *La Gazelle*. And a star is about to be born.

Midafternoon, we took a break. Monsieur Petit ran out for a few minutes and returned with fresh yogurt, a long skinny baguette, a bottle of Sancerre and two glasses. While we ate and drank, I raised the subject that had been nagging at me.

"It doesn't seem very erotic," I said.

"Right now, you are only learning the steps, the movements. You are like an actor learning the lines of a play. First you must memorize, until you can do the dance without thinking. Only then comes the interpretation, the power, the emotion, the brilliance." He smiled naughtily. "The sex."

The image of Eddie's paintings, the monumental erotic landscapes, flashed into my brain. It seemed to me that those had been works of pure passion from the moment his brush first caressed the canvas. Imagining the physical acts that must have inspired him pained me immensely. I drove the images out of my mind and forced myself to focus on the task at hand.

I continued to have doubts; the clinical step-by-step learning process seemed utterly passionless. Still, Monsieur Petit appeared to know what he was doing. I decided to trust him. We went back to work.

I'll say this for the French: they've got a good thing going with this wine-at-lunch business. A half bottle didn't decrease my efficiency one bit. On the contrary, with my inhibitions suppressed, I learned even faster. A few times, I even felt brief flashes of genuine physical pleasure as I moved. Maybe there was hope for me yet.

By the end of the second day, I had learned the entire dance. Memorizing the act's climax—for lack of a better word—was surreal. Every throb, every shudder was . . . choreographed. I imagined that porno stars must feel like this. *Sorry, that wasn't hot enough. Can you come again—only louder this time?*

Monsieur Petit must have sensed my doubts. "Do not worry," he reassured. "Tomorrow, we add the music." Indeed, so far we had worked in silence, with only the little impresario's barked instructions and hand-clapped beats as a soundtrack. "Debussy will ignite the spark of your passion. Soon all of Paris will burn with desire for you."

His voice resounded with a confidence that I lacked. All I could do was wonder:

Would Paris burn for me, or would I go down in flames?

63

*E*ach day, another of Madame Renard's loyal grandsons stood watch. After Marcel was Bernard, and now, on the third day, it was Alain's turn. He was my youngest and cutest bodyguard so far, although he wore the same sunglasses and smoked the same cigarettes as his brothers.

Monsieur Petit was a few minutes late, so I waited at the base of the stairs.

"He was on the street this morning," said Alain suddenly.

"Who?"

"The man you are avoiding."

I had a flash of panic. "Does he know I'm here?"

"No." Alain took a long drag on his Gauloise. "He was around last night, too. Bernard didn't see him, though—we only heard the reports."

"Reports?"

"From Colbo. Chez Mimi. Groupe Fontenoy. Eldan. All up and down the street. He was going door to door."

"Did anyone tell him anything?"

"Of course not." He smiled. I imagined his eyes were twinkling behind his Ray-Bans. "They're all afraid of Grandma."

At that moment, the familiar little Mercedes pulled into the courtyard. Alain opened and closed the car door for me. Seconds later, Monsieur Petit was veering maniacally through traffic.

Eddie really was looking for me. I was angry. Scared. And . . .

flattered? The fact that he had been so close by made my heart pound. I was glad when we reached the dance studio.

Petit had been right: adding the music made an enormous difference. For the first time, I began to *feel* the dance rather than *think* it. The strains of *L'après-Midi d'un Faune* were languid and seductive; if I closed my eyes, I could almost feel the voices of the flutes and the oboes licking across my skin. Another half-bottle of wine at lunch put me even more in touch with the sensuality of the dance, although some part of my brain whispered to me that I shouldn't have to get liquored up to perform. By the end of the day, I was doing the entire act without interruption or correction, and when I finished the last time, I was sweating and my heart was pounding—and not entirely from exertion, either. Once again, I wasn't anywhere close to sexual climax, but the possibility seemed less remote every time I danced.

Apparently, I wasn't the only one who noticed my growing transformation. At the end of my final dance of the day, after I collapsed to the floor, spent, Monsieur Petit applauded. It was the first time he had done so. I looked up at him. His smile was wide and completely genuine. "*La Gazelle* lives," he said.

Throughout the entire ride back to my apartment, I was still glowing from his praise. I was so happy that, without even thinking about it, I found myself humming.

"*La Vie en Rose*," Petit said.

Oh, shit. He was right. That was the tune that filled my head. After a day filled with Debussy's amorous orchestrations, here I was humming the song from *Sabrina*. The one Eddie and I had danced to, our bodies swaying in unison . . .

The Mercedes swung into my courtyard and screeched to a halt. "You are ready," proclaimed the little man in the driver's seat.

"To perform?"

"No. Soon, but not yet. You are ready to see . . . the film."

Upstairs in my apartment, I confronted Madame Renard. "Did you know there was a film of my mother doing her act?"

She sat down abruptly. "No."

The news seemed to hit her hard. It had been a shock to me, too. In theory, I should've been delighted. Other than in a childhood so distant I couldn't recall it, in my entire life, I'd only seen my mother in still photographs: two back home in Somerville, the snapshot from Dixie, and the collection displayed around the Parisian apartment. Now, unexpectedly, I would have the opportunity to view her for several minutes, live and in motion.

So why was I filled with dread?

First of all, according to Monsieur Petit, the film was a recording of *La Gazelle* performing her notorious act, onstage at the *Folies Bergère*. She would, of course, be wearing her less-than-naked costume. And the act would end, of course, with its infamous orgasmic finale.

There are some things a girl just shouldn't see her mother do.

But there was more to it than that. Maggie Archer Stone had been dead and gone since I was eighteen months old. For most of my life, I hadn't known her at all, and I'd hated her for it. Now, in only the last two weeks, I had been introduced to her as if for the first time. Her figmentary existence had acquired flesh and blood. I didn't possess my own memories of her, but I had the recollections of others: Dixie, Claudine, Marie, Madame Renard, Monsieur Petit. Those recollections, and the photos, portrayed a real person who, to my surprise and great joy, I resembled and admired. In these few days, I had formed an impression of my mother that I could gladly carry with me for the rest of my life.

Now, though, I was about to see her almost in the flesh. She was already real enough for me; the film might make her *too* real. Perhaps we shouldn't invite our ghosts to sit so close to us.

Monsieur Petit had thought watching the film would add another dimension to my performance. *You cannot pass up the opportunity to learn directly from the master,* he said. Of course, he was right. I couldn't pass it up. I had agreed.

Tomorrow I would meet my mother.

64

*I*nstead of a shocking costume, she wore blue jeans, and an over-sized shirt undoubtedly borrowed from her husband. She wore a little too much makeup, but that was to be forgiven; the cancer was already advanced, and she did what she could to keep her face from showing the effects.

"Hush, sweetheart," she said. The baby hadn't cried, but she kissed and rocked it as comfortingly as if it had.

"Never forget how much I love you," she said to the baby. "Never forget how proud I am of you."

There were tears in her eyes. "I'm sorry," she said. "I want to stay. I've tried so hard. But I can't. I'll miss you so much." Now she was weeping openly.

"I love you, Linda."

That was my dream. I had waited my entire life for it. Now, it had finally come.

It couldn't have been a memory. I was too young.

But it was. It had come to me in sleep, but that didn't make it any less real. It had really happened, just that way. I was sure of it.

I wasn't afraid anymore of watching the film of my mother's performance. Whatever I might see, or not see, didn't matter. I knew now who my mother really was. I knew how much she loved me. Nothing would change that.

Monsieur Petit had set up an old super-8 projector and a small screen in the studio. The film had been taken, without sound and without permission, by an overzealous tourist from Budapest. His camera and its contents were confiscated before he reached the theater exit. The camera was returned; the film was not.

Petit didn't know why the film had not been destroyed. He knew, but wouldn't tell me, how it had come into his possession. He swore on his mother's grave that this was the only copy. I believed him.

The quality of the recording was poor. The light level was low, and the image jerked from time to time. Still, there she was: my mother. *La Gazelle*. Wearing a costume that only accentuated her nakedness.

She and I looked so much alike, I found myself blushing, as if I were the one whose body was exposed before 1,600 people.

As she moved, I felt my own muscles tense and flex in time with the unheard music.

Her pace quickened. Her movements acquired an intensity, an urgency. Her breathing seemed to grow ragged. Her motions grew wilder, frenzied. Suddenly her body coiled, then *released*, contracting again and again and again, until finally she collapsed to the stage.

The spotlight that had followed her every move like a stalker disappeared, and she vanished into blackness.

The small spool of film ran off the reel. The loose end sputtered until Monsieur Petit shut the projector.

"So," he said, looking at me questioningly. "Can you solve the mystery?"

I knew what he meant. *Was it real, or was it an act?*

I shrugged sadly. "The mystery is still a mystery."

"Ah. Well." He was disappointed, but tried to look on the bright side. "Perhaps it is just as well. Now it is you who will have all of Paris guessing."

We drove back to my apartment in silence. I didn't tell Monsieur Petit what I knew.

She was faking it.

I was absolutely certain. I had no doubt whatsoever.

Maybe it's because I looked so much like her. Watching the film was like seeing myself. I didn't just view it, I experienced it.

What I had seen, what she had done, wasn't real.

The knowledge made me profoundly sad. Sad for her. For my mother.

She had been famous, and infamous. The rich and the powerful had been her lovers. They had strewn her with gifts and gowns. The public had groveled at her size 11 feet. But it had all been based on a lie.

She'd spent fifteen years of her life just going through the motions. Pretending, for no other reason than to make somebody else feel good. And not only onstage. She had altered herself to conform to whatever her latest paramour wanted her to be. The Prince of Spain wanted a woman who fucked standing up and hunted pheasants for fun? Done. The Captain of Industry desired a lady who indulged his foot fetish while discussing the stock market? As you wish.

I wondered if she hadn't been the saddest, loneliest woman in the world.

And now, it seemed, I was about to follow in her footsteps.

$\mathcal{M}$y entire life was in complete turmoil.

In a matter of minutes, Eddie Atkinson had metamorphosed from the most complex, mysterious, fabulously desirable man I'd ever met into the most loathsome despicable lying pervert on the planet. I had wanted to know everything about him, even if learning everything took forever. Now I never wanted to see him again.

In a matter of minutes, my mother had fallen from the pedestal on which, after all these years of animosity, I'd just placed her. Now she was a broken idol, and all I could do was look sadly at the pieces. I had learned to love her, and I still had that—but now I had learned to pity her, and that was almost too awful to bear.

In a matter of minutes, my dreams of my own future on the stage of the *Folies Bergère* were revealed for the plastic fantasies they were.

I had come all this way . . . I had learned so very much . . . and yet, what did I have?

Before I could answer that question, Madame Renard tapped gently on my door.

"Yes?"

She opened the portal just a few inches and peered around gingerly. "You are upset."

"Come on in."

"You are sure?"

"Please." I'd be better off with company; her presence would keep me from dwelling on my own dismal thoughts. "How did you know?"

"By the sound. When your mother was upset, she stomped up the stairs exactly the same way."

Another way I was just like my mother. Now I wasn't sure if that was good or bad.

"You are upset because of a man?"

"Yes."

"And because of the dance?"

"Yes."

She shook her head and sat down on the chaise. "Just the same as your mother. These were her gifts, and her curse. Without the men and the dance, I think she would have had no troubles." The angle of the old lady's head shifted. "Then again, without the men and the dance, I think she would have had no joys, either. All the years I knew her, she never stopped trying to find balance, to have the best of both."

"Did she?" I don't know why I asked the question; I already knew the answer.

"No."

"Do you think it's possible?" I didn't know the answer to that one.

"Perhaps. Maybe for you it is possible."

"Why for me?"

"I think you are stronger than she was."

That came as a surprise, particularly given how devoted Madame Renard was to my mother. "You barely know me."

She shrugged. "Still, it is what I think."

The fact that she perceived in me a strength I didn't feel buoyed me, but only slightly; for the most part, I continued to feel overwhelmed. An idea occurred to me. "When my mother was upset—because of the men, and the dance—what did she do?"

Madame Renard offered to call me a taxi, or to have one of her grandsons drive me—Alphonse was on duty today—but I was throwing caution to the winds. I couldn't tolerate being chauffeured anymore: not in Eddie's limousine, nor Michel Petit's Mercedes. I wanted, even needed, to be moving under my own power.

I dug a pair of nylon shorts and a ratty T-shirt out of my back-pack. Then I slipped on my Bloody Mary-stained New Balances.

I was ready to run.

Madame Renard tried to give me specific directions, but I told her all I needed was the general locale of my destination. I'd get there eventually. Along the way, fate and the traffic lights would decide my route.

I had no idea if Eddie was in the vicinity. If he was, all he saw of me was a blur.

I hadn't run since I'd left Somerville. Danced, yes, but not run. The relentless pounding, the inevitability of it, felt good. I sliced through crowds of pedestrians. Dodged cars. Hurdled a badly parked scooter. Startled a dog walker with four Jack Russells in tow. The hyper little dogs made me wonder how Jack was doing back home. Jack, our dog. And Jack, my father.

My mother had consorted with princes and business tycoons. Yet she had married candlepin-bowling, hard-of-hearing, waistline-challenged Red Line engineer Jack Stone.

I'd learned that my mother had been many things, but nothing suggested that she'd been a fool. What did she know about my father that I didn't?

I kept running. Although the changing lights altered my path often, sometimes dramatically, still I gradually made my way south, toward the river, and then west. I cut through the Place de Colette, named for another former queen of the *Folies Bergère*. I wondered if someday someone would establish a Place de La Gazelle. For my mother's sake, I hoped so.

I crossed the Rue de Rivoli and followed a short tunnel that led into the grounds of the Louvre. To my left, the glass pyramid rose, surrounded on three sides by the old museum. To my right were spread the lovely Tuileries Gardens. I turned right. It was a glorious day, and the gardens were crowded. There were tourists with cameras taking endless digital pictures, and locals strolling, sitting, lolling on the lawns, even sleeping in the sun. I was the only one running.

As I flashed by the crowds, a few heads turned. They were looking at me. Not at the daughter of *La Gazelle*. Me. Lindy Stone. Let them look.

The wide path through the center of the Tuileries was covered with a fine white grit, almost like chalk, and I kicked up little clouds as I ran. I looked over my shoulder. The clouds disappeared as quickly as they formed. I wondered if I would leave any more trace of myself in Paris than that.

After another minute, I slowed, then stopped.

I had reached my destination.

The Musée de l'Orangerie is the museum that Claude Monet personally chose to display his masterworks, *Les Nymphéas*. The Water Lilies.

Perhaps you've seen Monets before. Even some of his Water Lily paintings. I had, at the Museum of Fine Arts in Boston. But you only think you've seen Water Lilies.

You ain't seen nothin' yet.

The centerpiece of the Orangerie consists of two huge oval rooms illuminated by natural light filtering down through the ceiling. The walls of each oval room are covered with what feels like one enormous, endlessly long, infinitely placid painting. In fact, between the two rooms, I think there are eight different paintings. The canvases are vast: seven feet tall, and painted seamlessly end to end, fully three hundred feet in all. As you stand in the center of the oval and rotate ever so slowly, you are simply surrounded by the water, the lilies, the light, the clouds, the drooping trees. If a frog had hopped across my foot, I wouldn't have been surprised.

No wonder my mother came here when she was upset. It was the most serene place I've ever been.

I moved from the first oval room to the second, then back, then back again. At first I tried to choose a favorite painting, then got lost in where one painting ended and the next began, realized that that was the whole point, and quit trying.

The paintings took my mind off my dilemmas. They didn't

advance my thinking about what to do next with my life, but they sure were soothing.

I was there for hours.

At some point, I finally realized there was more to the museum than *Les Nymphéas*. When I had entered, I'd been handed a small map, which I'd ignored until this moment. Now I inspected it and saw that the collection included works by Renoir, Cézanne, Picasso, and others. I decided to take a brief look through the rest of the exhibition rooms, then return for more peace of mind from the Monets.

I moved quickly. Nothing else grabbed my attention the way the Water Lilies had.

That is, until I stepped into a small gallery and found myself face to face with the painting of my mother.

I might just as well have described it as a painting of me, because it looked as much like me as it did my mother—but I'd been in Paris only ten days, and I was quite certain no one had painted my portrait.

In this room, the subjects of all the large paintings were women, every one of them long-limbed. Some of them were dancers, some society types. They were all dressed in the casual elegance of wealth, and all of their expressions were on the spectrum between indifference and tragedy. Their skin tones were rendered in shades of gray, making their moneyed trappings seem all the more somber.

The painting of my mother, though, was by far the saddest. She sat in a chair, leaning her head against one hand, as if at a total loss. She wore a flowing gown of blue and black that seemed to bare her right breast entirely. On her lap was an animal, entirely ignored, and so indefinite in detail that I couldn't tell if it was a dog or cat. The most heartbreaking aspect of the painting was my mother's face. Her black hair hung limply over her right eye. Her eyes were unfocused, staring off into nothing. She wore a little too much pink rouge, and her mouth was a thin expressionless line. She was the image of complete hopelessness, total capitulation. She had done battle with the universe, and the universe had won.

No wonder she'd left Paris.

I read the little plaque next to the painting. The words printed there came as a shock. The artist, Marie Laurencin, had died in 1956—four years before my mother had even arrived in Paris. The title of the painting was *Portrait de Mademoiselle Chanel*, and it was dated 1923. Despite the stunning resemblance, despite the expression of utter resignation that I knew reflected what my mother must have felt, this painting was of someone else.

Had Maggie Archer, Mimi, *La Gazelle*, looked at this very painting and seen it as a mirror of her soul? Had she read the utter despair on the face of poor Mademoiselle Chanel and realized that this would be her own fate as well if she stayed? Had this image given her the strength to break away from the artifice of her life?

I could only guess at my mother's reaction to this painting. But I knew my own.

I knew it was time for me to leave.

Heading back to the apartment, instead of running, I strolled. Having decided to leave Paris, at least I could take my time on this walk and soak in the city that I would almost certainly never see again.

As I sauntered through the Tuileries, several men stopped and stared at me, and a couple even whistled. I was the same girl who'd left Somerville barely two weeks earlier, and yet somehow I'd been transformed. Men found me attractive. Pretty. Beautiful, even. And, remarkably, I believed it myself.

I turned and gave a big smile to one of my oglers. *Live it up, fellas*, I thought. *You're never going to see me at the* Folies Bergère*, so take a good look now, while you've got the chance.*

On Rue Richer, instead of ducking into the passageway, I stopped in at Restaurant Montana Americain. Tex was so glad to see me, he nearly wept. Ever since I'd moved into my mother's apartment and signed on to the Madame Renard dining plan, I'd been ignoring Tex and the Montana. I sat down at the window table and ordered a bowl of chili. Sitting there in plain view, I could be seen by anyone. If Eddie was nearby, he couldn't miss me. So what—let him see me. Let him come. I was leaving, and on my way, I'd tell him a thing or two if I got the chance.

Eddie never appeared, though. I finished the chili, paid my bill, and kissed Tex on his cheeks, left and right. Then I headed into the passageway. I passed Alphonse, the grandson of the day, with a wave. He was the widest one so far, with the build of a wrestler, or maybe a bear. I pitied Eddie or anyone else who tried to get by him.

I trotted upstairs to the apartment. I had to make my flight plans, and pack. I dreaded telling Madame Renard.

Packing took longer than when I started my travels, as I'd gathered a few things along the way, but my wardrobe was still limited. I assessed my acquisitions: my mother's headdress, and her jeweled sandals. My shorts, halter top, flip-flops and bathing suit from Las Vegas. My two IKKS outfits, new shoes and boots. I decided to keep my mother's skinny black Audrey Hepburn outfit, but her other clothes that I'd worn would stay here in Paris.

I glanced over at her closets. I'd still only glimpsed the tip of her fashion iceberg.

Curiosity overwhelmed me. I had no intention of taking any of her gowns; I wasn't about to wear Yves Saint Laurent on my jaunts to the dog park with Jack. Still, it wouldn't do me any harm to look.

For the next hour, I unzipped garment bags and took an amazing journey through Wardrobes of the Rich and Famous. Dior and Balenciaga, Chanel and Cardin, Lanvin and Ungaro. I guess all these fabulous clothes hadn't made my mother happy—but they couldn't have hurt.

I opened the last bag in the last closet, and my heart nearly stopped beating.

There it was. The dress. The barely there dream of a decadent gown I'd glimpsed in the ancient snapshot that had launched me on my odyssey. The glittering costume that had tantalized me, inspired me, insinuated itself into my fantasies . . . and now, incredibly, it was here in my hands.

It was far more breathtaking in reality than in the tiny old black-and-white photograph.

The costume was fashioned almost entirely of narrow jeweled straps and a few carefully positioned feathers. Other than the feathers, the bottom of the dress was comprised mostly of a rhinestoned G-string connected to a glittering waistband. Above the waistband, the jeweled straps sprouted in a fan pattern, with two of the fans climbing to the shoulders and linking behind the neck. And, except for a few more sparkles and tufts, that was it. Yet it had an iridescence, an aura that seemed to fill the room.

Looking at it in person, I had the same reaction as when I'd first seen the snapshot: I wondered what it would be like to wear it. Initially, I'd considered that speculation ridiculous. Now, though, I was quite serious. I wanted to know how the fabulous costume would make me look. How it would make me feel.

There was only one way to find out.

I would try it on.

I shivered.

It was warm in the apartment, but I still shivered. I had showered, shaved, trimmed. Now I was completely naked. This garment left no room for underwear. Nothing comes between me and my mother's dress.

I stepped through the waistband and slid it up until it rested at the top of my hips. The G-string just barely covered me, and I do mean barely. Although I have no butt to speak of, every inch of it was right there for the world to see—at least, if there had been anybody but me in the apartment.

I slipped my head between the two fans that joined behind the neck, straightened up and adjusted the top. It was actually designed quite brilliantly. Even though there was almost nothing to it, it was built to provide lift and support. A girl with much bigger boobs than mine could have worn it and not sagged. As for me, well . . . I have to admit: it made me look *fabulous*. Like I was born to wear it. Born to get out in front of the world wearing nothing but this.

Of course, there was more to the outfit than just the dress. I stepped into the shoes: first the right, then the left. They were the highest heels I'd ever worn. They made me realize that I loved being tall. I looked in the full-length mirror. My legs looked amazing.

Finally, I lifted the headdress and, slowly, carefully, placed it on my head. I felt like I was attending a coronation, my own. It was heavy, but as soon as it was on my head it gave my body balance, focus, a center.

I looked in the mirror again. I was transformed. I was beautiful and shocking, simultaneously sexual and like an exotic creature out of a fairy tale. I had become something more than human—an unimaginably tall, slender, exotic goddess. Looking at myself, my breath was literally taken away.

Despite my stunning resemblance to the image of my mother in the snapshot, I didn't see her when I looked in the mirror. I saw only me.

Where was the girl I'd been only weeks earlier? Where was the gangly, skinny, awkward, lamentable loser I'd known myself to be my entire life? She was gone. She wouldn't be back, either—because whatever else might happen to me, I would always carry this image in my memory.

At that moment, I decided I would take this dress with me when I left. I had no intention of ever wearing it again. But in the weeks since I'd been launched on my journey, the dress and I had become bound together. It would forever be a part of me, so I'd might as well keep it. Plus, I was quite sure that I would face my share of grim moments in the future, and I knew it would be easier to bear them with this constant reminder of my own perfection nearby. No wonder my mother had kept this dress safe in her own closet all those years.

I regarded myself a moment longer, to burn the image into my brain. Then, carefully, I reversed the process. I lifted the feathered crown off my head and placed it gently back into its case; stepped out of the shoes, left and then right; slid myself out of the dress and hung it carefully back in its bag.

I stood there in the silent room, naked again. Now I was not shivering. I felt warm, comfortable, confident.

Suddenly, a thought occurred to me: *If I looked so extraordinary in my mother's showgirl costume, how would I appear in her famous, infamous headliner's outfit?*

I tried to picture myself sliding into *La Gazelle*'s breathlessly bare bodysuit once I'd returned home to Somerville—but the image simply wouldn't form in my head. There was no occasion I could conjure where such an outfit would seem appropriate. I couldn't even conceive of a room in our house where I might feel comfortable slipping on that decadent second skin. Here and now, though, the place and time were perfect.

The costume was a miracle of design. It had no seams that I could discern. It was a full-body piece, arms, legs and bodice; only the back was bare, and that opening was the only way in or out. I slipped my right leg all the way into the spidery silken shaft, until my bare foot emerged. I felt as if I'd just immersed my leg in liquid electricity. Tiny sparks seemed to fire my nerve endings. Quickly, I slid my left leg in so that it would feel the incredible sensation as well. I inserted my arms into the sleeves and adjusted the bodice so that it clung to my body. My nipples tightened, and for a second I had trouble catching my breath.

I wondered if maybe, just maybe, my mother hadn't been faking after all.

Then I thought back to the images I'd seen in the film, though, and I was sure. Yes, the costume seemed alive with its own stimulating force, as if all the lustful desires of all the audiences from all my mother's performances had been caught permanently in the silken web. But no. Regardless of how remarkable the garment was, how incredible it made me feel, my mother's act had still been an act. And if I were to re-create it, I would simply be reprising the artifice.

Still, it was an amazing thing to wear. If my mother's showgirl dress had made me look like a goddess, her headliner costume turned me into a gorgeous beast, the embodiment of animal sexuality. *La Gazelle*, indeed.

I heard Madame Renard's knock at the door. I had grown so accustomed to her that, quite forgetting what I was wearing, I said, "Come in."

She did—and, seeing me, dropped the tray she was carrying, together with a cup of tea she'd been bringing for me.

She was literally speechless. I'd never seen her in such a condition, and it concerned me. "Are you all right?"

"I . . . I'm sorry. You just . . . she . . ." Slowly, the blood returned to her face. She sat down, then instantly stood up again. "I'm sorry, Mademoiselle, but seeing you—I almost forgot. Monsieur—"

The little impresario bounded up the stairs and through the open door. When he saw me, though, he stopped as suddenly as if he'd run smack into a brick wall.

"—Petit is here," she finished.

adame Renard excused herself, leaving me alone with Michel Petit. He circled me slowly. His mouth was open. His eyes beamed.

Finally he spoke. "It is a miracle."

Nobody had ever called me a miracle before. "Thanks."

"The costume . . . how did you find it?"

Somehow, my journey from the *Moulin Rouge* and silent Marie to *Jazz* and mysterious Françoise seemed peculiarly personal, and none of his business. "I looked," I said.

"It is a miracle," he repeated.

"You said that."

"You do not understand. Your mother . . . she is alive. Here. In this room. In you."

Oh, but I did understand. "No, she's not."

He stopped circling me. "But she is." His personality shifted gears, into theatrical maestro. He clapped his hands twice, sharply. "Come. Show me. The jeté."

I looked around. This was, after all, a living room, not a dance studio. "Here?"

"Why do you wait?" He clapped again. "Now. Dance!"

What the hell. I knew I was leaving. If I could give Monsieur Petit a few more minutes of joy before breaking the news to him, why not? I danced.

The body suit felt good as I moved. I'm not talking about sexual stimulation; it felt natural, like a second skin. It was better than being naked, because it made me feel my own body without inhibiting it. I moved effortlessly.

I knew *La Gazelle*'s act by heart. With Debussy's ghostly siren song playing in my head, I performed most of the dance. Just when the movements were supposed to grow more frenetic, though, I slowed, then stopped altogether.

Petit frowned. "Have you forgotten?"

"No."

"Then what is the problem?"

"I'm not going to do it."

"Because you are shy?"

"No."

He looked at the furniture. "Because the lamp table is in the way?"

"No."

"Then why?"

I wasn't sure how to tell him. "I'm not my mother."

He seemed mystified. "But you are."

"No, I'm not. I look like her. Maybe I even move like her. But I'm not her. I don't know how she could do what she did, but I can't do it. I can't go out there and . . . lie. It's not real. It never was. I guess she could live with that. But I can't. I won't."

He didn't want to accept what I was saying. "You just need a little time. You will change your mind."

"I won't."

His expression darkened. "You want more money?"

Money? It had never occurred to me. "You don't understand. I won't do it. For any amount."

His expression changed. The notion that his dream was crumbling before his eyes yet again was finally starting to penetrate. He began to look desperate. "I will pay you more money."

"It's not about money."

"Then what?"

"It's wrong. It's . . . dishonest." I reached the bottom line. "It's not me."

"You will not dance?"

"No."

"Please?"

"No."

One after another, a series of expressions played over Monsieur Petit's face: disbelief, shock, anger, despair.

"I'm sorry," I said.

He stood there, wordless, motionless. Then, like a marionette whose strings have been cut, he dropped suddenly to his knees. He wrapped his arms around my legs and buried his face in, well, my crotch. Silently, he started to sob.

Thank God he's gay, I thought. *And thank God nobody else is here. Because it must look like he's—*

At that moment, the door burst open.

I couldn't believe who I saw there.

Eddie.

69

*A*pparently, I wasn't the only one who couldn't believe what I saw.

Eddie just stood there in the doorway, his mouth agape.

In a matter of seconds, I noticed so many things: He wasn't wearing a tie, and his collar was unbuttoned. His shirt was torn, his nose was bleeding, and his perfect hair was a mess. He was carrying what might once have been a bouquet of roses—only where the flowers had gone to was anyone's guess; all he held in his hand were long thorny stems. His perfect façade had been scuffed, pummeled, cracked.

Instantly, I knew what he had done. Somehow he'd found me—maybe he'd witnessed my most recent, uninhibited going and coming—and then he'd rushed the castle gate, fought the mighty troll who stood guard (sorry, Alphonse), and climbed the tower to rescue his princess.

I had never seen him look so handsome.

His eyes took in the strange scene playing out on the living room carpet. The tall woman—the tall *beautiful* woman—almost nude, wearing a shocking illusion of a garment that made her appear even more naked than if she had stood there in her bare skin. The small man kneeling on the floor before the woman, his face buried in the folds of her sex, his body shaking.

No wonder Eddie slammed the door shut and ran.

I heard his feet pound as he raced down the stairs. From the sound of it, he took them at breakneck speed, at least two at a time.

I tried to run after him. Unfortunately, Monsieur Petit was still twined around me like a boa constrictor, and he refused to let go. I shuffled toward the doorway, dragging him along. For a little guy, he was surprisingly heavy.

Finally I reached the door. I opened it, leaned into the stairwell and yelled.

"Eddie!"

I was much too late. The running footsteps had stopped echoing. All I heard was my own desperate voice reverberate up and down the stairs.

He was gone.

It took me several minutes to get Monsieur Petit to release his grip. I literally had to pry his fingers open, one at a time. Even after he'd let go of me, fully fifteen minutes more passed before I could persuade him to leave. Dreams die hard.

"You will change your mind," he said, over and over.

My answer was the same each time. "No."

"You will."

"I won't."

"You will."

"No."

Finally, he said, "I will come back tomorrow."

"Please, don't waste your time."

"Because you will not change your mind?"

"Because I'll be gone."

Something about the way I said that must have convinced him. He uttered only one more word: "Oh." Then he collected himself, smoothed his hair, buttoned his blazer, stood up to his full height, and, with great dignity, left my apartment.

Once the door was closed and locked, very carefully, I removed the costume of *La Gazelle*. I hung it on a padded hanger, knowing that Madame Renard would find it and would know exactly how best to clean it and store it away. The thought made me sad. She'd pack it up perfectly in a garment bag and hang it in the closet, awaiting my return. Only it would hang there forever. I wasn't coming back.

I removed my mother's glorious showgirl dress from my things and restored it to the place I'd found it. I placed the large headdress case up on a shelf, then added the bejeweled sandals to the collection of beautiful footwear. Maybe someday some fashion archeologist would discover these closets and puzzle over what mysterious creature had left such glamorous artifacts.

I looked into my backpack. There, together with the old jeans and T-shirts I'd brought with me from Somerville, were the clothes I'd acquired in Las Vegas: the dressy shorts, flowered halter top, flip-flops and bathing suit. They were lovely, but they looked like someone else, not me. I removed them from the pack and added them to the collection in the closet.

Still in my bag were the two IKKS outfits I'd bought at Galeries Lafayette, together with the complementary shoes and boots. I adored them, and they made me look . . . beautiful. Most important, though, they were all mine. When I wore them, I wasn't Audrey Hepburn, or Jean Seberg, or Dixie Belle, or Maggie, or Mimi, or *La Gazelle*. I was me.

I left them in my backpack and zipped it shut.

Then I called the airline.

70

I could have stayed. I knew where Eddie lived; I could've camped in front of his door and confronted him. He would've had no choice but to talk to me.

But did I really want to talk to him?

I couldn't shake the image of that curvy little blonde woman stepping out of the private elevator into Eddie's loft, then shedding her coat. She'd been so obviously at home there, so comfortably naked, and her sexuality was reflected so patently in his paintings. What could Eddie say that I'd want to hear?

So, I fled.

Continental Airlines had a flight out of Charles De Gaulle Airport at 9:55 the next morning. The flight was full, but they suggested I might try to go standby. I told them to put me on the list.

I slept badly. Every time I closed my eyes and started to drift toward sleep, faces kept flashing behind my eyelids: Dixie and Claudine, Marie and Françoise. Prince Don Marcos, Monsieur Garrond, Michel Petit. The sad woman in the painting. My mother. My father. And Eddie, in all his incarnations: perfectly suited, tuxedoed, barechested, bruised and bleeding. Too many people had led me to this precise moment, and their voices all clamored for attention inside my head. All I wanted to do was sleep, but they wouldn't quiet down enough to let me.

The next morning I was out of bed and showered before five. I donned a pair of skinny jeans and a black T-shirt, slipped on my worse-for-wear New Balances, hoisted my backpack onto my shoulders and grabbed Jack's bowling bag. I locked the apartment, then tiptoed down the stairs. I stopped at Madame Renard's apartment. I hadn't been able to find the nerve to tell her I was leaving. I hoped she would forgive me. I slid the key under her door.

Out on the street, the day was gray and cool. I was glad. It would have been harder to leave Paris on a perfect day.

The windows of the Montana were still dark. Having been spoiled by Tex, I wondered whether I'd ever be satisfied eating a cheeseburger and French fries anywhere else.

Since I'd been living as Madame Renard's guest, I had plenty of money for a cab, but I didn't even consider it. I walked the few blocks to Gare du Nord, back the way I'd come less than two weeks earlier. Two weeks, and a lifetime ago. I paid my eight euros, and in minutes I was on the RER for the half-hour ride to the airport.

As I entered the terminal, I remembered my old childhood game. For just a second, I had an urge to dash madly to my gate and learn whether or not I'd missed my flight. I looked at a clock. It wasn't yet 6:15; departure was more than three-and-a-half hours away. The urge passed.

I waited. Only at 9:52 did I finally learn that I'd made it onto the flight. I found my way to my seat: back of the plane, middle of the row. Whatever. At least I was leaving.

I was exhausted, and, lulled by the sound of the engines, I should've fallen asleep instantly, despite the lack of legroom and the fact that my seat reclined no more than three inches. Still, sleep wouldn't come. That crowd hadn't stopped chattering in my head. I leaned forward and opened the bowling bag, which I'd stowed under the seat in front of me. From it, I retrieved the black-and-white snapshot. Really, I didn't even need to look at it; by now, I had every detail memorized.

I scrutinized the tiny image of the girl who had been my mother. "Why did you send me on this journey, anyway?"

She didn't answer. Neither did the old lady on my left or the snoring teenager on my right. Some questions don't have answers.

Had it been to discover who I really was? For a while, I'd thought

I was headed in that direction. Then, however, I'd been stunned to realize that instead of discovering myself, I'd been imitating others, particularly my mother—and that in doing so, I was imitating an imitation. My role model had spent fifteen years of her life faking it: deceiving her public, her lovers, probably even herself. So what did that make me?

I closed my eyes and tried to visualize a place that made me happy—only to find myself dancing in Eddie's arms on the yacht sailing through the perfect Paris night. From the yacht, we'd walked to his loft, where the passionate direction of the evening had been brutally changed by the arrival of a naked blonde with big boobs and a lust for lust. So much for my happy place.

Perhaps I might be able to chase away all these massively depressing thoughts if I focused on something that required concentration. The first idea that came to mind was my mother's act. Once you've memorized a physical routine, it's relatively easy to repeat it in the flesh. Performing it entirely in your head, though, is considerably harder.

I started to go through the steps mentally. *I run across the stage at just such an angle, for eight steps. Then, I leap from my left foot onto my right. I hold the landing on the right foot for the count of three, then collapse suddenly—then just as suddenly, spring back up onto the balls of both feet. Arch the back, stretch out the arms, spread the fingers. Then clasp my hands to my chest.*

No, wait. I was supposed to throw my head back. Try it again.

I tried it again. And again and again. Each time, at a different point, I'd realize I was mistaken; my brain had deviated from the famous sequence, and I had to start over.

At first I was baffled. I'd learned the dance so quickly and easily. I'd known it perfectly. How could I have forgotten it so soon?

After a while, though, I began to suspect that I wasn't making mistakes at all. I wondered whether my subconscious wasn't . . . *fixing* the dance.

On one level, there was nothing wrong with it, and it didn't need fixing. *La Gazelle* had performed it the same way for fifteen years without interruption, to the apparent continued delight of Parisians and tourists alike. But all that told me was that the dance was right for *my mother*. Just because I'd learned to duplicate her actions didn't mean the dance was right *for me*. If it were mine, I'd do it differently.

I started to get some specific ideas. A flight attendant brought me a piece of paper and a pen, and I began to make notes. Of course, it was an entirely academic exercise—but the flight was eight hours long, so why not?

It made those hours fly. By the time the captain announced that we were beginning our descent, I'd had to ask the flight attendant for three more sheets of paper, and both sides of all four pages were covered with my scrawl. Some of my changes were minute, but several of them were very substantial, and one was absolutely fundamental.

That orgasm thing had to go.

It wasn't real, and I just wouldn't—couldn't—bring myself to do it. But that didn't mean the act couldn't be erotic. On the contrary: by eliminating the fiction, it seemed to me that every remaining movement would be true, and, consequently, all the more alluring. I had plenty of genuine sexuality to express; hell, just the thought of wearing that gossamer costume again made my nipples harden under my T-shirt. Relieved of the pressure of pretending to get off in front of 1,600 people six nights a week, I imagined that I could take my mother's act, refine it, tailor it to myself—and then watch out, Paris, because this time you're in for a *really* hot show.

I folded my notes and stuffed them into Jack's bowling bag. I had my act all figured out. Needless to say, I couldn't be *La Gazelle*. Maybe *L'Impala*. I laughed out loud at that thought. Anyway, I was all set.

Too bad I wasn't going back.

The flight landed in Newark, New Jersey. I hauled my backpack and bowling bag through customs and boarded my connection for the short hop to Boston. The moment the plane had finished climbing, it started its descent. We pulled up to the gate at Logan Airport exactly on time at 2:47 p.m.

By this point, my body had sailed past exhaustion to a point somewhere close to physical collapse. Fortunately the mass transit route home was hardwired into my DNA. Silver Line to South Station. Red Line to Harvard Square. I emerged from underground and found myself surrounded by the familiar red brick bustle of Cambridge, Massachusetts. This was the landscape of my entire life—and yet, even with my senses dulled by lack of sleep, I could tell that the territory had somehow grown foreign to me.

I trudged along, and the increasing dinginess might as well have been a sign: WELCOME TO SOMERVILLE. Another two blocks and my house appeared. It had always seemed small and drab to me, but now it was smaller and drabber. I mustered just enough energy to force my legs to drive me up the steps of the stoop. I unlocked the door and stumbled inside.

I intended to climb the stairs and collapse onto my bed, where, I was now certain, sleep finally awaited me. But my plan was thwarted, because Jack had suddenly appeared and stepped between me and the stairway. Jack my dad, not Jack the dog. I hadn't known my dad could move that fast.

"You're back," he shouted.

"Yeah."

"You didn't call me."

"I never call you."

"You were gone a long time."

"I've been gone a long time before."

"I was worried about you."

Now *that* was a conversation stopper. In my entire life, I'd never known Jack to utter those words. Finally, I regained the power of speech.

"You were?"

This time he was the one who couldn't talk. He gave me a hug. A huge bear hug. Another first: I couldn't recall ever getting such an embrace from him.

It was an awkward moment. In fact, he held me so long that I did the only thing I could: I hugged him back.

Now my recollection gets weird. Because as I remember it, he lifted me up off the floor, flung me over his shoulder, and carried me all the way upstairs like a confused firefighter hauling a victim into a house instead of out of it. Then, very gently, he placed me down on my bed, slipped off my running shoes, and covered me with a thin blanket. He drew the blinds in the room shut, turned out the light, and then—honestly, this is the way I recall it—he *kissed me on the forehead*.

Just before I was overcome by sleep, I wondered: *Have I wandered into the wrong house? And what has this man done with my dad?* Then oblivion swallowed me up.

When I awoke, it was almost noon. I'd slept for nearly twenty hours. I was starved. What I wouldn't give for Madame Renard to stroll in with my breakfast on a tray—or, failing that, fried eggs à la Tex.

I sniffed. My mind was playing tricks on me. I could swear I smelled bacon, and fresh coffee. Jack's idea of cooking breakfast is toasting Pop-Tarts and stirring Nescafé. Again, it occurred to me that I was in somebody else's house. But the room I'd awakened in was my own, so the only way to unravel the mystery was to get up and follow the smells.

Downstairs in the kitchen, I beheld a man who looked uncannily like my dad . . . and then again, not much like him at all. The face was the same, and he wore his perpetual ratty bathrobe. But he was clean-shaven, his hair was combed, and under the bathrobe, instead of boxers, he wore a proper pair of pajamas that I'd bought him years earlier but he'd always refused to wear. What's more, he was standing over the stove. Not only was he frying up bacon, he was scrambling eggs. And a gleaming new coffeemaker was steaming and gurgling.

I grabbed a mug from the cabinet and poured it full of coffee. The coffee wasn't as strong as in France, but pretty close. It was exactly what I needed.

Eyeing this strange incarnation of my dad warily, I sat down at the kitchen table. "What are you doing?"

He spooned a mound of eggs onto my plate, added four strips of bacon, and slid the repast onto the table in front of me. "Making breakfast."

"You never made me breakfast."

"So?" He handed me a fork. "Shut up and eat."

My hunger prevailed over my curiosity. I shut up and ate. Granted, it was just eggs and bacon—but *damn*, who knew he could cook? I wolfed everything down and Jack refilled the plate. Then I swear he went to the refrigerator and poured me a glass of orange juice. Thank goodness it was Tropicana; if he'd squeezed the oranges himself, I'd have called the authorities to come have him committed.

Finally, he sat down across from me. "Did I ever tell you how I met your mother?"

I put my fork down.

"Eat," he said.

Once again, hunger won out. I picked up the fork and resumed eating. With my mouth full, I mumbled, "Yeah. Prospect Hill Park. You were sitting. She was walking."

He half smiled. "No. I mean, how I *really* met your mother."

This time, curiosity beat hunger. "Talk," I said.

"So it's 1979. March third."

"That part hasn't changed."

"Let me talk. It's about four forty-five in the morning. I'm taking the train out of the yard. Nice quiet time. Sun won't be up for another hour-and-a-half, and the train's dead empty 'cause I don't make the first stop of the day until five oh five. I'm tooling along at about twenty-five, just getting the engine warmed up. All quiet on the western front. Then out of nowhere, sweet Jesus, out in front of me there's a lady standing on the tracks."

He now had my full attention.

"Split second, I hit the brake and sound the horn both. Pretty soon the scream of the wheels is louder than the horn. The lady doesn't move. She's lookin' calm as could be. Just doesn't move. I'm yellin' my head off, 'Move! Move! Move!' Course she can't hear me, I'm in the engineer's cab. I pull on that brake for all I'm worth. Train stops. And there she is, still standin' there. I swear, there's only about two feet between her and the train. Now she's lookin' right at me, through the window.

"I figure I've got six minutes max before the next train comes out of the yard and slams into my ass. I don't want to radio in about the lady, because first, that'll throw the whole day's schedule off, and second . . ." His voice cracked. He cleared his throat. "And second, she was the prettiest thing I'd ever seen. Just lookin' up at me, sad like that. So I do everything I'm not supposed to do. I open the door, jump out, hustle her up off the tracks and into the train, close the door, start the engine up again, gun it to make up for lost time, hit the first station on the stroke and do the whole day's shift, start to finish. Never told a soul.

"Course, seeing as how I found her standin' on the tracks just waitin' to get hit, I wasn't about to let her walk away and find herself another train to kiss. So I kept her with me the whole day, right there in that tiny little booth. You know what we said the whole time?"

I shook my head, no.

"Nothin'. Very first thing, I asked her, 'What the hell were you doing?' And she said, 'It seemed like the right thing at the time.' What do you say after that?"

Jack picked up my plate and fork, washed them and put them in the dish drainer. He'd never washed a dish for me, either. Then he poured me more coffee. "Anyways, after my shift was over, *then* we went to Prospect Hill Park. I bought her a meatball grinder and a Coke. She said she never had a meatball grinder before. I said she must not be from around here. She said oh but she was, she just never did. She liked it. Then we sat for a long time and didn't say much of anything else.

"Finally I asked her if she had a place to stay. First she said yes. Then she changed her mind and said no. So I told her she could stay here." Something must've registered on my face, because he said, "And don't go gettin' any ideas. I told her she could have the whole place and I'd stay with Tommy Connolly, but she said absolutely not. Anyways I insisted she take the bedroom, and I slept in the spare room—your room. I told her she could stay as long as she liked." He smiled, remembering. "I guess she liked it, 'cause she never left."

"When did you two . . ."

"About two months. Up 'til then, it was more like having a roommate. You know, division of labor. I'd give her money for groceries, she'd cook, we'd eat, I'd clean. 'Til one day in May.

"That's the day she changed everything."

$\mathcal{M}$y dad had never been much of a storyteller. Who am I kidding?—my whole life, he'd barely strung three sentences together at one time. Now, though, I was spellbound. "What happened?"

"We finished dinner. I cleaned the dishes, took the trash out to the can, came back in and washed my hands. She's sitting right here at this table—right where you are now. I can feel her eyes on my back. Finally she says, 'Jack, come sit down.' So I did. Then she says, 'You are the kindest man I've ever known. You've never asked one single thing from me. You've never asked me who I was, or told me who I should be. I think I've found the only good man on this whole planet.'"

I could feel my eyes starting to well.

"'And I'd be crazy to let the only good man slip away. So,' she says, I swear to God, just like this, out of the blue, 'Jack Stone, will you marry me?'"

I didn't want to disturb the memory, so I whispered. "What did you say?"

He looked at me like I was a madwoman. "What do you think? I said yes!"

"Did you love her?"

"Haven't you been listening? I fell in love with your mother the second that train stopped and I saw her lookin' up at me with those eyes."

"Did she love you?"

He thought about that one for a while before he answered. "You asked me that once. A long time ago. Do you remember?"

I nodded, yes.

"Back then, I told you I thought she did, and I hoped she did. Well, these last couple of weeks you've been gone, I've been thinkin' about that question a lot. And I've got a better answer. The answer is yes. Absolutely. You know how I know?"

I shook my head.

"Because she *acted* like she loved me. The way she used to look at me. The way she'd hold my hand just walkin' down the street, for no reason at all. The way she touched me when I missed a spot of shaving cream and she wiped it off. Everything she ever did told me she loved me. And she was the truest person I ever met. So yes. You bet she did."

The truest person I ever met. Was this the same woman who'd spent fifteen years faking it, on the stage of the *Folies Bergère* and in the intimacy of her bedroom with a parade of lovers? Was Jack simply her final deception?

As soon as that thought occurred to me, I knew it wasn't so. These last weeks, I'd wondered what on earth my beautiful, talented, famous mother had ever seen in sturdy, dull little Jack Stone. Now I knew: he was the only man who let her be herself. In turn, that was exactly who she'd been for him: herself. If her actions told Jack that she loved him, it was because she did.

Tears had already been streaming slowly down my cheeks, but now I began to weep.

Jack was mystified. "What's wrong?"

It was hard to get the words out between sobs. "You loved her—and she loved you—and she *died*."

His voice got quiet, which, for a man as hard of hearing as my father, is most unusual. "Yeah." He stared down at the tabletop. "About that." Slowly, by sheer force of will, he lifted his eyes to meet mine. "I'm . . . sorry. Losing Maggie was the worst thing that ever happened to me. And you . . . from the minute you were born, you were like another little Maggie." He smiled, but there was a lot of pain in that smile. "You shoulda seen the two of you. You were a perfect matched set. I never saw a woman take more joy from her baby than Maggie did from you." Now the smile faded. "Only then she got sick. Every day, she got worse. And every day, you looked more like her. When she died, I swear, it almost killed me. Every time I looked at you, it was a reminder of how much I loved your mother, and how she was gone." He lifted a shred of his ratty bathrobe. "You know why I don't throw this away? Because she gave it to me. Our first Christmas. It's one of the only *things* I still have from her." He let the robe drop. "Stupid me. Takin' care of a robe." He reached across the table, took my hand in his, and squeezed gently. "I was supposed to take care of *you*. That's what she wanted me to do. Only I didn't. Sometimes, just lookin' at you, it hurt so much. And I let my hurt be more important than you. Which I never shoulda done. So. I'm sorry. I hope someday you'll forgive me. And I hope she'll forgive me, too."

We sat like that for a long time: me crying, Jack holding my hand, both of us feeling like we'd just met, and grateful for the meeting.

Much later, after Jack cooked us both cheeseburgers for dinner— not as good as Tex's, but not too shabby, either—and we silently quaffed a couple of Sam Adams, I wondered what Dixie had thought would happen when she sent me that snapshot and the peacock feather. I know she was trying to help me discover the mother I'd never known. In that respect, I'd been far more successful than either of us had had any right to expect, unearthing unimagined complexities of character and unlocking precious memories about the incredible woman who'd brought me into existence. But now there was more. She'd also introduced me to my father.

Thanks, Dixie.

73

*D*ad and I settled into a better shared existence than we'd ever known. Don't kid yourself; after he got the apologies and hugs out of the way, pretty soon we were shouting at one another again. But most of the time the hollering was more good-natured than angry, and at least once every other day, he seemed to invent some reason to give me one of those huge bear hugs. I did my best to remember to call him *Dad* and save *Jack* for the dog. All this good nature must have confused the canine, who ran and hid under a chair every time a father-daughter embrace seemed imminent.

Naturally, we continued to watch Red Sox games together on TV, as we'd always done. For the first time, though, we actually spoke during the games. And, during the broadcast of the recent away series against the Yankees, I got up the nerve to express my opinion that Derek Jeter was a babe. After I cleared up my dad's confusion by explaining that guys can be babes, too, we had a half-hour fight about whether I'd been unforgivably disloyal by admiring the physical attributes of one of the Sox's arch enemies. It was great.

Once or twice, Jack—I mean, Dad—gingerly tried to inquire about what I'd learned in Paris, and, more particularly, why I'd left Paris and come back to Somerville. Thus far, I hadn't been very forthcoming. I knew I would tell him eventually, but I wasn't in any great rush. After all, it had taken Dad twenty-six years to fess up about my mother, so I felt no pressure to spill my guts in the first seventy-two hours.

"Was it because of . . . a *boy*?" he asked.

My dad and I have never talked about me and boys, or me and men, notwithstanding that I've been having sex since I was, well, younger than the Fifth Amendment requires me to admit. He really hadn't the slightest idea how to ask the questions.

"Yes, Dad. It was because of a boy." Other things, too—but if I was in no rush to talk to my dad about Eddie, I was happy to defer forever any discussion about my mother's notorious act and her wildly revealing costume. Happily, Dad was sufficiently uncomfortable having such conversations that he let the whole thing drop.

I picked up working again at Casa B's. As I confessed at the outset, I've never been much of a waitress, and I'm still not. I am, however, a *better* waitress now than I used to be. Why, exactly, I can't explain. I have no plans to remain a waitress for the rest of my life. Then again, I have no plans for the rest of my life, period—so in the meantime, while I'm figuring out what to do next, I'm trying to pay more attention to getting the orders right, and maybe even smiling. Oddly enough, my tips are better than they used to be. Go figure.

Waitressing at Casa B's has the added benefit of positioning me just downstairs from my beloved Brattle Theatre. I noticed a Billy Wilder retrospective on the schedule for July. *Sabrina* was on the program. I wondered whether I could bring myself to go.

A couple of weeks after my return, I was awakened one morning by Dad bellowing, "Hey, come down and see this!"

It was an unusual reveille. Waitress hours mean late nights, so I'm never in any rush to get out of bed early. And, having spent his career greeting the dawn, my dad values his sleep and respects that of others. I looked at my clock radio: it was eight twenty. *What was he thinking?*

He yelled again. "Come on!"

I pulled the blanket over my head, only to feel the house vibrate as he stomped up the steps toward my room. I heard the whine of hinges as the door swung open.

"Did you know," my father boomed, "that in Paris, France, it's against the law to paint murals on the side of buildings?"

"That's nice," I muttered.

"I figured you'd find that interesting, since you were just in Paris."

"Interesting."

Suddenly the blanket was yanked off me and I was flooded with daylight. Dad kept talking. "CNN has a fascinating story on right this minute. Seems the police in Paris are threatening to arrest some artist who's painting a mural on a building."

Before I'd gone to Paris, Jack—Dad—had never, to my knowledge, watched CNN or used the word *fascinating*. Even in my sleepy state, I continued to marvel at how my absence had apparently transformed him.

"It's a really nice painting," Dad observed.

"That's nice."

"Of a woman."

"Good."

"She's pretty much naked."

"Naked."

"Which I guess is pretty common in Paris. Naked ladies in ads, and on magazine covers, and whatnot."

For some reason, he just wasn't going to stop talking. I blinked my eyes and sat up. "Yeah. I guess that's right. So?"

"So apparently half of Paris wants to throw the artist in jail because he painted on a building. And the other half of Paris thinks he's a hero because supposedly it's a really good painting. Plus she's naked."

I tried to picture some creative yahoo splashing paint over one of those gorgeous old white stone buildings. I could certainly imagine the French getting up in arms about that. Then again, Parisians do love their art—and, as evidenced by the *Crazy Horse*, *Lido*, *Moulin Rouge* and the late lamented *Folies Bergère*, they love their naked women, too. I guess Dad was right. It *was* a pretty interesting story. Still, why did he have to wake me up?

"I *really* think you want to see this," he insisted.

Okay. Fine. Rob me of my precious sleep. Be that way.

He raced down the steps ahead of me. I'd never seen him move so quickly. "Hurry, it's still on."

I stumbled downstairs, rounded the bend and looked at the TV screen. There was Anderson Cooper's sleekly handsome face. He was talking, but I missed the words. Because behind him, in the background, loomed the painting. It must've been at least fifty feet high. And, although it was quite graphic, I must correct one of Dad's observations: the woman in the painting wasn't actually naked. I know this for an absolute fact.

Because the woman in the painting was me.

74

This was not like the painting at the Orangerie. Yes, that work bore a striking resemblance to my mother and, consequently, to me, too—but ultimately, it was a painting of someone else.

No, this hugely revealed woman flashing her most private attributes at the City of Light was unquestionably Lindy Stone, daughter of *La Gazelle*, former resident of Rue Richer. In a word, *moi*.

I say the woman in the painting—yours truly—wasn't actually naked because the mural depicted me wearing my mother's transparent silk bodysuit. As painted, though, I didn't look like I was wearing a costume; rather, the subtle veining pattern that slithered throughout the garment had, in the painting, become part of my skin. That effect, coupled with the massive scale of the work, the vibrant colors and the masterful artistry, made me look more than human, like some mythical goddess of erotic love. My body seemed like a force of nature; my breasts were graceful hills, and the bend of each elbow and knee was a valley shadowed in mystery.

I had seen such paintings before, although none had been so monumental. They'd hung on the walls of Eddie Atkinson's loft. But there were two critical differences between those paintings and this one. The body depicted in those paintings was unmistakably that of another woman; the physique that filled the huge mural was mine. And the paintings in Eddie's loft had never depicted the subject's face; here, the face was prominent, bold, beautiful—and again, it was mine.

Across the bottom of the painting a single word spanned the entire width of the building: *désolé*.

Sorry.

Anderson Cooper was wrapping up his story. "Apparently it wasn't enough of a risk that Atkinson quit his high-paying job in the name of art. Now it's up to the authorities, and maybe the Parisian public, to decide whether his bold creative statement will cost him not just money, but his freedom."

Several thoughts crashed into my brain simultaneously.

Eddie had relinquished the rewards of his Harvard education and quit his investment banking job in the name of art.

He was risking jail by painting me on the side of that building.

He had painted me—wonderfully—entirely from memory.

Dad interrupted all of those thoughts. "So, young lady, what do you have to say for yourself?"

I couldn't help myself; I laughed out loud. I'm sorry, but that's the sort of question you'd expect from the father of a fourteen-year-old who just broke curfew for the first time. And throughout my entire curfew-breaking, rule-breaking, law-breaking life, Jack Stone had never once asked me that. It took a fifty-foot naked mural in Paris to turn him into everydad.

He was still waiting. "Well?"

"That's quite a painting," I said.

"It sure is. I suppose there's an explanation?"

"Kind of."

"Kind of. Okay, how's this: I'll supply the coffee, and you supply the explanation?"

I looked at his new coffeemaker. "You're gonna need a bigger pot."

It was dinnertime when I finished. And I told my dad the *short* version.

"Well," he said.

"Well?" I swear, I half expected him to say *You're grounded*.

Instead, he asked a question. "What do you plan to do about this?"

"Which 'this' are we talking about?"

"All of it. You. Eddie. The blonde. Your mother's act. The naked painting."

"I told you, I'm not naked."

"Try explaining that to Paris."

For the first time I could remember, I asked my father for parental advice. "What do you think I should do?"

He turned the question right around at me. "What do you want to do?"

"I don't know."

"Sure you do. You just told me."

I did my best to recall the last nine hours, during which I'd spoken almost nonstop. I couldn't remember the part where I told him what I wanted to do. "Remind me."

"Who's the blonde?" he asked.

"I don't know."

"Exactly!" Dad pounded the table and my coffee cup jumped. "Do you love this Eddie guy?"

"I don't know."

"Exactly!" He pounded again. I grabbed the mug before its cold contents spilled. "And what about that act—do you want to do it?"

"Not Mom's way." As the words left my mouth, I realized it was the first time I'd ever uttered the word *Mom*.

"Of course not. *Your* way."

"I don't know."

"Exactly!" This time I also lifted Dad's coffee cup, out of fear the pounding would launch it off the tabletop.

"You keep saying that. What's your point?"

"My point is, you don't know the answers to any of the most important questions. If you sit around here on your skinny ass for the rest of your life, you'll never find out."

"So what should I do?"

"What you've gotta do."

75

I didn't tell anyone I was coming: not Madame Renard, not Monsieur Petit, and especially not Eddie. I wanted to confront him without warning, and I wanted his reaction to be completely spontaneous.

As before, I took public transportation from the airport and walked from Gare du Nord to Rue Richer. When Madame Renard opened her door, she wept unashamedly. It was the second best *welcome home* I'd ever received—behind only the post-Paris reception I'd gotten from my father, the remarkable man I'd shared a house with my entire life but never really known.

Over the old woman's protestations, I carried my backpack upstairs myself. I opened the door to the apartment that truly was my home. While Madame Renard waited, I peeled off my travel clothes, gave them to her for laundry, and donned the black silk robe that hung waiting for me.

"Will there be anything else, Mademoiselle?"

"Yes, please. I'm going to shower now. Can you call Monsieur Petit and ask him to be here in an hour?"

She clapped her hands together. "He will be delighted!"

"Maybe not. But it'll be an interesting conversation, that's for sure."

I was right. The conversation was interesting.

"You have returned!" the little man crowed.

"I have."

"And you have come to your senses!"

"I have."

"So you will do your mother's act!"

"Not . . . exactly."

Much agitation followed. Some of it was quite colorful, in a gutter-profanity sort of way. Monsieur Petit was clearly surprised by a few things.

He was both scandalized and impressed that I could swear as well in English as he could in French.

He was appalled that I would not defer to his creative judgment.

"You still need a headliner, don't you?" I asked.

"Yes."

"Then it's my way or the highway."

He speaks pretty good English, but that phrase was beyond him. I didn't bother to try to translate it. He'd figure it out soon enough.

And, he was entirely taken aback by my notion that I was at liberty to alter my mother's act. "You cannot rewrite the Holy Bible," he said.

"Nobody's going to pay a hundred euros a ticket to see the Holy Bible on the stage of the *Folies Bergère*."

He admitted that I had a point.

I asked him if he'd heard the news about the building-high painting of me in my mother's costume.

"Of course," he said. "All of France has seen it."

"Free advertising," I suggested.

He scowled. Mostly, I think he was annoyed that he didn't think of it. Because immediately, I could see the wheels start to turn in his head. After a few moments, his eyes got very wide. "I have it," he declared. *"Folies Désolés!"*

"I don't understand."

"It is the title for our new revue." He waited for comprehension to dawn on my face; when it didn't, he explained. "In the history of the *Folies*, the title of every revue has had the word *Folie* or *Folies*, and a total of thirteen letters. The title of the painting is *désolé*. So, now, we have the title of our new extravaganza!"

I thought about it. Roughly translated, *Folies Désolés* means *Sorry Craziness*, or maybe *Sorry Folies*. "It doesn't make any sense," I concluded.

"No," Monsieur Petit acknowledged. "But it will make millions!"

With a new title and the prospect of millions dangling before him, Petit was willing to consider my radical notion of an orgasm-free performance. "You must still convince me," he stated on his way out the door.

"I will," I replied. And I knew I would.

I strode proudly through the streets of Paris. I'd chosen to wear my black IKKS outfit, the one with the patterned T-shirt, tailored waistcoat, and long slender skirt with the crumpled silk hem, finished off with my black boots. I looked fabulous, and I knew it.

As I walked, heads turned. I'd purposely fixed my hair exactly the way Eddie had painted it. Even though I was fully clothed, more than a few passersby recognized me as the woman in the mural. Several times, people called out *Désolé!*, as if it were my name rather than Eddie's apology. Approving murmurs followed me all the way to the cobblestone lanes of the Île Saint-Louis.

I reached the massive, ancient wooden doorway to Eddie's building. I wondered what to do. There was no doorbell, no intercom. I had crossed the Atlantic only to be thwarted by a door.

Then the door swung open.

76

I looked inside the courtyard, but there was nobody there. Still, this was why I was here. I stepped in and closed the huge portal behind me.

I walked past the garden I'd only smelled the night I'd been here. The roses were enormous, and together they formed a palate of pinks any artist would be proud to capture on canvas. I spotted one flower that had already bloomed its fullest. In a day or two it would be dying. I pinched it off its stem and took it with me.

Across the court, the elevator sat open and waiting. The key was already inserted into the top slot, waiting for me to turn it. I did.

When I stepped into the loft, the very first thing Eddie did was kiss me. Passionately, desperately, for how long I have no idea. Yes, I had come here for an explanation—but that would wait. Explanation or no, he desperately wanted to kiss me, and I desperately wanted to be kissed.

Finally we stepped back and looked at one another. I realized how much I had missed him.

I handed him the rose from the garden downstairs. He held it up to his nose and inhaled deeply. Then he smiled and said, "You're not the police."

"No."

"I thought you might be."

I spotted a small video monitor near the elevator. I hadn't noticed it on my previous visit. He'd seen me on the street; that was why the door opened for me. "You knew I wasn't the police."

He shrugged. "Guilty as charged."

"Are they really going to arrest you?"

"Maybe."

"Don't you have a lawyer?"

"Several. That's why they haven't arrested me yet."

I looked at what he was wearing: black jeans and a tight T-shirt. His dragon tattoo was clearly visible at his neck. His feet were bare.

"You quit your job," I said.

"So you heard."

"The whole world heard."

"I didn't care about the whole world," he said. "I cared about you."

Okay, that wasn't an explanation, but it sounded pretty good to me anyway.

"Why did you quit?"

"I spent my whole life lying. Lying to my clients. Lying to myself. I didn't want to lie anymore." He looked at the nearest canvas, which was bare. "Doing this lets me tell the truth."

"Can you afford to tell the truth?"

He smiled. "For a little while. Until my savings run out, anyway."

"Wait a second," I said. "You lied to me."

His brow furrowed. "No, I didn't."

Was he going to deny it? "Of course you did. You said you never brought a woman up here before."

"And?"

"That was a lie."

"No, it wasn't."

"Who was that blonde?"

He smiled. *Smiled*. The nerve of him. "Sylvie? She's not a woman."

"I beg your pardon. Yes, she is. I've seen the evidence."

"I mean, she's not a *woman*." He waited for me to grasp the distinction. I didn't. "She's my model."

Like that meant anything. "And?"

"As far as I'm concerned, she's not a woman, she's a model."

"And?"

He stepped back and pointed at the huge paintings that covered his walls. "What do you see?"

"Her."

He shook his head. "What *don't* you see?"

Hard as it was for me to confront the carnal images, I studied them. I saw her breasts, her thighs, her back, her waist, her ankles, her shoulders. I already knew what was missing. "Her face."

"Exactly. I've never painted her face."

"Why not?"

"Because she's just my model."

He seemed to think that explained and excused everything, but it didn't. "If she's *just your model*, how come you had sex with her?"

"What makes you think I had sex with her?"

I looked around the loft. Naked voluptuous Sylvie filled canvas after sensual canvas. "What about these?" I asked, pointing to the paintings.

"What about them?"

"They're so . . . erotic."

"So?"

"So how could you possibly paint such erotic paintings of her if you never had sex with her?"

"Maybe I'm just a really terrific painter."

"You *are* a really terrific painter."

"Thanks. Have you seen your painting yet?"

"Only on TV."

"It's much better live. Did you like it?"

I blushed massively. "I loved it."

"Pretty erotic, huh?"

"I'll say." Had somebody turned the heat up in here all of a sudden?

"See? I've never had sex with you, either. Didn't stop me from painting that painting."

Okay, so maybe the paintings didn't prove anything. "Wait a second! I *know* you had sex with her. She practically said so."

His brow furrowed. "What are you talking about?"

The memory was painful, but it was burned into my brain. "She asked you, *Are you going to do just her? Or both of us together?*" I began to get angry at him all over again.

Which made it all the more incredible to me when he started to laugh.

"*W*hy are you laughing?"

It took Eddie a while to stop. When he did, he wiped his eyes and said, "She was asking if I was going to *paint* you, not have *sex* with you."

Oh, come now. Did he really expect me to believe that?

I guess my skepticism was obvious, because he kept talking. "I've been painting Sylvie for years. She knows me pretty well by now. She knew I'd never brought a *date* home. So she assumed you were another model."

Hmm. I guess that was possible. Maybe I had simply imagined the worst. Then I remembered how Sylvie had stroked my cheek, the way she had licked her lips. "But she was coming on to me! And don't try to tell me I was imagining that." I've been hit on enough to know it when I see it—and even though the hitters have been almost exclusively male, trust me, Sylvie wasn't subtle.

"Oh, no, that wasn't your imagination. She was definitely hitting on you."

"So?"

"So." Again, Eddie appeared to think he'd explained everything perfectly. When he perceived that I was still agitated, though, he stopped and thought. I could practically see him assembling the pieces in his head, trying to figure out what it was I didn't get. Finally the light dawned and he smiled broadly. "Oh, yeah," he said. *"Sylvie is a lesbian."*

The moment he said it, I knew it was true. Everything made sense. No wonder she was hitting on me. In a way, I guess I should be flattered.

Okay, maybe not.

Anyway, much more important, it meant Eddie wasn't a filthy horrible lying pervert after all.

"Did you notice anything special about your painting?" Eddie asked me.

"It's fifty feet tall."

"Besides that."

"It's painted on the side of a building."

"Besides that."

"I'm naked."

He shook his head. "It's *you*. That's what's special about it."

I still didn't understand. "Well, obviously it's me."

"Why is that obvious?"

"Because the woman in the painting has my face."

He clapped his hands together. "Exactly! I painted your face."

Really, he and I were going to have to start communicating better. "And?"

Suddenly Eddie's voice dropped almost to a whisper. "I never painted a woman's face before."

"What?"

"Never. Just bodies. The faces never mattered to me." He reached out, took hold of my hands and pulled me close. "But you . . . you're different. You matter. That's why you're my first." He swallowed hard. "My only."

This time I kissed him. The kiss lasted even longer than the first one.

I heard a siren wail in the distance. Eddie's body tensed, and he pulled away from me. He was genuinely scared. The siren got closer and closer. Eddie seemed to hold his breath. Then down below us, on the street along the river, a police car raced by without stopping. The siren trailed away.

I thought for a moment. "They won't arrest you," I finally said.

"How can you be so sure?"

"It can't be a crime to paint the poster for the new revue at the *Folies Bergère*."

He looked at me, mystified.

"Trust me."

"Are you sure?" He sounded hesitant, but I could tell he wanted to believe me.

"I'm sure."

"Okay, then. I trust you." Before my eyes, his entire body changed, relaxed. He was giving himself over to my care. It felt wonderful.

"You won't have any trouble paying the rent, either."

"Why not?"

"*Folies Désolés.*"

"I don't understand."

"Do you trust me?" I got up close to him. Very close.

"Completely."

"Good. I'll explain after." I began to peel off his T-shirt.

"After what?"

"After we get naked."

We got naked fast.

The explanation had to wait a while, though. After all, Eddie and I were two talented, artistic people. Together, we sure were . . . creative.

After the third time, Eddie and I cuddled up in his bed. I wondered:

Do I love this man?

I wasn't positive yet—although I was as far down the road to love as I'd ever been. And I was sure going to stay on this path with him and see where it led us.

I thought about my mother: the beautiful, sad, strong, loving woman who had helped me find my way to this place and this moment. She had labored her whole too-short life to find the perfect balance between her dance and her man. Ultimately, she'd found a truly good man: my dad. But she'd never been able to have them both.

Now that I'd returned to Paris, found my own dance, and united with Eddie, maybe—just maybe—I could.

But two things I knew for certain.

I was the truest person Eddie ever met.

And with him, I'd never have to fake it.

𝕷𝖊 𝕸𝖔𝖓𝖉𝖊

Théâtre: a spectacle is reborn, and a star is born

It was an opening night for the ages. They were all in attendance: Mistinguette, Chevalier, La Baker, Babette, Fernandel, La Gazelle. Also Gyarmathy, Petsch, and Derval. Not in the flesh, of course; they are all a part of history. But history was in full attendance last night, as the spirits of the *Folies Bergère*'s grand past were undoubtedly present and seated in the prime seats to witness as the most famous music hall in the world reopened and history was made anew.

Folies Désolés. The name has been on the lips of every Parisian ever since the appearance of its brilliantly provocative and highly illegal mural. The name means nothing, which is to say, it means as little and as much as every *Folies* spectacle to precede it.

The new revue is everything a *Folies* show has ever been, and more, and then more still. Under the expert conception and direction by M. Michel Petit, the tableaux are more beautiful, the singers more tuneful, the costumes more featherful, the dancers more graceful, the clowns more hysterical, and the nudes more plentiful than those of any *Folies* show in memory. Reputedly, the staging cost not one but six fortunes, and every euro is there on the stage.

And yet, how sad for the singers, the dancers, the clowns, and, yes, even the lovely nudes. Because no one in the capacity audience came to see them. No, the crowds were there for the woman in the mural, whose striking visage and breathtaking physique nakedly propositioned us all. *Come see me*, her towering image seemed to demand. *I dare you not to.* And with such a challenge, which of us could stay away?

Who was this goddess of temptation? The secret was quickly revealed. She is Lindy Stone: none other than the American daughter of our own beloved Mimi Archer, *La Gazelle*. Rumors that she would recreate her mother's legendary and infamous act fueled a frenzy of ticket sales, at prices heretofore unknown.

Promises that the new nymphet would not only reprise *La Gazelle's* act, but improve upon it, resulted in an unprecedented six-month advance sellout.

But is Lindy Stone worth it? Does she honor, and perhaps even surpass, her theatrical (and erotic) heritage? Is she truly a star for the ages of the *Folies Bergère*?

Yes. Oh yes. Oh God yes. Oh God oh God oh God yes! Yes . . . yes . . . oh, oh, oh God . . . YES! YES! YES!

(A moment, please, while I smoke a cigarette.)

Because the spontaneous manner in which *La Gazelle* earned her immortal nickname is the stuff of legend, the opening night crowd came prepared. After the climax of Lindy Stone's astonishing reinvention of her mother's act, dozens of theatergoers rose to their feet, each calling out the name of some exotic beast or bird, all hoping to christen the new star with her stage name. But everyone is too late. It seems she is already, and will forever be, known as *Désolé*: the caption coined by celebrated outlaw artist Eddie Atkinson, whose depiction of his muse captured not only the imagination of Paris but the heart of his subject. Oh, lucky man.

The rest of us will simply have to keep coming to see the show.

After all, we can dream.